T0129415

Finishing school failed to turn them into proper society ladies. Now these four friends vow to remain single until they find suitors worthy of their love and devotion . . .

Betrothed to a man she has barely met, Lady Faith Landon calls upon her three best friends—the self-proclaimed Wallflowers of West Lane—to help uncover the secrets of her mysterious fiancé. Her suspicions are aroused when she learns that he has recently returned from France. Is he a traitor to his country? The truth is quite the opposite. Nicholas Ellsworth, Duke of Breckenridge, is a secret agent for the English Crown who has just completed a risky mission to infiltrate Napoleon's spy network.

After his adventures, Nicholas craves the peace and quiet of the country and settling into domestic bliss with his bride. Until he discovers Faith's deceptive investigation. How can he wed a woman who doesn't trust him? But a powerful spark has ignited between Nicholas and Faith that could bring about a change of heart. Faith seizes her second chance to prove to Nicholas that they are a true love match but his past catches up with them when three French spies come to exact revenge. Surviving rather than wooing has become the order of the day . . .

Visit us at www.kensingtonbooks.com

Books by A.S. Fenichel

The Wallflowers of West Lane
The Earl Not Taken
Misleading a Duke

The Everton Domestic Society
A Lady's Honor
A Lady's Escape
A Lady's Virtue

Forever Brides Series
Tainted Bride
Foolish Bride
Desperate Bride

The Demon Hunter Series
Ascension
Deception
Betrayal

Published by Kensington Publishing Corporation

Misleading a Duke

The Wallflowers of West Lane

A.S. Fenichel

LYRICAL PRESS
Kensington Publishing Corp.
www.kensingtonbooks.com

LYRICAL PRESS BOOKS are published by
Kensington Publishing Corp.
119 West 40th Street
New York, NY 10018

All Kensington titles, imprints, and distributed lines are available at special quantity discounts for bulk purchases for sales promotion, premiums, fund-raising, educational, or institutional use.

Special book excerpts or customized printings can also be created to fit specific needs. For details, write or phone the office of the Kensington Sales Manager: Kensington Publishing Corp., 119 West 40th Street, New York, NY 10018. Attn. Sales Department. Phone: 1-800-221-2647.

Lyrical Press and Lyrical Press logo Reg. U.S. Pat. & TM Off.

First Electronic Edition: September 2020
ISBN-13: 978-1-5161-1052-0   (ebook)
ISBN-10: 1-5161-1052-8   (ebook)

First Print Edition: September 2020
ISBN-13: 978-1-5161-1055-1
ISBN-10: 1-5161-1055-2

Printed in the United States of America

For Dave, my constant hero. My heart.

Acknowledgments

Thanks to my wonderful group of women friends who keep me focused and forging ahead: Karla, Gemma, Juliette, Naima, Kristi, Corinne, Maggie, Tif, Laura, Mina, Farah, Robin, Sheryl, and Mona. You ladies are my rock. None of this would happen without your sturdy shoulders to lean on. To our men and women serving in the military and their families. Thank you for all you do.

Chapter 1

The last person Nicholas Ellsworth expected to find at his good friend Geb Arafa's dinner party was Lady Faith Landon. Yet there she was, Nicholas's fiancée, maddeningly pretty and equally aggravating. She fit perfectly with the lush décor and priceless artifacts in Geb's parlor. "Lady Faith, I had not expected to find you here. In fact, you and your friends' presence is an astonishment."

"I hope you are not too put out. It seems Lord and Lady Marsden have become fast friends with Mr. Arafa, and that friendship has extended to the rest of the Wallflowers of West Lane." Despite his desire to be rid of her, Faith's soft voice flowed over him like a summer stream and he longed to hear that voice in the dark, in their bed. The way her curves filled out the rose gown set his body aflame and there seemed nothing he could do about it.

He shook away his attraction, reminding himself that this was a sneaky, manipulative woman whom it had been a mistake to attach himself to. The fact that he longed to find out if her honey-brown curls were as wild as they promised, despite her attempts to tame them into submission, shouldn't matter. Nor should his desire to get lost in her wheat-colored eyes and voluptuous curves. This was a woman made for loving.

Lord, he hated himself. "I wonder that your being here with those friends is not some dire plot in the making."

He had reason to be suspicious. When he'd first arrived home from France, in the spring, she and her friends had engaged in spying on him and trying to ferret out his past. It was intolerable. He should have called off the engagement, but the thought of ruining her for good society didn't sit well with Nicholas. Instead he'd offered her the opportunity to set him aside, but she had refused to do so as of yet.

She frowned, and was no less stunning. Her full lips longed to be kissed back into an upturned state. "We are here because Mr. Arafa invited us. He's your friend. I'm surprised he didn't mention it."

Nick was equally bewildered by Geb's silence on the matter of Faith and the other members of the Wallflowers of West Lane. He had met them on several occasions during his feeble efforts to get to know Faith. Her instant suspicions that he was hiding something may have led to her friends' actions, but he still couldn't let the slight die. Though he did admire the strength of the friendship between Faith and the three women she'd gone to finishing school with. They were as close as any soldiers who fought and died together. Even if they called themselves "wallflowers," there was nothing diminished about any of the four.

"He is not required to give me his invitation list." It pushed out more bitterly than intended.

Those cunning eyes narrowed. "I think you would like it exceedingly well if he did."

That she wasn't wrong raised the hair on the back of Nick's neck. He had not been able to keep many friends over the years. His work for the Crown had made that impossible. Now his friendship with Geb Arafa was in jeopardy as well.

He bowed to her. "I do not always get what I want, Lady Faith."

Head cocked, she raised one brown eyebrow. "Don't you, Your Grace?"

Geb chose that moment to stroll over. His dark skin set off his bright tawny eyes, and though he dressed in the black suit and white cravat typical of an Englishman, there was no mistaking his Eastern background. "Nicholas, I'm so glad you are here. I thought you might be held up with politics."

Nicholas accepted his offered hand. "I finished my meetings and came directly."

Smiling in her charming way, Faith's golden eyes flashed. "I shall leave you gentlemen to catch up."

Both Nicholas and Geb bowed and watched her join her friends near the pianoforte.

"She is a delightful woman, Nick. You should reconcile and marry her." Geb ran his hand through his black hair, smoothing it back from his forehead.

Not willing to let his attraction to Faith rule his decisions, Nicholas forced down the desire seeing his betrothed always ignited in him. "She is sneaky and devious. I shall wait for her to give up and call off." "I would have thought such character traits would appeal to you." Geb lowered his voice. "After all, you are a spy with much the same qualities. You might consider speaking to the lady and finding out the details behind her actions."

"Why don't you just tell me what you know, Geb?" It was obvious his friend knew more than he'd disclosed thus far. Nicholas asking for more was futile. If Geb was going to tell him more than he already had, he would have done so months ago when he'd first informed him that Poppy and Rhys, now the Earl and Countess of Marsden, were investigating his character. Being spies meant that Geb and Nick kept their own counsel most of the time. As an information broker, Geb was even more closemouthed than most spies. He only offered what was necessary to complete a contract or, in this case, to inform a friend of something less than critical.

"I am not at liberty to divulge that information." Geb's white teeth gleamed.

"I didn't realize you were so keen on keeping a lady's secrets," Nicholas teased.

Grabbing his chest, Geb feigned a knife to the heart. "I would never tell tales of a good woman. There have been a few ladies of our acquaintance who were not reputable, and those who are part of our line of work whose secrets I had few scruples about divulging."

"Indeed." As much as he wanted to be angry with Geb for befriending Faith and her friends, he couldn't manage it. The truth was, Geb was quite discerning about who he called friend.

During the time he'd spent with them, he couldn't help but like them as well. They were the most spirited and brightest women he'd ever known. He recalled a beautiful blonde in Spain who had tried to put a knife between his ribs, and shuddered. At least he didn't think these Wallflowers were out for his blood, just his secrets. What he didn't know, was why they were so keen on divining his past. He might be a fool to think them innocent. His trust of a sweet face in the past had nearly gotten him killed.

Geb nudged him out of his thoughts. "Talk to the girl."

Glancing at where Faith stood drinking a glass of wine and talking to Poppy Draper, Nicholas mused over if they were plotting their next attempt to invade his privacy. "Perhaps later. First, I would like a glass of your excellent cognac."

"Avoiding her will not make your situation better," Geb warned, his rich Egyptian accent rounding the words and lending a sense of foreboding.

"The lady will decide I am not worth the trouble and find herself a less complicated gentleman to attach herself to."

Nodding, Geb said, "I'm certain that is true. She is too lovely for half the men in London to not be in love with."

Nicholas wished that thought didn't form a knot in his gut. He also longed for a day when Faith wouldn't enter his mind a dozen times. She had gotten under his skin before he'd even met her, and he couldn't rid himself of her spell. Even knowing it had been her mother and not the lady herself who had written to him when he was in France hadn't dulled what he knew and liked about Faith Landon.

"One day you shall have to tell me how you came to this, my friend." Geb signaled for Kosey, his servant.

The extremely tall Egyptian wore a white turban and loose black pants and a similar blouse. He carried a tray with two glasses of dark amber cognac. "Dinner will be ready in ten minutes, sir. Will that please you?" Kosey spoke English in an Eastern way, which made the language warmer and less harsh to the ear. It gained looks from some of the other guests, but Nicholas liked the formal, old-fashioned speech.

"Very good," said Geb.

Nick observed the gaping of the other guests. "Why have you invited these snobs to Aaru, Geb?"

"Flitmore has some items I wish to obtain and Humphry has proved to be a good source of information about certain parliamentary discussions."

"I trust you would never use such information against my beloved country." A knot formed in Nick's gut.

"No, but I might try to sway other members of your government. I like to know what is happening in my adopted country, Nicholas. That is all. As a foreigner, I have no say. This gives me some needed control." Geb grinned.

Nick held back a scolding that would do no good.

"Do not look at me so ill. I merely use information to my advantage just as everyone else does. I will share bits with them or buy back pieces of Egyptian art. It will harm no one."

Kosey moved to the door where he waited for word from the cook that dinner was ready to be served.

Lord and Lady Flitmore gaped at Kosey. Perhaps it was his height as he towered over everyone in the room. It might have been his odd clothes. Whatever it was, their shocked regard needled at Nicholas.

Faith stepped between him and the couple. "Lady Flitmore, it's nice to see you again. I heard your daughter Mary would be here tonight, but I've not seen her. I hope nothing is wrong. I know how she can get into mischief."

Lord Flitmore coughed uncomfortably. "Mary had some trouble with her gown and is coming in a later carriage. She will be here any moment."

As if on cue, a footman announced the arrival of Lady Mary Yates. A slim woman with red hair and flawless skin sauntered into the room. Pretty in the classical way, her long, thin nose appeared in a perpetual state of being turned up at everyone and everything. Hands folded lightly in front of her, she walked directly to where Faith stood with Mary's parents. In a voice without modulation, Mary said, "Mother, Father, I'm sorry to be late. I hope no one was waiting on me."

The lack of any emotion in Mary's voice made it difficult to tell if she was sincere or just saying what was expected of her. "Thank you for sending the carriage back for me."

Lord Flitmore pulled his shoulders back and beamed at his daughter. "Dinner has only just been announced, my dear girl. Please say hello to His Grace, the Duke of Breckenridge."

Mary made a pretty curtsy and plastered a wan smile on her rosy lips. "How do you do, Your Grace?"

Bowing, Nick couldn't help but notice the look of disdain that flitted across Faith's face. "A pleasure, Lady Mary. I'm pleased you could come tonight. Do you know Lady Faith Landon?"

Another curtsy and a smile that likened to a wolf, and Mary said, "Lady Faith and I went to the Wormbattle School together. We have been acquainted for many years. How are you, Faith?"

Faith raised a brow. "Very well, Mary. You are looking fine. Your parents tell me you've had some issue with your gown this evening."

Mary's gown was dark blue and threaded with gold. It pushed all her assets up to the breaking point of the material at her breast and flowed down, showing off her perfect figure. She blushed. "Just a small issue that my maid and a needle and thread resolved easily enough."

The ladies leered at each other.

Clearing his throat, Lord Flitmore said, "Mary, let me introduce you to our host."

"Of course," Mary agreed, and with a nod to Nick, all three Yateses left the circle.

Faith watched after Mary but had schooled her features to a pleasant expression that no one could have noted anything amiss from. Nick had many questions, but none of them were any of his business.

"Shall we go in to dinner?" As they were officially engaged, Nick offered Faith his arm and they preceded the others into the dining room.

The long table had rounded corners and was draped in white linen. Fine china leafed with gold, and highly polished crystal and silver, made the setting gleam under three fully lit chandeliers hanging overhead, and with four standing candelabras placed in all corners of the room. The high-backed, dark wood chairs were cushioned with a pale blue damask. It was decidedly English, and extremely elegant, to appeal to Geb's guests.

At the head of the table, Geb welcomed everyone formally to his home before launching into a story of being on a sinking ship, and the diners were riveted despite the fact that most of them would not invite an Egyptian man of no known rank into their own homes. Faith smiled warmly at Geb, and Nick wondered if she were different. Would his friends, regardless of their origins, be welcomed to her table?

He shook off the notion. He would not be going through with marrying Faith Landon, no matter how much he desired her or how kind she pretended to be. She had betrayed him with her spying, and he wouldn't have it.

Another exception to the apparent prejudice against Geb were Rhys and Poppy Draper. The earl and his bride genuinely liked Geb and had become fast friends with him after being stranded at his house in a storm.

"Did you swim to shore from that distance, Mr. Arafa?" Poppy's blue eyes were wide and her dark hair and lashes made the color all the more demonstrable.

Geb's cheeks pinked and he laughed. "I'm afraid nothing so heroic, my lady. I was hauled out of the ocean by a small fishing vessel. My lungs were full of water and I caught a terrible ague and spent three weeks in a Portuguese hospital."

They all laughed with Geb.

Rhys Draper took a long pull on his wine. "I would be willing to bet you were the most interesting thing those fishermen plucked from the Atlantic that day. And you were damned lucky. Not only could you have drowned, but if this had happened a year later, you might have been caught up in Napoleon's invasion."

"Indeed, luck was with me that day and many others." More sober, Geb gave Nick a knowing look.

Nick noted his friend's careful use of *luck* rather than invoke the name of the Prophet in a room full of Christians. Knowing how religious Geb was, Nick knew what he was thinking. They had experienced many adventures together, and luck, Allah, or God had seen them through some things that at the time, seemed impossible.

The footmen served the soup.

Nick noted that many of the guests poked at the fine broth, vegetables, and bits of tender beef, but didn't eat. The Yates family were among those who would not eat from the table of an Egyptian but would be happy to attend, since Geb was a good resource for many business dealings. Not to mention the depth of Geb's pocketbook.

Faith, Poppy, and Rhys ate with gusto. Perhaps more than was natural, and Nick decided they had also noticed the rudeness of the other guests.

Besides the Yateses, Sir Duncan Humphrey, his wife and two sons, Montgomery and Malcolm, were in attendance as well as William Wharton and his wife. All were well respected among the ton and had obviously not come for the food or company. They didn't speak other than the occasional thank you.

On Nick's right, Faith sipped the last of her soup and turned to Mary. "You didn't like the soup?"

"I'm not hungry. I'm certain it is quite good." Mary narrowed her eyes at Faith.

"It's really too bad, it was the best I've tasted." Faith smiled warmly and turned her attention back to Geb. "Poppy told me how wonderful your cook is and now I can taste the truth of it."

"You always did have a great love of food, Faith." Mary's voice rang with disdain and she peered down that thin nose at Faith's curvaceous figure.

Poppy looked ready to leap across the table and do Mary physical harm.

A low laugh from Faith calmed the situation. "I suppose where I am fond of a good meal you are fond of a good bit of gossip. We each have our hidden desires. Don't we, Mary."

It was a warning, but Nick didn't have enough information to know what was at stake.

Mary bit her bottom lip and narrowed her eyes before masking all emotion and nodding. "I suppose that's true of everyone."

A flush of pride swept over Nick. He had no right to feel any sense of esteem for Faith's ability to outthink another woman and put her in her place. Yet, he couldn't help liking that she had not been bested by a bigoted daughter of parents who would attend the dinner party of a man they clearly didn't like, but wanted something from.

Turning his attention back to Geb, Nick noted his friend's amusement at the social volley going on at the table. Geb smiled warmly at Poppy as she changed the subject to the delectable pheasant and fine wine.

By the main course, Nick had given up on the other end of the table and was ensconced in a lively conversation among the four people around him. Rhys was well versed in politics and they discussed the state of coal mines. Faith and Poppy both added their opinions, which were well thought out and more astute than he would have thought for ladies of their rank. Perhaps he should rethink his views of what ladies ponder in the course of a day. Clearly it was more than stitching and tea patterns.

Geb, too, ignored the reticent group at the far end of the table and joined the banter. When Kosey announced that cake and sherry were being served in the grand parlor, Nick was disappointed to leave the conversation.

As soon as they entered the parlor, Flitmore cornered Geb about the sale of several horses, and Sir Duncan wanted to know when the next shipment of spices from India would be arriving.

Stomach turning at their duplicity, Nick escaped to the garden.

Geb had torches lighting the paths. The gardens here were one of Nick's favorite places in England. They were orderly and wild at once. White stones lined the lanes meant to guide one through the low plantings. It was a maze but without the threat of becoming lost. The fountain at the far end broke the silence of the pleasant autumn night. Soon winter would turn the garden into a wasteland and a good snow would give it the feel of an abandoned house.

Nick sighed and walked on.

"Are you determined to be alone, or might I join you, Your Grace?" Faith called from only a few feet behind him.

He must be losing his training for her to have sneaked up behind him without notice. "Is there something you wanted, Lady Faith?"

She stepped closer. Several curls had freed themselves of her elaborate coif and called out to Nick to touch them. "It is a lovely garden." She glanced around and smiled.

"Yes. Geb has taken bits from all his travels and placed them in his home and this garden. I think it brings him comfort."

Faith's golden eyes filled with sorrow. "Do you think Mr. Arafa is lonely here in England?"

"It is never easy to live amongst a people not your own." Nick considered all the time he'd spent in France, Spain, and Portugal and how much he'd missed the rainy days in England and people who understood his humor.

"The Wallflowers are very fond of Mr. Arafa. We have not entertained much, but I will see that he is added to our invitation list. Perhaps a circle of good friends will make him feel more at home." She'd placed her index finger on her chin while she considered how best to help Geb.

Adorable.

He needed to be free of this woman. "You didn't say what it was you wanted, Lady Faith."

Frowning, she walked forward and down the path. "Must I have a reason to walk in the garden with my fiancé?"

Leaving her to her own devices and returning to the house flitted through his mind, but it would cause gossip and he was curious about her reason for seeking him out. "We are hardly the perfect picture of an engaged couple."

"No. That is true. I wanted to apologize for any undue strain I may have caused you by trying to find out what kind of character you have."

"Is that your apology, or shall I wait for more?" he said when she didn't elaborate.

She stopped and puffed up her chest. Her cheeks were red and fire flashed in her eyes. "Why must you be so difficult? Even when I'm trying to be nice, you find fault. The entire situation was mostly your doing. If you had been open and honest, that would have been an end to our query and none of the rest would have been necessary."

Even more beautiful when she was in a temper, he longed to pull her into his arms and taste those alluring lips. He was certain just one tug would topple all those curls from the pins that held her hair in place and he could find out if they were as soft as they appeared. It was maddening. "I hardly see how it was my fault. You and your friends spied on me and involved Geb, which is unforgivable."

As soft and lovely as she was, a hard edge caught in her voice. "I suppose, then, you will not accept my apology. I see. Well, in that case, I'll leave you to your solitude." She turned to walk away and stopped, eyes narrowed into the darkness beyond the gardens, which were surrounded by tall evergreens.

Following her gaze, Nick saw nothing, though the hair on the back of his neck rose. "What is it?"

"I felt eyes on me, as if someone was watching." She shivered and continued straining to see in the shadows.

"I'm sure you are imagining things." He dismissed her worry.

That hateful glance fell on him before she plastered false serenity on her face. "Perhaps."

He preferred the disdain to the untruthful agreement. Why he should care when he wanted nothing to do with her, he didn't know. "Shall I escort you back inside, Lady Faith?"

"You are too kind, Your Grace, but I can manage the journey on my own." With a curt nod, she stormed away from him toward the house.

Unable to look away, he admired the gentle sway of her hips until she climbed the veranda steps and went inside. Lord, how he longed to hold those hips and slide his hands up to that slim waist, and so much more. He shook away the wayward thoughts before he embarrassed himself with his desires.

One thing was certain, Faith Landon would be his undoing.

Chapter 2

"I really don't know what to do," Faith said on a long sigh.

Faith loved Tuesday tea with the Wallflowers of West Lane. It was a time set aside when they all talked and vented their problems. It had been a tradition since Aurora married and moved into her horrible husband's West Lane townhouse in London.

Luckily the Earl of Radcliff had been killed when cheating a gambler at a less than reputable establishment. His death had freed Aurora, but the scars remained.

With or without that terrible character in their lives, they still met every Tuesday for a long, relaxing tea. Several months ago, Poppy had married Aurora's brother Rhys, and he had joined them and been named an honorary Wallflower.

Rhys was a welcome addition and always added a bit of fun to the conversation. His rakish days behind him, he'd settled into a lovely life with Poppy and never looked back. His golden-boy good looks still turned heads in the ballroom, but Rhys only saw his wife and none other.

Rhys turned a serious eye on her. "To be honest, Faith, I'm surprised you haven't just called off and let that be the end of it. Breckenridge has given you leave to do so and been a good sport and gentleman by not calling an end to the engagement himself. He's protecting your reputation."

"Mother would be furious. She's already quite in despair over my behavior. Well, what she knows of it." Faith cringed at the lectures she'd had to endure the last few times she'd seen her mother. Living at the West Lane house made it more tolerable. Still, she hated to be at odds with Mother.

"I don't think your mother is why." Mercy was curled up on the chaise with her feet pulled under her willowy figure. Her green eyes flashed with merriment, and she twirled a strawberry-blond curl around one finger. Her yellow dress was a direct compliment to the butter yellow and blue décor.

Faith shrugged. "I was just starting to find him interesting when he found out about our investigation."

Aurora patted her silken blond hair back into place. She had dropped all pretense of mourning the beast she'd been married to, and was in a lovely royal-blue day dress. People talked that it had only been eight months since her husband's death, but she'd had enough of black and brown frocks. "Do you think you would like to marry him, Faith? I mean, despite his reluctance to tell you what he was doing all those years out of the country? We still know almost nothing about his character, beyond the fact that he seems nice on the surface."

"No," Faith answered quickly. "I won't marry him under the current circumstances."

Mercy laughed and pushed her spectacles up on her nose. "It seems the two of you are in agreement then." She sobered. "There would be some scandal if you called off without an offer from another gentleman, but we can survive a bit of gossip. You would recover."

Frustrated, Faith plucked at the end of her ruffled sleeve. "I don't like the way any of this has gone. I wanted to know him before I married him or rid myself of him. Is that so much to ask?" She hopped up from the settee and paced to the window.

The parlor faced the street, and the rainy day had kept most people inside. Still, there were a few hearty souls trudging down West Lane with their umbrellas held high. The weather was a reflection of the disaster she'd made of her life.

"What do you want?" Rhys asked.

Turning, Faith faced her closest friends. They would do anything for her and she would do the same. All four women had been sent away to finishing school in Lucerne due to bad behavior, and the three years growing into young ladies had been a pleasure because of the friendship they'd forged. Nothing would ever separate them; not marriage nor distance. They were the Wallflowers of West Lane. It had been the luckiest day in Faith's life when she met these three on the way to Switzerland. She shuddered when she imagined having to survive the Wormbattle School for Young Ladies on her own.

"If I could just get him to listen, really listen. I mean, without all the other noise about what we've said and done. I want him to tell me what kind of man he is and answer some basic questions about his life. I want to tell him what I want from life and have him hear me. I know men don't care what women want, but I refuse to be a doormat." Faith's breath had sped up with her desires. She calmed. "If I could take him away somewhere, where he would be forced to listen—" She laughed. "I sound like a madwoman." Mercy tapped her chin. "No. A bit desperate, but not mad. How could we convince the Duke of Breckenridge to go somewhere private, out of the city, where you might talk to him uninterrupted for a few days?"

Faith threw up her hands. Maybe there had been a better way to handle this arranged marriage her mother had devised, but she still couldn't think of how. If only Nicholas had simply answered some questions rather than remaining silent on every subject in his past. "It's impossible."

"Not necessarily." Rhys sat forward from where he had been ensconced in an oversized chair with Poppy.

Tugging on his shoulder, Poppy forced him to face her. "What's going on in that head of yours, husband?"

"A bit of a scheme is all."

Aurora narrowed her eyes and rubbed her palms together. "What kind of scheme?"

Unfolding from the chaise, Mercy rose up to her full height and went to Faith by the window. "Come sit and let's figure this out." She wrapped her arm around Faith's shoulders and coaxed her back to the grouping of seats set up for conversation.

Sitting on the chaise with Mercy, Faith sighed. "What did you have in mind, Rhys?"

"Well, Poppy tells me that the best way to judge a man's character is to see how he treats servants and animals," Rhys said.

Poppy grinned wide. "I had no idea you were even listening to me back before we liked each other."

The two had been at odds for years before they fell in love. Looking at them now, one would think they had always been together.

He kissed Poppy's cheek. "I always listen, my love."

Faith couldn't help rolling her eyes. "What Poppy said is true. A man who is cruel to people in his employ, or animals, is not to be trusted."

"It's important to know if he has a temper as well." Aurora's previous playfulness was gone.

Mercy said, "A temper merely means he is passionate. It is whether that temper is violent and out of his control that is important."

Aurora nodded. "Agreed."

Stroking his chin, Rhys considered the qualifications. "A gentleman is trained to hide many things in public. If you want to find out the kind of man he really is, you will have to be alone with him and put him in a difficult situation. Are you willing to go that far, Faith?"

It was outrageous to spend time alone with a man, no matter the situation. To not have a chaperone would ruin her reputation. However, marrying a man whose character was a mystery was far more dangerous, as Aurora had shown them all. Desperate for some way to resolve the matter, Faith asked, "How do we get Nicholas to go along with this?"

"He won't," Rhys said. "We would have to trick him and trap him somewhere."

"Good Lord," Poppy screeched. "You were incensed by the idea of spying on him only last spring, and now you want to lure him into a trap?"

"I don't see how else Faith will be able to find out what she wants to know." Rhys stood and rubbed his chin while pacing the rug.

Aurora tapped her fingers on her knee. "Do you think Mr. Arafa might be of some help?"

"Would he help?" Mercy's eyes were wide behind her spectacles.

Rhys considered it.

Poppy said, "He might. He admires Faith and thinks her a good match for his friend. Also, he feels bad for having told Nicholas about our spying. He didn't expect him to react so intensely."

"Poppy and I will go and speak to him and see what he thinks." Rhys returned to his seat. "You'll need to find an animal of some kind to test him with."

Mercy clapped. "The downstairs maid, Kathy, just brought in a stray puppy. I'm sure she wouldn't mind your taking over his care."

"That dog is a menace," Aurora said.

A wicked smile lit Mercy's face. "He'll be perfect to test that anger we talked about too."

Faith hadn't heard about the puppy. "I will go and speak to Kathy after tea and meet the puppy."

"This is madness." Faith must have lost her mind to even consider spending time alone with Nicholas.

Rhys shrugged. "If you think it goes too far, Faith, then we'll forget the entire thing."

"I can't live with the current status of things," Faith said. "I need to know if calling off is the right thing to do rather than the only thing to do."

Poppy nodded. "So what we need is a location away from town that we can lure Nick into, and if you are there alone, he would be ungentlemanly to leave you stranded."

"Stranded!" Aurora stood. "You mean we are just going to leave Faith at some strange location and hope the Duke of Breckenridge is a gentleman? We can't just take it on goodwill that he will stay and protect her. He might take her virtue and leave her with no protection. What do we know about him beyond our suspicion that he is a spy?"

Shaking her head, Poppy sat on the edge of her seat. "I don't think so. He is a reasonable man. He was very cordial to Rhys and me when we went to see him after our spying incident was discovered. He wasn't happy with us, but he let us in and spoke to us. He was kind, and I dare say, even friendly."

Rhys nodded. "I'm not sure I would have been so gracious in his shoes."

"But does that mean he won't take advantage of a woman alone in the country?" Aurora wrapped her arms around her middle.

"He does not strike me as a man who would want a woman who was not willing." Rhys's cheeks and neck pinked.

Faith couldn't blame him for being embarrassed when speaking about such a subject with four women. She was certain her own face was berry red. "I'm willing to take the chance. He may have secrets, he may even be working for the government, but I don't believe him a monster, Aurora."

Mercy drew a breath and pulled herself to her full seated height. "Then that's settled. We go on with the madness of finding a country house where we can strand Faith and His Grace for a set period of time. The rest will be up to you, Faith."

A foreboding knot settled in the pit of Faith's stomach. "I think it is the only way to satisfy my sense of right and wrong with regard to Nicholas."

Aurora sat and leaned back against the cushion. "If you are sure, you have my full support, Faith. Should I call for more tea or have we had enough for today?"

"I can't drink another cup." Poppy curled into Rhys's side.

"We should be getting home." Rhys smiled at his wife.

Faith said, "One last thing, and it's regarding Mr. Arafa."

"What about him?" Rhys narrowed his gaze.

Nicholas said something about his being lonely here in England. I thought perhaps when we entertain here at West Lane, we might be inclined to invite him. I like him, and Poppy and Rhys have become good friends with him.

"I have no objections." Aurora smiled. "You three have spoken so much about him and I've only met him once. I would like to get to know him better."

Poppy frowned. "I was disgusted with the others at the dinner party."

Rhys patted her knee. "They are typical hypocrites. They come to his home to wheedle information or money from him, but the color of his skin offends them so much they won't eat his food. It was abominable."

"And you know none of them would dare invite him into their homes." Faith wished she could have slapped Mary Yates and her parents silly.

Aurora sighed. "I can't promise that people within our circle won't behave the same. I can only be sure of those in this room being kind to Mr. Arafa."

"Perhaps that will be enough." Faith hoped it would be.

Chapter 3

Three weeks later
Parvus Castle
Shropshire County, England

By the time Nick arrived at Parvus Castle the light waned in the west. He'd ridden steadily, stopping only at dark, for more than three days after receiving Geb's note of an urgent matter. Geb might have finally gotten him the names and locations of the French spies he'd been researching the past year.

At the front drive, a young boy took Nick's horse to be cared for. There were rarely many servants at the small castle, which was used mainly as a hunting lodge or to get away from life for a while.

Knowing there was no butler, Nick didn't bother to knock. Besides, he was tired and badly in need of a warm fire and a good draught of brandy. He banged open the front door. "Geb!"

Brushing off the snow from his coat, he tossed the wet outerwear on a bench by the door and stomped the mud from his boots.

A shuffle of movement came from the salon.

A white ball of barking fur loped into the foyer and jumped on Nick's legs.

"Who are you?" he asked in a softer voice. "Has Geb gone and gotten himself a puppy?" Nick knelt to scratch behind the pup's ear.

Nick stood, and the puppy continued his happy yipping and followed along as they drew closer to the salon.

"Geb?" Nicholas turned into the salon and froze.

Nick blinked several times as if doing so might erase the vision of Faith sitting in Geb's hunting lodge. She was as lovely as the first time he'd seen her, though less formally attired in a pale green day dress. Several brown curls had escaped and hung around her heart-shaped face.

Gathering his wits, he stepped inside, careful not to stomp on the puppy, who continued his elation. Nick searched for Geb in the large salon before turning back to Faith. "Where is Geb?"

"Mr. Arafa is not here." Her voice was soft and melodious, while she was wide-eyed and clasping her hands so tightly, her knuckles had turned white.

Was she afraid of him?

"What are you doing here, Lady Faith?" Nick loomed over her.

She craned her neck and looked at him. "Mr. Arafa has loaned me the use of this castle for a fortnight."

A level of anger that only Faith could conjure built inside Nick. "Geb sent me a message. He said it was urgent I meet him here immediately."

Standing, she forced him to step back. Though it didn't keep her from having to look up to him. She might be bold, but she was petite. "I'm sorry we were forced to deceive you, Your Grace. It was necessary for you and I to have some time together where you cannot ignore me."

"Are you saying you talked Geb Arafa into deceiving me as well?" Nick continued to blink. He was certain at some point his friend would pop out from behind some door, tell him it was all a bad joke, and explain why Faith was at Parvus.

"It was necessary and he was very kind to comply." She pursed her lips and pulled her clasped hands to just under her ample breasts.

His gaze fell to her splendid décolletage before he could help himself.

Turning away, he stormed to the window. None of this was possible and yet, here she was with no sign of her friends or his. A steady snow had fallen for the past twenty minutes and the ground was coated already. "I can't even imagine how you have coerced my dear friend to go along with your schemes. It is clear that you have powers of persuasion that I have underestimated."

He expected her to appear smug when he turned, but her slumped shoulders and bowed head didn't look pleased with herself. She looked contrite and ashamed. "I wish there had been another way. I tried to speak to you at Mr. Arafa's dinner party, but you wouldn't give me a chance. Besides, I want more than to apologize for spying on you."

What he should have done was leave immediately. Curiosity kept him rooted to the floor near the large window. "What do you want now?" It came out harsher than he intended, but he wasn't sorry. This infernal woman had duped him for the last time. He would go back to London and tell her mother the engagement was off. Let her reputation be damned.

The puppy sat between them and swiveled his gaze back and forth. His black eyes were curious in his puffy white fur. A few black spots on his floppy triangular ears were his only markings.

Stepping closer to him, she met his gaze. "It is what I have always wanted, though I have not gone about it in the best way. I want us to get to know each other and then decide if we might suit. This means you must be willing to tell me something about yourself that has happened in the last five years and lower that mask you insist on wearing."

The idea that she saw he wore a mask disturbed him. It was some comfort that she couldn't see through it. Yet that, too, put a knot of unease deep in his belly. This woman would be the death of him. "I have no intention of marrying a woman whom I cannot trust. You have gone out of your way to take that trust and batter it to a pulp. You have shown your character to be sneaky, underhanded, and ruthless. Why would I want to tell you anything?"

Sorrow welled in her golden eyes before she could mask the emotion.

Despite his dislike of the woman, and his frustration over his attraction to her, he wished he could take back the words that hurt her. Damn it all.

She returned to her seat, picked up the book on the table, and schooled her features to reveal nothing more. "I see. Then I suppose you will wait out this storm and be on your way, Your Grace."

The dog trotted over and lay down on her feet.

Looking out at the snow, Nick sighed. He couldn't leave until the snow stopped. Perhaps by morning, the weather would clear. Surely, he could survive one night with Faith Landon without succumbing to whatever spell she put on men like Geb. He sat in the wingback chair across from her. Noting the book, he asked, "You read Descartes?"

"I read everything." Her chest lifted and fell in a deep breath that distracted him from his stance of not liking her.

It really was unfair that she should be so impossible yet so beautiful.

"What is the dog's name?" He snapped his fingers and the ball of fur loped over.

She lowered the book. "Rumpelstiltskin, but I just call him Rumple."

Lifting Rumple into his lap, he gave the puppy a scratch behind the ears. "I suppose that means you're a bit of a troublemaker and always up to mischief."

Rumple cuddled in closer and exposed his belly for more attention.

"You like dogs." A hint of a smile tugged at her full red lips.

He shrugged and thought of the hunting dogs, Milo and Merry, that he'd grown up with. "I like well-behaved dogs that have a purpose."

Once again Rumple's attention was drawn from one to the other.

Eyes narrowed, whatever she was about to say, she abandoned. Her expression changed to serene indifference. "Shall I call for tea or do you need to rest before dinner?"

He'd not heard a footstep or any indication that whoever was chaperoning her was about to join them. The castle was silent save for Rumple, who whined as he chewed on Nick's hand. "Who is here with you?"

A warm blush bloomed on her cheeks. "No one."

Confused, Nick must have misunderstood. "What do you mean? How did you get here?"

"Rhys and Poppy brought me, but they have gone to their country home a few days' ride from here. I have a lady's maid and there is a cook. The castle has a young boy acting as the groom, whom you probably saw when you rode up. Jamie also serves as the houseboy. I'm told there is a groundskeeper, but I've yet to see him."

"You must be mad to come here by yourself. You'll be ruined. Have you no care for your reputation?" It was not to be believed that a member of the ton would put herself in a situation where she was alone with a man not her husband. "People will think you a tramp."

She cocked her pretty head. "Is that what you think?"

Putting the puppy on the floor, he stood. "I don't know what to think. You never do what a proper young lady should."

"Don't I?" Placing Descartes on the table, she folded her hands in her lap and studied him.

"No. Any other woman of your station, when told they are to marry a duke, would simper and fawn over her intended. You acted as if I'd handed you down a death sentence."

"Is simpering and fawning something you are fond of?" She kept her voice even, but a spark of anger flashed in her golden eyes.

He couldn't help it, he loved to see her emotions fired up. "When I introduced myself at that ball last spring, you scolded me for introducing myself, then acted bored when we danced. When I wouldn't answer your inappropriate questions, you became angry and stalked off."

"You didn't answer my question."

So drawn in by her growing temper and how well she held it in check, he'd forgotten for the moment what she'd asked. Retracing the conversation, he remembered. "Simpering and fawning...Not particularly."

"Then why would you want me to have done so?"

"I didn't. I don't." She had trapped him with his own words. "I just meant you don't respond to things in a common way."

"And you don't like that? You want me to be like the rest of society and conform to expected behavior?" She closed her eyes for a moment, then stared down at the rug, thinking the matter over. "It isn't likely that I could do that even if I wanted to."

"That is not what I want. I don't want anything. It is merely an observation."

"I see." She lifted Rumple, who curled onto her lap and closed his eyes.

"Why wouldn't you just call off and be done with me, Faith? Why go to all this trouble and possible disaster for a man you don't like?"

A girl of perhaps sixteen, with brown eyes and light brown hair poking out from under a white cap, stepped into the room. She crossed to the table and picked up the tea tray. "Shall I fetch more tea for the gentleman, my lady?"

Faith looked at him.

He shook his head.

"No, Thea. You probably have enough to do getting dinner prepared. It seems His Grace is not hungry."

Thea's eyes went wide and she made an awkward curtsy before rushing out of the room.

"I heard the old cook retired," Nick said. "Just as well. Hopefully that little girl won't poison us."

Faith idly scratched Rumple behind the ears while the puppy slept. "I hadn't realized you'd been here at Parvus Castle before."

He hated himself for being jealous of the mutt on her lap. He longed to rest his head against those thighs and have her thread her fingers through his hair. Wishing he could dismiss his desires wouldn't make it so. He shook away the thoughts and focused on what she said. "Geb uses it as a hunting cabin. We have come here several times to get away."

"You have known Mr. Arafa a long time?"

"Are you interrogating me again, Lady Faith?" The hair on his arms prickled with the old feeling of an adversary trying to get the better of him.

She put the dog in the crook of her arm and stood. "I was trying to have a conversation with you, Your Grace. However, it is clear that is not possible currently. I will see you at dinner."

Nick watched her stride out of the salon. Her head high and shoulders back like a queen.

The woman was mad to have arranged this, and he was insane to still be standing on the property.

He couldn't just leave her alone with the storm, and he would be a fool to leave in the midst of such weather. This early snow was damned inconvenient.

Pulling on his coat and hat, he went in search of the one person on the property who might actually know what was going on. At the back of the small wilderness behind Parvus, a shed had been converted years ago for the groundskeeper.

Nick pounded on the door and tucked his hands under his arms. The temperature was dropping as night fell. "MacGruder, you in there?"

The door flew open. "There's no need to break the door in. I'm not twenty, you know. It takes a minute to get out of the chair at my age."

Jacob MacGruder had been at Parvus since he was a boy, and fifty or more winters had passed since them. His leathery skin was scarred and marked by time and his bony hands swelled at the knuckles. The scraps of hair on his head had gone full white, but his steel-blue eyes were still sharp and fierce.

"I thought you might have gone deaf in the years since I last saw you."

MacGruder grunted. "I thought you might have got yourself killed with that nonsense on the Continent, but Master Arafa assured me you were still alive. Come in before you freeze me to death."

Doing as he was told, Nick kicked the snow from his boots and hung his overcoat on a rusted hook near the door.

A fire burned in the rough hearth and soon dispelled the cold from the opened door.

"The master sent a letter that you would be joining the little miss. I thought I'd seen everything, but this is something new. You being courted by a fine lady like that." McGruder's laugh was like grated steel.

"Is that what she's doing?" The idea that Faith would try to woo him, sent a pleasant thrill through him despite his decision to be done with her.

MacGruder shrugged. "The master just said the lady had need of Parvus, and I was to see that no harm came to her. He said you would be joining her and would behave like a gentleman. Since Cookie left, there's been little good food to be had."

"Cook was a menace in the kitchen. She could kill hogs with the swill she served." Cringing at the memory of the terrible food from past visits, Nick sat on a low stool near the fire. "What else did my friend say in that letter?"

A shrug. "That the girl, Thea, would cook, and the boy, Jamie, would help out where needed. She's a fair cook. I sampled the fare yesterday and again at breakfast. I'm happy to not have to cook for myself."

"Why am I here?" Nick said it mostly to himself, but needed to know.

"The little lady wanted you here, so you're here. The master must think highly of her to have gone along. Caught a glimpse of her when she arrived with her friends. She's a pretty little thing. Only brought one small trunk and a few books with her. Sensible that. Why did she need to lure you here, is what I want to know."

"She didn't." Nick ran his hands through his cropped hair.

"You'll be leaving after the snow blows through then." There was a knowing lilt to MacGruder's tone.

Nick stood and walked to the other side of the one-room residence. A bed was half hidden by curtains in one corner and the other had a small stove and sink with one cupboard. He stood by the sink and stared out the small window into the snow. "If I leave, she'll be here alone until her friends can be contacted and return for her. That could be a week's time at least."

"She's a grown woman. I'm sure she can manage with a handful of servants for a few days. If something happens, we'll send for the magistrate. He could be here in two days." MacGruder peered over his shoulder at Nick.

Shaking his head, Nick couldn't figure out how she had such a hold on him. She'd been rude when he'd first met her, and haughty at times. Then she'd sent her Wallflower friends to spy on him. She always asked questions he wouldn't answer and she never acted like he was a duke. "I thought all women wanted to marry a duke."

"But not this one?" MacGruder was far too intuitive.

"I don't know. It seems she wants to know the man behind the title." His stomach growled and he regretted turning down tea, which likely would have come with biscuits at least.

"I'm liking her more and more."

"My life is not for public display." Nick slammed his hand on the edge of the sink, cutting the palm. Blood seeped from the tiny wound.

MacGruder got up much faster than one would have thought possible. He grabbed a towel from the cupboard and handed it to Nick. "Don't drip blood on my floor."

Nick pressed the cut and held tight.

"It seems to me"—MacGruder paused—"you'll have to trust the woman you intend to marry, or why bother? If you just intend to marry someone to breed sons for you, you've picked the wrong lady. Now, that's just my opinion."

"Once she finds out the kind of man I really am, she'll wish she had run from the start." Wishing he could change the past wouldn't make it so.

Deep creases marked MacGruder's frown. "You did what needed doing. No one likes the memory of war, but many of us live with it just the same."

The old groundskeeper had been a batman in his youth, and served several officers before being wounded and returning home.

"She'd be better off with some simple gentleman, with little to regret besides a bad gambling habit." Nick wished it wasn't true, but his past always came back to haunt him.

"Best to let the lady decide if that's the case. Women have a sense about such things." MacGruder ambled toward the door and opened it. "You'd better get yourself back to the house before you miss dinner. Maybe clean up some too. You smell like a horse."

Nick laughed. "Glad you're still alive, old man."

Raising a brow, MacGruder said, "I imagine my time will come soon enough. Now you go and be nice to that lady. She's gone to a lot of trouble to get you here. The least you can do is listen to what she has to say."

Nick rushed through the snow. Why had she gone to all this trouble? Perhaps he should take MacGruder's advice and listen. Maybe he could forget his past and be the kind of man a woman like Faith needed.

Chapter 4

It was full dark and the snow still fell steadily. Faith waited in the salon, but hadn't seen Nick since walking out on him a few hours earlier. She shouldn't have lost her temper. It had been a perfect opportunity to ask questions, but he was so stubborn.

She sipped a sherry, but she had never cared for the drink. She only took a glass because it was expected. It was the reason she did a lot of things in her daily life, to fit in and be accepted. She took no pleasure in most of them.

Tricking Nicholas into meeting her at Parvus Castle was another matter. She felt wicked and right for her attempt to find out if they suited. Sighing at how backward her thoughts were, she took another sip of sherry.

Since there was the probability that Nicholas would leave as soon as the storm passed, Faith had dressed in her finest gown for dinner. She'd not packed a great many formal clothes, but the shimmering gold silk gown matched her eyes and showed her figure to its best advantage. She'd forgone any lace around the low neckline in favor of letting her breasts push up in what she hoped was an enticing way.

Of course, she'd been sitting with her back straight and her chin arched up toward the fire for fifteen minutes, waiting. The pose had her back and neck aching, and Nicholas had not shown himself.

Putting down the crystal glass, she pressed her hands into the deep red cushion of the settee and arched until the pain in her lower back lessened. Closing her eyes with the pleasure of releasing stiff muscles, she sighed.

A low moan from the doorway startled her eyes open.

In a black suit with a crisp white shirt and cravat, Nicholas stood just inside the room, his expression so calm and indifferent that Faith must have imagined the sound of a moment before.

She stood and curtsied. "Good evening, Your Grace."

"Lady Faith." He bowed. "I hope you haven't been waiting long."

"Not long," she said.

A white bandage wrapped his hand. "Have you injured yourself?" she asked.

He shrugged. "Small penance for my bad temper. It's little more than a scratch."

Curious, but respectful of his obvious desire to downplay his injury, she asked, "Did you find something to entertain you this afternoon?"

He crossed to the cart in the corner, where brandy and sherry had been set out with several glasses. He poured himself a glass of brandy. "I visited with the groundskeeper. I have known him for several years and he is an interesting character."

Faith had yet to meet Mr. MacGruder, but she would make a point to seek him out as soon as the weather improved. Perhaps he could lend some insight into her duke's disposition. Though, the fact that a duke would go to visit one of the servants was a good sign. "I have not had the pleasure of meeting him as yet."

"MacGruder was impressed that you traveled with only one small trunk." Nicholas smiled to devastating effect.

Steeling her heart against the effects of his good looks, Faith took a breath. "I am not as needy as some ladies, but I am not without the need of creature comforts. I brought what was necessary for my own happiness."

She thought he might ask what things she'd brought, but he sipped his brandy and considered her without remark.

"Cook tells me dinner will be ready shortly."

With a nod, he sat across from her. He always chose the seat farthest from her, as if she might give him the plague. "I'm curious to see if she is a better cook than the last. MacGruder thinks so, but he is happy to leave the responsibility of feeding himself to another, regardless of the palatability of the fare."

Faith laughed. He'd made a joke, an actual joke. Perhaps that was a step in the right direction. "We shall see."

"Is the sherry not to your liking?" He gave a nod toward her abandoned glass.

If she expected him to tell the truth, she would have to do the same. "I do not care for sherry."

"Then why did you pour it?" He lifted both brows.

Taking a deep breath, she thought of how best to answer without sounding like a ninny. "Young ladies are supposed to enjoy a sherry."

Nicholas leaned forward. "And…" he prompted.

"And I try to fit into society's guidelines at least on the surface." She did sound like an idiot.

"Luring me here was not very conformist." He relaxed against the wingback chair's cream damask and watched her with the intensity of a hawk summing up his prey.

Her heart pounded and she pressed on. "No. That is the real me pushing her way through. Drinking sherry and being polite to people like Mary Yates is the person my parents sent me away to school to become. I want to make them happy, so I try to appear as the daughter they wished for."

It was impossible to tell if he was frowning because of what she revealed or for some other reason.

Jamie popped his head in the door. His freckled face was washed clean and he'd put on a brown jacket. His dusty brown hair was still mussed and long, but he smiled and tugged on his new finery. "Dinner is served."

Standing, Faith smiled at the boy, who puffed out his chest and grinned. "Well done, Jamie."

Jamie's chest puffed up even more and he stood straighter.

Offering his arm, Nicholas led them across to the dining room. He tousled Jamie's hair as they passed the salon door and smiled warmly at the child.

"I've taken Rumple to the kitchen so he won't be botherin' you while you eat."

"That was very thoughtful of you, Jamie." Faith delighted in the youth and enthusiasm of both Jamie and Thea. It was nice to be around people unwearied by life.

The table had been set for two, with one place setting at the head and another to the right.

Nicholas stopped a few feet away from the settings. "This is your party, Lady Faith. Which would you prefer?"

She pointed to the chair on the right. "This will do, Your Grace."

He held out the chair and leaned in as she sat. "Perhaps we might dispense with the formal titles since we are alone here at Parvus?"

Once he was seated, she settled her pulse and asked, "What would you prefer to be called?"

"Nick would do nicely, if you don't find the notion too upsetting."

Thea arrived with a tray, which she placed on the sideboard. Then one at a time she served them each a bowl of soup that smelled divine. The aroma of spices and rich meats filled the dining room.

Nick's stomach rumbled loudly. He laughed. "I believe I regret not accepting your offer of tea this afternoon, but now that I see this, Cook, I'm glad I waited. It smells delicious."

Blushing, Thea made a quick curtsy and rushed from the dining room.

The soup tasted as good as it smelled. The bits of meat might have been venison, but they were tender and must have been cooked for hours to have created the rich warm flavors along with salt and thyme.

"This is delicious," Faith said.

Nick's eyes were filled with the delight of the rapturous soup. "I don't know that I've ever had better."

"Then Thea's cooking is superior to the cook who retired?" She couldn't help her joy at seeing him so pleased with the food. It made her wish she had cooked it herself. It was strange to suddenly want to please him, or anyone beyond her parents.

"Compared to this, Cookie's offerings cannot even be called food, Lady Faith." He chuckled and took another spoonful of the soup.

A warmth flushed her cheeks at the reminder of his offer to use familiar names and the fact that the food had made her forget to accept his offer. "Faith. You may call me Faith."

The rest of the meal was equally scrumptious. It was so good, Faith's plan to learn more about Nick had gone forgotten until a lovely pudding of plums and honey was set before them. "I suppose I should apologize for luring you here?"

With his spoon halfway to his mouth, he stopped. "Only if you are sorry, and I think you may have already done so."

She couldn't look away from the wonder on his face as he ate the warm, sweet confection. The sight tightened things inside Faith that she hadn't known existed. "You were too angry then. I thought perhaps now, you might accept my regrets and perhaps an offer of friendship to begin again?"

Putting down his spoon, he stared a long moment. "You want us to be friends?"

"It would be a start." It was hard to breathe when he gave her his full attention. Miss Agatha Wormbattle had always warned her to be careful what she wished for, and finally she understood what her old schoolmistress was talking about. Nick's full regard was daunting and churned up desires she'd not considered.

"Tell me why you arranged all of this. And not some pretty story you use to make this seem normal. The real reason." He folded his long elegant fingers together and laid them on the edge of the table. Relaxed, but ready to flee at any moment. Nick was like a tiger ready to do whatever was necessary for his survival.

Setting her spoon on the table, Faith considered his question. He already knew more about her than she knew of him. She'd given much away when she told him about the sherry. "I'll tell you anything you want to know, but you must promise to answer my questions as well."

The corners of his sensual mouth turned down and he focused on his hands for a long moment. "There are things about me and my past that are best left in shadow, Faith."

It was more than he'd ever shared before. At least he wasn't pretending his past was that of a normal sedentary duke of the realm. "I can see where this might be difficult for you. Perhaps you should answer any difficult questions honestly but simply. I can wait for details for when you and I have established some trust."

Lifting his head, he met her stare. His dark lashes made the blue of his eyes deeper, and emotions made them more intense. "Tell me why you brought me here, and then I shall decide if I wish to play your game of questions and answers."

She supposed someone would have to give a little, and it should be her since she had tricked and manipulated him. "I can be quite stubborn."

"Is that your response?" He rolled his eyes.

"No. I'm only saying that my stubborn tendencies get in the way of good behavior at times. When my mother told me I was to marry a duke, I should have been elated, but I knew nothing about you. She had been communicating for months and not mentioned anything about it. Then suddenly you were in London and we were to marry." Faith wasn't sure how to continue.

"Do you not wish to marry?"

"I would like to have a family."

He hesitated. "Was there something about me you disliked?"

"Not in the way you think. This is a long story, Nick. Perhaps we should return to the salon." Her stomach knotted at the memories and confidences she was about to relate.

Rising, he gave an encouraging smile before helping her out of her chair. They walked together into the salon and Faith sat near the fire. The storm still raged and left the castle cold and damp. Jamie had built a fine blaze and she was glad to rub the chill out of her arms.

Nick sat in the chair opposite and waited.

Rumple bounded into the salon, barking and tail-wagging.

Jane, the lady's maid Faith had brought from West Lane, rushed in after. "I'm sorry, my lady. He got out of the kitchen and wouldn't stop hunting for you."

The ball of fluffy puppy jumped into Faith's lap and she laughed, avoiding his enthusiastic kisses. "It's all right, Jane. Leave him here. I'll take him up to bed with me."

Jane hesitated. "I had hoped to put the boy to bed. He's quite exhausted."

Nick said, "I will see the pup has his time outside before we retire."

"Thank you, Your Grace. If you need anything, I will be helping Cook in the kitchen and to settle the house for the night."

"We're fine, Jane. Thank you." Faith waited until her maid fled before she settled into scratching Rumple's ears and returned her attention to the past.

"To give you the honest answer you deserve, I have to tell you things that are not really my place to divulge. I will ask that you keep these confidences to yourself." Faith worried over the wisdom of trusting a man who kept his own life under such a tight veil, but there was no way to be honest and not tell him everything. If she only told her part of the story, he would never understand.

"Secrets are something I am quite good at keeping, Faith." He had the good grace to give her a brief smile.

"You already know that my friends—Mercy, Poppy, and Aurora—and I all went to the Wormbattle School for Young Ladies in Switzerland. It's an unusual way to educate a daughter and it was meant as a punishment for my willful behavior as a girl. It turned out to be the best three years of my life. When I met those three, everything fell into place. I was happy.

"Aurora had a letter in our final weeks at school. Her father had arranged for her to marry the Earl of Radcliff. We were all very excited about the first of our group to get married and it was a lively ride home."

Nick observed her intently as she told her story. She couldn't tell if he was picking apart her story or just curious.

She drew in a long breath and steadied her heart. Her movement gave the tired pup in her lap cause to wiggle about, so she placed him on the floor near her feet. He settled on his paws with a yawn. Faith brushed the fur from her skirt. "Within a fortnight, Aurora was married. A month later, we all knew what a terrible mistake it had been. That was the first time Bertram Sherbourn struck Aurora. It was a battered wrist and a bruise under her left eye. She was embarrassed and blamed herself for his bad behavior.

"The rest of us, blamed him. We couldn't protect her, and the beatings grew worse. Bertram drank most of the time and gambled incessantly. Those hobbies took him out of the house, for which we were grateful.

Then he would come home and rape his wife and beat her bloody. There was no way to stop it and all we could do was put her back together and call the doctor when needed."

"That animal should have been horsewhipped," Nick mumbled, his fists clenched on his thighs.

"Yes, well, men can get away with a great deal when a wife is considered property and the character of the man leads him to believe that is all she is." Faith had to take several breaths to gain control of her temper. She'd cried out all her tears for Aurora over the three years of her marriage; Faith had no more on that subject.

Nick remained silent and attentive, seeming to understand she needed a moment to gather her wits before she could continue.

"When that monster died last year, we all relaxed for the first time since their wedding. Aurora had survived, at least in body. We also made a pact that no other Wallflower would suffer her same fate."

He sighed. "I can see how your mother arranging a marriage to a man you'd never met might have caused you some trepidation. I would never hit a woman." His face registered something ugly. Some memory he'd rather not have conjured. "At least as long as she was not trying to do me harm."

"There is more than one way to destroy a person, Nick. We wanted to know what kind of a man you are, and you foiled our plans at every turn. All I know about you is that your parents are both dead and you spent most of your childhood fishing and hunting at your estate in Hertfordshire and you attended Eton."

He nodded. "That is a sad story and explains why you, Poppy, and Rhys investigated me, but it doesn't quite answer my question of why you brought me here."

"That is where my stubborn streak comes in. If I called off, Mother would be furious and possibly never forgive me. Father already thinks me worthless, so his anger is not relevant. When you discovered our plan to ferret you out, I was just starting to like you. I was angry you left Mother's house party for some bit of business that you were unwilling to even hint at. When you became so enraged over our investigation and wanted me to call off, it showed a gentlemanly quality. You could have ended things and ruined me, but after all these months, you didn't, and I'm too stubborn to end the engagement without finding out who you are."

His voice was low and thoughtful. "And if you find out I'm more monster than man?"

"Are you?" Heart lodged in her throat, the words croaked out.

Blowing out a long breath, Nick deflated. "I have things in my past that might make you think so."

"Like a woman you might have struck who was trying to do you harm?" She repeated back what he'd said and wondered if he'd meant to tell her that much.

A sad smile didn't touch his eyes. "My sins are far worse than that, Faith. You might be better off with some nice viscount or earl who will cover you in silks and speak of fashion and the goings-on at court."

"If that is so, why did you arrange a marriage to me, with Mother?" Fear coursed through Faith. She didn't know if she was afraid of him or afraid losing him would be a mistake. Something about Nicholas Ellsworth drew her in and terrified her at the same time.

"I needed a wife. You had gone to the Wormbattle School, and I thought you might be unconventional. I hate the idea of a wife who is like every other dimwitted debutante in London. Your mother's letters were very persistent. I thought you had written some of them and she had only posted them. I'm somewhat embarrassed to admit that now."

"Mother must be quite desperate to marry me off. I'm sorry that she misled you. I never saw those letters and knew nothing of yours until a week before we met at the ball." Chest tight, she said, "If you still want me to end our betrothal when you leave here tomorrow, I will write a letter to that effect. Then if you would be kind enough to let Rhys and Poppy know to come and fetch me, this will be over for you."

"Will it be over for you as well?" He sat on the edge of the chair like he might leap up at any moment.

"You shouldn't trouble yourself about me. This was all a terrible, foolish mistake. It was unfair of me to try to drag information from you, which you do not wish to share. My stupid need to please my parents kept me from refusing you from the start, and then my curiosity and attraction muddied the waters. I got so caught up in finding out who you are, I mistreated you. For that I am truly sorry." Faith rose to say good night. The exhausted pup gazed up at them, sad faced.

Jumping to his feet, Nick met her between the two chairs. "If you are leaving because the idea of my jaded past frightens you, I understand. If you wish to call off to save yourself from a man whom you cannot like, this too I can accept." He ran his hand from her shoulder to her elbow as light as a butterfly's wing. "However, if you are leaving because you think I dislike you, or that I am still angry, I would beg you to stay."

Rumple jumped up to see what the fuss was about and kept close to Faith.

Faith struggled to draw breath. Nick's closeness made her head spin and her stomach quiver in a most pleasant way. "I'm not afraid of you, Nick." "Good." His smile was sweet, though sadness still touched his eyes. "Because I would never harm you, Faith."

She wanted to seem worldly, but her voice quivered. "If I stay, I'm going to ask you questions you won't want to answer."

"I know." He held her elbow with the lightest touch and his thumb caressed the sensitive inside skin.

Longing for more of his touch, she cupped his cheek. "Will you tell me about your past?"

"Probably not, but that doesn't mean I won't tell you about myself." He chuckled.

Maybe it would be enough.

Chapter 5

Nick was a complete fool. He'd been so angry when he'd found Faith alone at Parvus, he nearly road out into the storm. Sitting with her in the salon and hearing why she had done it all, he longed for more time with her.

She sighed. "Perhaps you might tell me what you plan to do with your time now that you have returned to London?"

Lord, she was a better diplomat than many in the service whom he'd known. "I have several investments that have gone unattended during my absence. I've spent the past few months sorting through papers and studying accounts."

"Will you be staying in England, or do you plan to travel again?" Faith kept her tone steady, but her eyes shone with intelligence and a scheme.

Knowing she was trying a new way to discover his past, he still couldn't muster any animosity. Her persistence was amusing and oddly endearing. "If things remain calm on the Continent, I was considering a trip next year to see if my investors have survived."

"Wouldn't penning a letter be easier?" Her gaze was shrewd.

"Perhaps." He laughed. "But not as much fun."

Faith nibbled on her thumbnail and narrowed her eyes. "I have surmised through my investigation that you were in France on behalf of the Crown. Can you at least confirm that?"

It was a slippery business to give half information. Still, he didn't wish to lie and he hated the idea of ending the evening. "My capacity was unofficial."

She stared him down, her lips twisting unhappily. "The Wallflowers and I have further speculated that you worked in some kind of espionage. It would explain your reluctance to impart *any information*." When he didn't react she continued. "The real problem is not knowing on behalf of which government you worked. I can wish it was our own Crown, but that does not mean that was the case. Are you an English patriot, Nick?" His heart pounded. What a clever woman she was. She and her Wallflower friends had learned or assumed a great deal. Now she asked a question that he could answer without lying. "I am a great patriot to the country of my birth."

She cocked her head. "Were you born in England?"

A guffaw overcame him. "I was. In Hertfordshire, to be specific."

"Well, that is good news. Can you tell me one thing you did while serving the Crown?"

"There is a great deal of assumption lining your question, Faith." He steadied his breath. Instinct told him to run, fight, or hide when faced with an interrogation.

"Perhaps, but my question stands." She was even more lovely when she smiled.

He shifted forward in his chair and lowered his voice. "Not much of what I did while abroad fills me with pride."

Following his lead, she sat forward too. It brought them close enough to touch, but she didn't reach out for him. "Was it all bad? Was there not one thing you are proud of?"

It was painful how fervently he desired her touch, but he would not take what was not offered. She deserved better than him, he knew. Perhaps it was that fact that had sent him into such a rage over her spying on him.

"You will not answer?" Deep sorrow in her eyes, melted his resistance.

Searching through the plunder of his memories, he grasped for a tale he wouldn't be ashamed to tell her. "There was an abbey set afire in a small French village. The nuns and several orphans were trapped inside. I remember the smoke thick and choking as it poured from every window. Three nuns yelling, in French, from a third-floor balcony were surrounded by six crying girls. People ran in every direction to avoid falling embers as the roof caught fire.

"I thought of my assignment, and the consequences of being late or failing altogether. I knew I would never live with myself if I didn't try to help them. In the stables I found a length of rope and draped it over my neck and one arm. The mortar was old around sharp gray stone. I dug my fingers into the crevices and scaled up the building.

"Once inside, the heat bombarded me. I tied off the rope to the balcony rail and a metal sconce embedded in the mortar near the door. I told the nuns to pray it would hold. Two at a time, the girls wrapped their arms around my neck and I climbed down with them. One nun ventured down on her own. I went back and took one more.

"My energy spent, I could hardly stand, let alone go back for the last nun. Yet I gripped the rope. A farm boy of maybe eighteen, took the line from my hand and climbed to rescue the final nun." He could still feel the pain of his overextended lungs. "The Spanish abbess had been killed and the building set afire by French troops as an example of what happens to traitors. The boy and I hid the nuns and their wards in the woods until the French army moved on."

She wiped a tear from her cheek. "You were a hero."

"Not to my superiors, who chided me for missing my..." He hesitated. "Appointment."

With a strong touch, she reached out and clasped his hand. "To three nuns and six children who were innocent, that day you were their hero."

"I suppose that is something." He held tight to her small, delicate hand.

"I think it is everything." Faith shivered, turned her head, and looked out the window.

"What is it?" He followed her gaze, but saw nothing but snow and darkness.

"I suppose it's nothing, but I've lately had the strangest feeling someone is watching me. I felt it first when we were in the garden at Mr. Arafa's home, then several times in London the week that followed, and just now." Faith rose and walked to the window before tugging the drapes closed.

Nick pulled the cord for Jamie, but at the late hour the boy was already in bed and Thea poked her head in the door. "Yes, Your Grace."

"Can you check all the doors and see they are bolted for the night?" It was probably nothing, but in his experience, it was better to err on the side of caution.

Thea's eyes were wide, but she nodded and rushed to do as he said.

Alone again, Nick walked to Faith but didn't touch her. She had gotten under his skin and he didn't know how he was going to walk away. Even knowing she'd be better off without him, he wanted her. "It's probably nothing, Faith."

She drew a shaky breath. "You're right, of course. Just an uncomfortable feeling." Her smile was wide but fake and didn't touch those intriguing eyes that showed a touch of green in the firelight.

Heart pounding, he longed to draw her close and taste her lips. "It's late, my lady. Perhaps you are tired."

With a sad smile, she nodded. "I'll see you in the morning, Nick. Thank you for the talk." Leaning on her tiptoes, she pressed those lips that he coveted to his cheek, then left the salon.

Rumple ambled after her with sleepy eyes.

Unlikely he would find sleep for a long time, Nick poured himself a brandy and stared into the fire until it had nearly burned down.

* * * *

Nick had received a note in Faith's swirling hand to meet her in the hothouse for luncheon. He had not seen her at breakfast, and somehow she had managed to elude him all morning. Parvus was a petite place—in fact, the name meant *small* in Latin—so how she had avoided him was a mystery. His own longing to catch a glimpse of her, was unsettling.

There was a fleeting moment when he'd first woken and saw the blue skies, that he considered getting on his horse and riding toward London. He would stop at Geb's home near the city and give him a severe thrashing for his interference.

Then the memory of Faith touching his hand, and understanding his joy and shame at the abbey, swamped him with warmth. He couldn't leave her alone for so many days until her friends returned. He even considered carrying her to town and putting her in a coach to make her way home. It would be sensible and not ungentlemanly. Still, he could not bring himself to do it.

She had set up this elaborate and unconventional seclusion, and the snowstorm seemed like a sign that perhaps she was in the right. He would take the situation one day at a time.

He rounded the side of the house and found MacGruder placing a bag in his mule-drawn cart.

The groundskeeper took up the reins. "You look better today. Perhaps the country air is good for you."

Nick couldn't help liking the old curmudgeon. "Where are you off to?"

"I go once a month to see my niece in town. Lillian MacGruder is her name, should you need to reach me. Since you look to be staying with Lady Faith, I saw no reason to delay my visit. I'll be gone two or three days. In winter there is little for me to do in the garden and it does my heart good to see Lillian. She makes me a fine tea for my aching joints." He smiled warmly.

"Enjoy your visit," Nick said, and waved him down the lane.

Continuing around the house, he walked down the path to the hothouse. The south-facing wall was almost entirely glass, allowing enough light to warm the inside where plants grew as if it were summer. When he'd been in Spain, he'd loved the warm winter while also missing the cold damp of England and home.

Inside, he followed the sound of shuffling and crystal clinking, past orange trees and other warm-climate plants that had been brought inside to winter over, until he discovered the source.

In a light blue day dress, Faith flitted and fussed with the small round table set in the center of a circle of yellow rose bushes. She was like a bluebell among the thorny bushes, lovely and delicate.

She told Thea, "You have done an outstanding job. Thank you."

The cook spotted him and her eyes went wide as she cleared her throat and blushed.

Faith turned, and a shy grin spread across her face. "I see you found our luncheon spot."

"Your note was very helpful," he said and approached the table. "That will be all, Thea. Thank you."

With a curtsy, Thea took up her skirts and rushed toward the exit.

Faith's smile remained fixed as she poured two glasses of wine. "I hope Mr. Arafa will not mind, but I discovered he has a rather fine wine collection in the cellar. I procured a bottle for our meal."

He accepted the glass of deep red wine from her. "He will probably never notice as he does not drink spirits and only keeps it for friends to enjoy."

A bead of wine lingered on her lip for a moment before the tip of her tongue poked out and licked it away.

Nick's groin tightened at the sight, and he closed his eyes and tasted the rich contraband wine. Lord only knew how Geb managed to procure French wine during the war, but he could get anything he wanted; the political state was unimportant for his purposes.

Once he pulled his desires back in check, Nick opened his eyes and surveyed the table. China and silver had been brought to the hothouse as well as cold chicken, meats, cheeses, and bread. "Have you arranged a picnic, Faith?"

She beamed with pride. "I saw no reason to allow winter to deter me when this oasis exists here at Parvus."

"And I thought Geb had lost his mind when he built this glass monstrosity. I shall have to admit my mistake." Nick stepped closer and pulled out a chair for Faith.

Once she was seated, he rounded the table and sat facing her. "Thank you for making such an effort. I do not deserve such fussing."

She cocked her head. "Of course, you do. We all do, Nick."

"Who fusses over you, Faith?" He'd meant it to tease her, but her sad expression made him immediately regret his question. "I'm sorry. I did not mean to offend you."

Forcing a smile, she shook her head. "I am not offended. It is just that I have not warranted a great deal of pampering in my life. My greatest accomplishment was getting myself sent away to school so as not to embarrass my family beyond repair. I did have a nanny, who was quite good to me."

Her head was cocked in thought, searching for one pleasant memory of her youth that might have been gratifying.

It was ridiculous to want to flay her parents for their negligence, but there it was along with the sudden urge to do something to make Faith feel special.

"One of the things I liked in the description of you, sent by your mother, was the fact that you had been a student at the Wormbattle School. It gave me hope that you were not conventional and might not despair at my manners."

A long sigh deflated her. "And I was horrible from the start."

"I should have waited for a proper introduction. Storming across the ballroom and introducing myself was impertinent. I thought myself above such conventions just because I have a lofty title. You were right to put me in my place. Perhaps if I had acted like a gentleman, we would not have come to such a pass and become estranged." He'd thought about this many times since they first met.

Faith leaned in and placed her wine on the table. "May I tell you a secret?"

"Of course." Curiosity had him bursting.

"I wasn't really put off by your introduction. I was just terrified of marrying a man whom I didn't know. Fear is the one thing that always makes me fail. I wish I was more like Poppy."

Perhaps Faith's notion of getting to know him through his friends wasn't so far-fetched. He helped himself to bread and cheese. "Tell me about your Wallflowers."

She nibbled on the bread. "Wallflowers don't gossip about each other."

"That seems a wise practice for maintaining a friendship, but I'm not asking for gossip, only to know them better and perhaps you as well." He smiled, hoping it would charm her as it had charmed many other women in his past, for both pleasure and business.

"What do you want to know?" She took a chicken leg from the platter and pulled a morsel free to taste.

There was so much attention spent on one small bit of food, he realized this was part of Faith's makeup. She paid close attention to detail in everything. The picnic in the solarium was a great example, and she had done that for him. A spark of delight ignited inside him. "How did you gain the title of Wallflowers?"

She sighed. "Mary Yates."

"What does Miss Yates have to do with it?"

Chewing another bite of chicken, she stared out the wall of windows. The view was full white from the snow covering the garden outside, and the flowers within paled in comparison to the reflecting sun. "Mary Yates was a year ahead of us at the Wormbattle School. She had gathered her friends long before Poppy, Aurora, Mercy, and I ever arrived. They were a vicious pack of girls, embittered by their parents' choice to send them away. I can't really blame them for that. It turned out to be the best thing for me, but it hurt when Father announced he'd had enough of me and was sending me away."

"I can only imagine. Of course, I was sent to Eton, but it is expected for my sex to go away to school, and I went home during breaks." He wanted to reach out and comfort her old hurt, but it wasn't his place, and he didn't want her to stop her story.

"We never had breaks. It was a three-year sentence from the start. Mary resented her situation and seemed determined to make everyone around her suffer her unhappiness. She decided the four of us were the perfect targets since we had just arrived and become such fast friends.

"On occasion Miss Agatha, the headmistress, would arrange a ball with a nearby boys' school, St. Simon's. These balls were hugely anticipated and meant to be both educational and amusing. As soon as the young men arrived, Mary made her rounds, telling everyone that we were bores and they should keep their distance. There were some other cutting remarks, but I'll keep those to myself. Mary has her flaws, but she also has her own set of problems as an adult."

He marveled at how kind she was, even to a woman who did not return that kindness. Mary appeared spoiled and intolerant. Even her beauty had not persuaded Nick to like her.

Faith continued. "As a result, not one boy asked any of us to dance. After the ball, Mary called us Wallflowers."

"I thought you all were fond of the title."

Smiling, Faith was a bright star among the flowers. She shone brighter and with more beauty. "We love it. Even as girls we thought it a fine moniker. We didn't care about balls and silly young men. By the next ball, we were all asked to dance and even had a few proposals before we left school. Of course, none of us took those offers seriously.

"When Aurora married and we began meeting for Tuesday tea at her home on West Lane, we added the address to our name."

It was a show of strength and resilience to turn a hateful moniker into something grand that had held these women together through trial and tribulation. He couldn't help but respect them. "Tell me one thing you admire in each of your friends. Surely that cannot be considered gossip."

A wisp of a smile tugged at her kissable lips. "I will make you an offer, Nick. I will answer your query about my friends and perhaps something about myself, if you will tell me about the woman you may have done harm to."

Suddenly Nick couldn't breathe. "What woman?"

"The one who made you hesitate when you said that you would never strike a woman. I surmise that in certain cases you would harm a member of my sex, and I would like to know precisely what those circumstances are. I realize it is not in your nature to tell anyone anything, but we are alone here. I will not repeat anything you confide to me." She raised one brow and used the corner of her napkin to dab at her lips.

Lord, he longed to kiss those lips until she was too breathless to ask him any more questions and no longer cared about his past. She was right about his nature, but if this was the woman he wanted, he would have to trust her. The notion made him sick to his stomach.

Chapter 6

Faith had played her hand. It was a risk. She didn't know if he wanted her secrets enough to share his own, and she was certain that hers could not compare to whatever he would tell, but she needed to know something before she fell completely in love with him. The danger of that was quite real.

Putting down his bread, he stared at the plate for a long time. "You may regret knowing such things, Faith. I told you that I am not proud of many things I have done."

"I feel you must let me be the judge of that." Her pulse pounded, but she refused to remain silent and risk hating him for his deeds sometime in the future. It was better to know now than regret later.

"MacGruder said much the same thing." He chuckled and gazed up from the table. "Can you promise me that what I tell you will remain between us?"

A swarm of butterflies warred in her belly, but she had to know. "I will keep your confidence."

Cloud cover had rolled in since they'd been eating, and a light snow made a *tink tink* on the sloped glass roof. It wasn't the storm of the day before, but gave the hothouse a more private feel and deadened any noise from outside.

"This is not a pretty story." He took a deep breath, nibbled a bit of meat to stall for time, and met her gaze. "As you have cleverly surmised, I worked for the interests of the Crown while traveling abroad. My journey took me to many places and even back here to England several times over the past five years."

He rubbed the back of his neck and stared out the steamed windows at nothing. "I landed for a time in Vienna. It is a lively town and already possessed by Napoleon by then. I had been in service for a year and thought myself worldly. Unfortunately, I met a woman more worldly than I."

When it appeared he would not go on, Faith asked, "What was her name?"

"Léonie." He breathed it out more than said it. "She was perhaps two or three years older than I, and extremely beautiful. There was a wisdom about her that attracted me as no woman ever had. Of course, I knew I could never marry such a woman, without family or title, but when I told her this, she didn't care."

He laughed. "I thought myself to have found the perfect mistress. We were far from home, where my father could disapprove or my mother would ever hear gossip. Léonie didn't care about marrying a man with a title, and I was infatuated, with the enthusiasm of youth."

Faith wanted to be so sophisticated that she wasn't bothered by Nick's past exploits. She tried to eat some of the lovely meal before them, but her appetite was gone. The thought of him liking or perhaps loving this Léonie stirred jealousy, an emotion she'd never before experienced.

Nick reached across the table and took her hand. "Shall I stop, Faith? You asked for this story, but if you are not comfortable with the telling, I shall desist."

Forcing a smile, she said, "I'm fine. Please, go on."

With a final squeeze, he released her fingers. "Léonie and I were inseparable for many months. It was perfect. Until one day I saw her on the street with a man who looked suspiciously like a French spy I'd been sent to watch. When I confronted her, she became incensed and went into a rage in her native tongue. It was a year later, when I'd mastered the language, that I finally understood the vulgarity she'd spewed that day.

"In my ignorance and desire, I allowed that it was not the same man. We separated for a few days and when we came back together it was filled with forgiveness and passion."

Stomach in a knot, Faith was sorry she'd asked, but she didn't want him to stop. She had to know what happened and get a sense of this man.

Obliviously, Nick continued. "Blissful that our relationship had survived a disagreement, I fell into a deep sleep. An hour later, voices in the common room of our apartments woke me. A chair scraped and a man spoke in hushed tones. My first response was worry for Léonie, but then I heard her voice as well. She didn't sound afraid. Her tone was low, conspiratorial.

"Caught up in my rage, I stupidly flung the bedroom door wide." He shook his head and ran his fingers through his cropped dark-brown hair. "They were only shocked for a moment before one of two men ran at me. I must have been quite a sight, wearing only a nightshirt. I managed to evade the attack, causing him to stumble and crash to the floor. The second man ran out the door. I expected Léonie to do the same, but she stayed. Brandishing a short sword, she charged toward me.

"Gone was the beautiful woman who'd bedded me an hour before. She was transformed into a vicious killer. Her blond hair was wild and loose and her eyes filled with hate. She said, 'Why couldn't you just stay in bed? This would all be over in a few days and you could have walked away.' I had no idea what she meant, but as her blade impaled my chest, it didn't matter."

Faith gasped.

Nick chuckled and rubbed his chest just above his left breast. "I wouldn't have thought her so strong, but she ran me through. An inch lower and I'd have been dead in an instant. The man who'd stumbled when I moved, got up off the floor. The only weapon at my disposal was jutting from my body. I pulled it out and slashed him across the throat. Wide-eyed, he grabbed his gushing throat and collapsed to the floor."

"Léonie wailed out a cry, and I turned toward the sound. She ran directly into her own sword, still in my bloody fist." Head hanging, Nick cradled his face in his hands. "I called the surgeon, but there was nothing to be done for her. She cursed me until she died."

For several seconds, Faith couldn't utter a word. He blamed himself for Léonie's death, but it had not been his fault at all. She had gotten what was coming to her. Fiercely protective, Faith wanted to tell him, but instead asked, "What of your wounds, Nick?"

His eyes burned with regret and self-loathing. "The surgeon mended me and nothing internal was damaged. It was a miracle."

Despite his sarcasm, she agreed with the words. "It was that. Where did you go from Vienna? Surely you didn't stay in the city after such an ordeal."

"Clever girl." He smiled warmly at her. He sipped the wine from a crystal glass. "No. I returned to England to recover right here at Parvus. Geb and I had been friends for six months. It was only meant to be a business arrangement, but there is something about him that makes me trust him above all others. My parents were alerted to my condition and came here for a few weeks. The food nearly killed me, but my wound healed."

"And your heart?" She held her breath.

His long look pierced her soul. "As I said, nothing ever touched my heart. At least, not where Léonie was concerned."

Unable to look away from his eyes the color of the morning sky before the sun was fully risen, she met his stare and prayed she could find her voice again. Clearing her throat, she said, "It must have been terrible for you to be betrayed in such a way."

He shrugged. "An occupational hazard, I'm afraid."

"But you have given up that life, have you not?"

A forlorn smile and he studied at his hands in his lap. "Tell me about these Wallflowers of yours."

She wanted to weep at the sight of such sorrow. Instead she let the joy of her friendships tug her out of her gloom. "You said to tell you one thing I admire in each of them." Faith loved the women she'd met at school. She believed there was the family you were born into and the one you gather for yourself. In the case of the Wallflowers of West Lane, they were as much family to her as her own mother and father, perhaps more so.

"Shall I start with Poppy?" she asked.

"She is the one I know best. I could not dislike her despite my desire to do so after finding out about the spying." He shook his head, a pleasant grin transforming him and making him breathtaking.

"Poppy is fearless. Well, that's not exactly true. She may fear a thing, but she never lets that fear stop her. In fact, I think when she finds herself afraid of something, she immediately sets out to climb that mountain."

Nick offered his hand as he stood. "And what of you, Faith? Are you brave?"

Accepting his offer, she stood and, hand wrapped in his, they walked through the flowers and plants being kept vibrant out of season, for their delight. Several full-grown orange trees had been potted and bore fruit inside the warm environment. "No. I am afraid of many things and not nearly as brave as Poppy. She never conforms to make anyone happy. It is marvelous."

He wrapped her hand around his arm while keeping his hand atop hers. "I think you underestimate yourself. There is nothing wrong with wanting to please people."

"Perhaps." Though she doubted the truth of it. She did manage to get her own way most times. After all, she had stolen away from the city to lure Nick to a secluded castle, and they were getting to know each other. Mother and Father would be apoplectic if they knew.

"What about Aurora? Do you admire some trait of hers?"

"Most people would say her beauty is her most appealing trait." Faith shook her head. "They would be wrong. I mean to say, Aurora is quite beautiful. She is perfectly formed with good height, while not too tall or short, and her figure is perfectly balanced. She has exactly what society looks for in a lady. Perhaps that is why she manages to make the ton think she is just like them. Maybe that is why she could hide what Radcliff did to her. She is the strongest person I've ever known. No amount of horror changed her from the wonderful person she is. Radcliff couldn't break her spirit and, by God, he tried."

"Then it is her strength of character that you admire?" Nick wound them around another small grove of orange trees potted near the back of the building. They were only there to keep warm until spring when they would be dragged back outside to flourish and produce flowers.

"Yes. Aurora never wavers." Her friend was like a golden statue, always the same. Always dependable.

"That's good, because if it was her figure, I would have to tell you that while Lady Radcliff is lovely, your figure is spectacular. Every curve begs for a man to look and touch." He said the last in a sultry voice.

Her insides quivered with the satisfaction of knowing he liked the way she looked. She was not what the ton admired, but his wanting to touch her made up for the slights she had endured over the years. "My mother would beg to differ. She prayed I would get my figure from her side of the family, but I am much like my grandmother on my father's side."

"I would not wish to disagree with your mother, so I will stay silent on the matter. Is your grandmother still alive?" He changed the subject.

Nodding, she thought of Grandmother. "She lives in Sussex. I visit when I can. She is funny and brazen in many ways. She and I have always gotten along famously."

"I should like to meet her." They rounded the front of the hothouse, but Nick turned them inward away from the glass wall and through a forest of tropical trees. "That leaves Mercedes."

"Mercy, like Grandmother, uses humor to barrel through any situation. I don't know how she manages it, but she finds something funny in nearly every moment of life. I also wish I could play any instrument as well as she plays no less than six."

"Six?" He stopped and faced her.

"Oh yes. At last count, she had mastered pianoforte, harp, flute, clarinet, lute, and some stringed instrument that her aunt had brought in from Spain. I love the sound of that one. It's low and sensual somehow." She blushed at her own musings. "Do you know it?"

Pulling her to a stop, he faced her, cradling her face in his hands. "It's called a guitar and it can be quite sensual, as you said. I met a man in Porto who played so well, the ladies swooned."

Unable and not wanting to look away, she moistened her dry lips. "I have never swooned, but I think I would like to hear him play."

"Perhaps one day we will journey to Porto in better times." Leaning down to her height, he pressed his lips to hers. Making no demands, he just let their lips touch. Faith sighed against his mouth. She hadn't even known she was waiting for his kiss, but she would never have enough. Wrapping her hand around his neck and lifting on her toes, she pulled them closer together. Her entire body quivered with need for more of him.

Nick's arms wrapped around her and pulled her tight against his chest, nearly lifting her off her feet.

She gasped and he plundered her mouth with his tongue. The outside world disappeared into obscurity and there was only Nick and his glorious mouth making her want more than a nice lady should, but she didn't care.

Feeling his desire pressed hard against her, she tightened to him. Her center pulsed for contact, hoping he felt the same and satisfied when he groaned in pleasure.

He traced from her jaw, down her neck to her shoulder, and each kiss set her more aflame.

"Nick." The voice coming from her was unfamiliar, filled with passion and need.

"Good Lord, Faith. Say it again." He trailed a path of kisses back up to just behind her ear.

Her knees buckled, but he held her in place. "Nick," she repeated obediently.

Crushing her to him, he nuzzled her hair. "You will be the death of me. I don't know how it happened, but I have completely forgotten how angry you made me and can think only of your sweetness."

She laughed against his chest. "My sweetness is fleeting. I'm just glad I had Thea keep Rumple in the kitchen. Lord only knows what he would think of this."

Smiling down at her, he brushed a wayward hair back from her forehead. "Everything is a game to a puppy."

As she drew a deep breath, she shuddered. There was an intensity in the air around them that prickled her skin. She took a step out of his arms. "You mentioned your parents. I know your father has passed, since you are duke. What about your mother, are you close with her?"

"Sadly, Mother did not survive the year after Father died." His solemn reply spoke of a man who'd admired his parents.

"I'm very sorry. Was theirs a love match then?" It was so strange to hear of dukes being deeply in love with their wives. Most married to have children and increase their standing either financially or politically.

They kept love at arm's length. The majority took mistresses as well. Her stomach heaved and she fought down the disgust.

Nick reached out and took her hand. "They loved each other, but the marriage was arranged. They were married quite young and had known each other as children. My sister, Countess of Dunworth, is older by three years. She tells me they were always touching and kissing even when she was small."

"It sounds quite magical to have a love so true that your mother could not go on without him. I'm sure you miss them a great deal." She let him lead her forward until they were only an inch apart.

He kissed her fingers. "I do miss them. Mother and I were particularly close. For a while I was angry with her for leaving, but I've come to understand that my father provided her zest for life. Without him, she withered."

Faith's heart broke for the couple who had created Nick and loved so truly. She brushed a tear away. "Would you like more wine?"

A cold wind blew through the hothouse, indicating the door had been opened. Faith had told the meager staff that they were not to be disturbed, so something must be wrong. "Thea? What is it?"

A man with a round face, ruddy cheeks, and an odd accent stepped around the large potted orange trees into view. "I'm afraid it isn't your cook, my lady. She and the other two are safely locked in the cellar."

Nick's grip tightened and he tugged her behind him. "Charles, what on earth are you doing here?"

Another man, tall and good-looking with sharp features and cruel eyes, stepped from behind the trees. This man sounded well educated but distinctly French. "We are here to settle a debt, old friend."

"Joseph, this is a surprise." Nick's voice could cut glass.

Faith gripped his arm and his muscles were tense as a bow pulled back and ready to fly. They might be playing the part of friend for the moment, but these were dangerous men. "I did not know we were to have company. May I offer you gentlemen some wine?"

A third man, dressed in the English style and with an elaborately tied cravat, joined them. He had a scar above his left eye and the blacks of his eyes nearly disappeared, leaving only the palest blue. He and the man Nick called Joseph were tall and lean. "I'm afraid that is not what we came for, Miss Landon. You may not know this, but you have aligned yourself with a fiend."

All three appeared smug, and the rigidity in Nick's stance screamed warnings of danger. Unsure how to continue, Faith kept to what she knew. In three years at Miss Agatha Wormbattle's school she had learned to act a lady and keep her true thoughts to herself. One could plot and plan without anyone knowing. "I'm sure you're mistaken. This is the Duke of Breckenridge."

"Yes, so I've heard. Yet I knew him as Count d'Armon and I'm sure there were other names as well," the third and most frightening man said. His French accent rang with disgust.

Nick sneered, then stepped fully in front of Faith, blocking her from the view of the others. "And how many names have each of you gone by, Jean-Claude? I can think of at least three for Charles alone."

The higher voice of Charles rang out. "We trusted you, Nicholas. You were my friend and you betrayed us. Surely you didn't think we would let you walk away and return to your elaborate life."

"I did what I had to do for my country. It is no different than what you each have done." Nick tried a more reasonable voice.

Jean-Claude pulled a pistol from inside his gold-trimmed coat. "I'm sure you believe that, my friend. However, you cannot betray us and get away with it. The emperor might forgive you as it is wartime, but I never shall."

Reaching behind him, Nick pulled her close to his back. "What do you want then, an apology?"

Jean-Claude's laugh sent needles prickling at the back of Faith's neck.

"No, Your Grace," Jean-Claude said, his voice sweet and sultry. "We demand blood."

Chapter 7

Nick knew one day his past would come back to haunt him, but he never imagined it would be so soon, and he certainly never intended to put anyone else at risk.

The war still raged on the Continent, yet here were three of Napoleon's best spies, in England for the purpose of taking him to task. It was madness. Nick searched for some way to get Faith and the servants out of this mess, but with all three adversaries armed as they pushed him and Faith down hallways to the cellar, he could see no immediate escape.

His best option for reasoning was Charles, but he'd have to wait for the right opportunity.

One lamp lit the dusty cellar where Geb stored his wine. In the corner Jane, Thea, and Jamie huddled together on the floor. Jane stood when Nick and Faith were pushed through the heavy oak door, while Thea and Jamie remained shaken, with their arms wrapped around each other.

Faith rushed into Jane's arms. "Did they hurt you?"

"No, my lady. They were less than polite, but they did not harm any of us." Jane's eyes were filled with worry.

Kneeling in front of the two youngsters, Faith cupped each of their cheeks. "It's going to be all right. Soon those men will get hungry and they will take all three of you to the kitchens. You will keep your heads down and cook for them. No one need be heroic. Just do as you're told until His Grace finds us a way out of this."

Nick hoped she wasn't putting more faith in him than he deserved. "Good advice and you're right. They will need to eat. They've also locked us in with the wine supply, which means by dark, Charles will be down here looking for drink."

The cellar was not as large as the entire castle; it was perhaps thirty feet across and twenty long. One side had wine bins filled with bottles and barrels. Cool and temperate all year long, it was the perfect place to store wine. A dirt floor and no furniture gave no comfort. The thick door had a heavy steel lock to keep the wine safe and them sealed in.

At least they had been given a lamp. Nick hoped candles would be replaced before they were thrust into total darkness.

Standing and facing him, Faith put her hands on her hips. Those unusual eyes of hers were narrowed on him. "Who are they, Nick?"

"Where is the puppy?" Nick avoided the question, but he also knew if anything happened to the dog, he was in real trouble.

Jamie said, "The round-faced man took a liking to Rumple and has kept him above."

With so much to worry about, the expression of concern on everyone's faces over a scrap of a puppy should have been farcical. However, even Nick had come to love the little fellow in one short day.

"You look worried," Faith said. "Do you think they would harm an innocent puppy?"

Lying wouldn't do anyone good. Enough lies had been told by him and on his behalf. Nick was through with lies, though he suspected he'd come to the epiphany too late. "I don't know. These are ruthless men who have little moral fiber. Charles is not vicious and has a great love of animals. Hopefully that will be enough to keep Rumple safe. However, keep in mind that Charles is here to do me harm over misleading them, when he himself works for both the French and Austrian governments as a spy. You can imagine, his sense of decency is skewed."

"And what of yours?" Faith had not come close to him since they'd entered the cellar. Standing several feet away, when he stepped closer, she backed up.

Nick stopped his approach. "I have already told you that most of what I have done during this war, I am ashamed of. However, if I was asked to do it all again, I most likely would. I believed my actions were necessary for the safety of England and I still know that to be true."

"But?" She was too clever by half. She saw his duplicity without him saying anything. Was it just Faith or had he lost his ability to be a good agent?

Backing up to the wall, he sighed and leaned against the cold stone. "But those men upstairs were my friends. Despite the fact that I was sent to infiltrate their circle, I did more than that. I befriended them. They told me things they would only tell a close confidant, and each one of them has a right to be furious with me. This makes them unpredictable."

"Surely, Charles would be less so if he too is harboring duplicity." She studied him for a long moment before approaching. She leaned next to him, then slid down to the floor.

Nick sat next to her, relieved that she was not too disgusted with him to be close. It shouldn't matter if she hated him. His problems were epic in comparison to the regard of a woman, yet it was important she not hate him. "Charles Schulmeister, or Karl, as he was born, will do whatever is necessary to survive and accumulate money. If he goes against Jean-Claude and Joseph, he will mark himself a traitor and they will either ruin him or kill him."

"I see." She studied her hands. "That would motivate him to go along with whatever the plan might be." After a long pause, she watched him. "Are they going to kill you, Nick?"

He laughed because it was the only thing he could do. There was no sense weeping over his life choices. It was only a shame that his cousin William would inherit. He'd never cared for that bore. "Yes, probably. But not right away."

Her face lit up. "Mr. MacGruder will send for help. He must have seen some of what happened in the hothouse or garden. Surely he'll notice something amiss by nightfall."

He hated to dash her hopes, but he'd already promised himself no more lies. "MacGruder went to see his niece in town. He won't return for days. They probably saw him leave and thought it a good time to act this afternoon. When MacGruder returns, perhaps he can send a note to Geb and you will be rescued. Still, Geb is at least a three-day ride and four days back with any kind of army. We shall have to be smart and stay alive on our own, my dear."

Deflated, she went back to staring at her hands. "I will be extremely vexed with you if you die, Nicholas."

It was madness to care about such things when his own death was probably hours away, but it warmed his soul to know she wanted him alive. "Wouldn't my untimely death be the perfect solution? You would be free to find a good man to marry, and with the added benefit of my regard. I imagine you would be in high demand after an appropriate mourning period."

"Don't be disgusting," she bit out and gave him a scolding stare.

He pulled her hand from her lap and kissed her soft knuckles. "I am deeply honored by your concern, Faith."

If the servants had not been across the way, she might have kissed him. She looked from his lips to his eyes and back again before pulling her hand free and glancing away. "Tell me about the other two."

Longing for that kiss was reckless and immature, but still he wanted to taste those sweet, full lips again and again until she was breathless. It took a force of will to steady those untimely emotions and push them aside. "Joseph Fouché wanted to be a teacher. He went to Paris to study and got caught up in the excitement of the revolution. He was charmed by none other than Robespierre himself. However, when his mentor heard of some atrocities he'd committed for the benefit of France, they had a falling-out and Joseph lost his faith. He is quite dangerous and smart. He keeps an extensive catalog of all royalists, and it is probably particularly vexing to him that I managed to elude his list."

"And the one with the hateful glare?" Faith shivered and rubbed her arms.

"Indeed. It's a fine description. Those eyes have frightened hundreds of resisters and royalists. Jean-Claude-Hippolyte Méhée de La Touche. He is by far the most dangerous to be in a room with. He was meant to follow in the footsteps of his surgeon father. Born in Meaux, there was an uproar when at the age of twelve he left for Paris. Not long after that, he was imprisoned. He has reinvented himself many times and swindled many people and governments, including our own."

"You say that as if you admire him." She had taken on that scolding tone again.

"He is clever beyond any other person I've ever known. He saved my life once as well. If the politics had been different, he and I might have been good friends. As it is, I have made a deadly enemy and put you and those three innocents in danger." Frustrated, Nick rose and crossed to the servants.

He crouched in front of Thea, and the girl's eyes widened and her lips quivered. Speaking softly to ease her worry, he said, "Thea, it is growing close to the supper hour. They will come to order you to cook. You must tell them you cannot manage without Jane and Jamie. Feed them your best food and be silent. They will be so happy with the meal, they will keep you all on the servants' level."

Thea gave a nervous nod. "I'll try, Your Grace. Are you sure you wouldn't like me to poison the lot of them?"

He liked this child. "No. Best not risk it. If one abstains, we'd be in a real mess. Feed them well and stay safe."

Clutching his coat sleeve, Jane demanded, "What of you and my lady?"

He put his hand on top of hers. "I will have to think of something else for our salvation, Jane. I promise to do all I can to protect her."

Meeting his gaze directly, Jane said, "That had better be enough, Your Grace. The Wallflowers will haunt you into the next life, if anything happens to Lady Faith."

Servants rarely spoke so boldly, but Nick couldn't blame her. "I shall expect full retribution as I will never forgive myself should she or any of you be harmed."

Jane nodded and pulled her hand away.

The key scraped in the lock.

Nick stood against the wall near the wine. He leaned and crossed his arms over his chest. It was easy to fall into the old habit of being relaxed even when he knew his life might end in the next few hours. He hoped to form a plan while his old friends ate and drank. If he was lucky, the lure of good food and wine would hold off his execution for the night.

The door swung open. Charles stepped in, brandishing his sword. He pointed the blade at Thea. "You. Upstairs and get cooking."

Wide-eyed and trembling, Thea rose. "I'll be needing the help of the others to make a proper meal, sir."

Charles narrowed his eyes and looked Jane and Jamie over. "Fine. All three of you get to the kitchens. Do not think you can escape or send word out of this house. I will kill the lovely Lady Faith should any action other than cooking be taken by any of you."

All three scurried to the door. Charles grabbed Jane's arm. "Bring wine, girl."

Jane scowled, but turned and walked to the wall of wine.

Nick plucked three fine bottles from the bin near him and handed them to Jane. If she came back later for more, he would know the spies were drunk and they were all likely safe for the night.

Taking them, Jane gave him a hard look and a nod before rushing up the steps after Thea and Jamie.

"Charles, don't you find it hypocritical for you to punish me for my duality when you work for both the French and Austrians?" Nick remained relaxed against the wall.

Already ruddy, Charles's complexion reddened like a berry and he puffed his cheeks. "I could just slit your throat and keep you quiet, Nicholas. But I suspect the threat of killing or maiming the lady will be enough to keep your mouth closed."

Nick lifted his hands in surrender. "I merely asked the question."

"Do not test me, Nicholas. I know you think me less than the others, but I have managed quite nicely. I would have let you go, but Jean-Claude and Joseph were adamant you had to pay. As I have no loyalty to you…." He shrugged as if the rest of his sentence was obvious.

Nick supposed it was. Charles had no real loyalty to any person or country. His only allegiance was to himself. "Enjoy your supper. Cook is quite talented. You'll want to keep the minimal staff to feed you. Don't be quick to temper. They are quite young, but they will serve you well."

Faith had remained near the far wall, but stood during the encounter. "I hope you have not harmed my dog." Like a queen with all the power, he might have been dirt under her feet rather than her captor.

Looking aghast, with open mouth and shocked eyes, Charles said, "The puppy is under my care. No harm shall come to the sweet boy. I am not a monster."

"His name is Rumple and he is fond of fowl. If Cook prepares hens, you might be kind enough to give him some scraps."

Charles bowed. "I will see to his feeding, my lady."

Bestowing a slight smile on him, Faith said, "Would a candle or two to see us through the night, be too much to ask?"

The only candle in the cellar had burned halfway down and would leave them in the pitch dark long before anyone came for them in the morning. Charles studied the candle for a long moment. "I will arrange enough light for the night."

"Thank you." She curtsied.

Looking contrite, with his head bowed and eyes searching for how he'd been swindled, Charles narrowed his brows and exited.

Once the lock had clicked, Nick waited several beats before crossing to Faith. "That was excellently done."

"I do not like total darkness. I hope he keeps his word." She shuddered.

Nick pulled her into his arms. "I hope so too. I'm sorry, Faith. I made enemies and now I have put you and those children in danger. Suddenly everything I did in the name of England seems foolish. It never occurred to me I would be putting anyone else in jeopardy."

The scent of flowers and crisp winter air hung in her soft riotous curls. He breathed deep and held the memory. He would need pleasantries to hold on to with the horrors that were to come.

She might have read his mind. "Do you think they will hurt you?"

Releasing her, he stepped back. "Yes. They will try to gain information about English agents. They must find a way to make their ignorance of my treachery worthwhile. The food and wine may hold them off until morning. Perhaps a little longer with the effects of the drink lingering. You must not give the impression you care overmuch for me. That shouldn't be too difficult."

Faith's eyes softened and she cupped his cheek. "I care about what happens to you, Nick. I would not have lured you here, if I didn't care. I wish I'd never done any of this. It is my fault they captured you with no means to defend yourself. Not even a proper footman to whack one of them over the head."

"None of this is your doing. They would have gotten to me eventually regardless. In a few days, MacGruder will send for help and you will be rescued. Or they may just leave here once they have what they want from me." Nick's sigh was filled with regret. It wasn't really a surprise that his life had come to this, but it was still disappointing. He would have liked to see what life with Faith might have been. Never dull, he was sure of that.

Her hands were fisted at her hips again. "Are you resigned to your own death then? Have you no intention of fighting back?"

"I will do all that I can to stay alive, my lady." He caressed her cheek and the soft skin along the side of her neck. "I am quite motivated to find out all there is to know about a certain Wallflower."

"Just a few days ago you wanted nothing to do with me. Now your life is in danger and I'm to believe your feelings have changed." Curiosity laced her words and she leaned into his touch, cocking her head and gazing up at him.

Lord, he wanted her. "I don't believe my feelings have changed since the moment I vexed you at the ball where I first set eyes on you. That is not to say, you didn't make me exceedingly angry and wary about our contract. However, my trepidation was comforted by your honest explanation for it all. I never guessed what you had been through and am ashamed for not having asked rather than reacting so zealously."

Sensing his hesitation, she prodded. "And?"

Nick kissed her forehead and kept his cheek on her soft flesh a moment longer. "And I was terrified that I didn't deserve you, and as these last few hours have proved, I was correct in that."

"I don't see that." She leaned in and let her curvaceous body mold to his.

How he had come to need so much from anyone in so short a time, he didn't know, but he needed more from her. For so many years he needed nothing and no one but himself and his wits. Now, this slip of a woman ruled his head and his heart. "What do you see?"

"I see a man who did what was necessary in war and his conscience won't let him rest. If you felt nothing about your actions, Nick, it would be far worse. That would mean you had lost your sense of right and wrong. I imagine it is a difficult thing to learn throughout your youth that it is wrong and a sin to harm another, and then be thrust into war where you are ordered to do just that. There must be many men suffering with this struggle to balance the two once they no longer have a war to fight."

"Are you always so empathetic, Faith?" Unable to stop himself, he wrapped his arms around her again and rubbed the chill of the damp cellar from her arms and back. Lord, she fit against him perfectly with every curve pressing in all the right places.

Snuggling into him, she wrapped her arms around his back. "I suppose I have a habit of looking at things from several sides. I could even see Mary Yates's point of view for a long time."

Happy to change the subject and keep her warmth pressed to him, Nick asked, "How could you make her mockery of you and the others right?"

"Not right so much as understandable. Mary's morals are skewed by years of bad parenting, but she found a place at the Wormbattle School that was elevated and important. When Aurora, Poppy, Mercy, and I arrived, already a strong force united, she was threatened and lashed out. It was as if we had cornered a tiger."

Nick was not as forgiving. "And how do you explain away Mary's behavior toward Geb?" Despite not agreeing with her, he could spend a lifetime holding her close and breathing in her warm floral scent.

Faith's spine went rigid. "That is unforgivable. She, her parents, and the rest of those fops, should be ashamed. Unfortunately, they don't have the mental capacity to see the error of their ways. Mr. Arafa is ten times the person of any of them, but they see only his differences and find them abhorrent. It is pure ignorance that leads to such hate."

"I noticed that Rhys, Poppy, and yourself treated Geb as an equal." Pride swelled inside Nick as it had the night of Geb's dinner party.

She pushed away and stared up at him, shocked. "Of course. If we didn't like someone, we wouldn't accept an invitation to his home. Besides, our regard is not dependent on either finances or the color of a man's skin. Wallflowers know about being excluded and would never be the cause of that kind of harm."

Drawing her close again, his admiration grew tenfold. "I'm liking Wallflowers more and more."

A long yawn drew her body tight before she relaxed. "It has been quite a day."

Nick took off his coat and spread it on the floor by the wall. He drew her down to sit atop the thick velvet and sat beside her. "You will need your sleep, Faith."

She rested her head on his chest as he wrapped his hand around her shoulder. She sighed against him. "Won't you be cold without your coat?"

"I will be fine. Rest now. Tomorrow will be another long day." He hid his shudder over the horrors he suspected would befall him in the next few days, and reveled in the softness of her body against his.

"I suppose wishing we could just stay like this forever is childish." She closed her eyes.

"No." He kissed the crown of her head and sent up a prayer that she would not suffer for his sins. "It is never foolish to wish, Faith."

Chapter 8

Faith had been grateful for the candle and bread when Charles Schulmeister and Jane arrived in the morning. Her stomach grumbled, but she refused to eat the last two pieces. Charles had taken Nick away when he and Jane had brought her food. If they didn't feed Nick, she wanted to have something for him.

It had been hours or maybe it was days. There was only the burning down of the candles to mark the time. The six-hour candles told her she'd been alone for nearly twelve hours, but she would have sworn it was twice that long.

Shuddering at the thought of what they could be doing to Nick for twelve hours, she prayed he was still alive. He had to be. This was all her fault. If he were killed or even damaged, she would be to blame. She'd not thought about his safety when she made her elaborate plan to bring him to Parvus. She'd known her own fate could be total ruin, but it had not occurred to her that Nick might have enemies who would love to find him alone, unarmed and without friends.

She closed her eyes. There was no way for her to know such a thing. Still, how would she live if she lost him? A tear escaped and she brushed it away.

A clink of keys forced her to sit up and await whatever fate might have in store. A shadowed figure approached. Faith didn't recognize the gait or shape of the man. She pressed against the wall.

"My lady, don't be afraid. It is Jacob MacGruder. I've come to take you out of here." There was tenderness in his whispered Scottish accent. His haggard, wrinkled face shone in the light. Bright eyes stared at her as he offered his hand to help her up.

Faith's legs ached from disuse, but she pushed to her feet. Relief spread through her along with gratitude. "And the others. Are they safe?" MacGruder shook his head and put his finger to his lips. He glanced nervously back at the door. "I can't get to the servants and they have His Grace on the main floor."

Faith stopped. Her feet were rooted to the ground while panic welled up inside her gut. Despite the churning inside her, she kept her voice low. "I'm not leaving them behind. They told Jane and the others that they would kill me if they tried to run. What will happen to them if I go?"

"His Grace would want you safe. I can get you out. I wish I could take them all away, but I can't, my lady. You must come now." He pulled her forward.

Ripping out of his grip, Faith stood her ground. "I cannot leave them to die while I am rescued. Go and fetch the magistrate, Mr. MacGruder."

His gaze shifted to the open door. "The magistrate went to London. I can't get word to him quick enough to help; besides, he's a bit of a dimwit. I can get you out and we must go before they discover I've come back."

"Then fetch some local men to join the rescue." She searched her mind for some way out for all.

MacGruder shook his head. "There is no one who will risk their neck for a man they don't know. His Grace only visits rarely and has spent no time in town. I'm willing to take the risk, but no one else will. Come now, miss. You must come quickly." He reached for her arm.

Backing away, Faith sat on the coat Nick had left for her comfort. "If I go, they will kill someone as an example. It will likely be the boy, Jamie. I cannot leave. I will not leave Nick to die while I am saved. I could not live with myself. I would prefer death to a life of utter regret."

He turned his head up to the ceiling, and gave a desperate whisper. "Miss."

"Ride to Aaru, fast as you can. Tell Mr. Arafa what is happening. Pray we survive long enough." She stared at the groundskeeper, heart pounding.

His shoulders slumped. "You are a special lass. I'll give you that." He shook his head. "Stay alive or he'll never forgive me, and he's going to be mighty furious with you as well."

She nodded.

Still shaking his head, MacGruder left, locking the door behind him.

Faith closed her eyes to pray that he made it out of the house undetected. He would be three days to Aaru and then at least that long to return, maybe more with soldiers. She slumped down to lie on the coat. It smelled of Nick and she breathed deep, letting that bit of him comfort her.

Opening her eyes revealed nothing. The cellar was thrown into total darkness as the candle guttered out while she had prayed. She closed her eyes again and hoped Nick was still alive.

Unable to bear the darkness with her eyes open, she kept them shut when the key sounded in the lock. When the hinges creaked, she risked opening her eyes.

Faith blinked until her vision cleared and adjusted to the candlelight from the three-tiered candelabra in Jane's hand.

Tears welled in Jane's eyes and glinted in the flames.

"I don't have all night, girl." Charles's thick accent sounded from the steps.

Jane rushed in and quickly placed one of her candles in the cellar lamp. She blocked the view of the door and knelt in front of Faith with a basket. "I've put a few bits of meat and cheese in, my lady." She pulled something wrapped in a rag from her pocket and tucked it in the side of the basket. Her tears spilled over.

"Thank you, Jane."

Behind Jane, the sound of moaning forced Faith to return her gaze to the door.

Charles deposited Nick on the floor with a thud and a loud groan. "You should just tell them what they want to know, Nicholas. It would go easier for you. They would still kill you, but you wouldn't suffer so. I hate to see you tortured like this."

Stumbling to her feet, Faith tried to reach Nick.

Jane gripped her arm and righted her. "Slowly, my lady. It has been many hours since you've eaten and you are weak."

Pure hatred for the round-faced Austrian burned through Faith.

Nick's face was bloody and swollen. Blood stained his white blouse and his back heaved with the exertion of breathing.

Charles took a step back at her glare. "The boy is bringing water so you can clean him up, and ale for drinking. He is stubborn. If he would give them the information, it would go much better for him."

Gently, Faith put her arm around Nick but kept her stare on Charles. "You may save your explanations, sir. They are wasted on me."

Jamie arrived with a bucket of water in one hand and a carafe of ale in the other. The water sloshed over the side, but he was careful to ease the carafe down without incident.

His eyes were red rimmed.

"Are they kind to you, Jamie?" Faith didn't know what she would do if those animals had hurt a boy. She might not be able to stop herself from charging at the one in her presence.

"Yes, my lady. I played with Rumple until he fell asleep and I've been helping Jane and Thea in the kitchen." The boy glanced warily at Nick, who attempted a smile, but it was more grimace.

"It's okay," Nick ground out. "My lady will clean me up and I'll be almost good as new. It looks far worse than it is, Jamie."

Faith hoped it was true, but suspected the reassurance was for the boy's sake alone. "That's right, Jamie. You just do as you're told and all will be well."

Charles nodded. "I will protect them as much as I can, Lady Faith. I'm not a monster."

Standing despite her stiff joints and muscles, Faith narrowed her gaze at him. "A man who stands by while others do terrible things is still a monster, *monsieur* or *herr*, or however you think you should be addressed. Your duplicity in all things disgusts me."

Shame washed over Charles's face before he straightened his shoulders, turned and walked out. "Come. If you don't want to be locked in with them, come."

Jane squeezed Faith's arm, took hold of Jamie's hand, and rushed out the door.

A moment later the heavy door slammed and the key turned in the lock.

With as little pressure as possible, she cradled Nick's face and turned it up to hers. Swollen and covered in blood, she couldn't tell how bad his injuries were. "Do you think you can help me get you over to sit against the wall?"

It was barely a nod, and even that made him grimace, but he looped his arm around her shoulders and pushed to his feet. It was only a few steps to reach the spot that Faith had made hers while she waited. The lamp sat a few feet away, and once she'd helped him sit, she moved the light closer. Bringing the water bucket close, she knelt beside him. "Do you think anything is broken?"

"No, sweetheart. It really does look worse than it is." His voice was little more than a croak.

She handed him the carafe. "Drink."

Two sips and he put the ale down.

Remembering the rag that Jane had tucked in the food basket, Faith pulled it free. Inside were two extra candles. She would see that Jane had a raise in wages when they got home. The thought of the candle going out again terrified her. She put the extra candle in back of some wine casks and returned to Nick with the rag.

Gently, she wiped away the blood around his mouth. He must have bitten his tongue or cheek, as she found no cut to account for the bleeding.

Once his chin and neck were clean, she pushed back his matted hair and got her first good look at his eyes. The right was completely swelled closed with a gash above the brow.

He peered at her through the slit in his left eye. "I must be quite a sight."

"You have looked better, but I think your face will heal." She dabbed at the cut, which had stopped bleeding and didn't appear too deep. The water was cool and would do the swelling good as well. "What did they want to know?"

Nick leaned his cheek into her hand. "Just things about what the English are up to."

Satisfied that she'd done all she could for his face, she put the rag in the bucket, squeezed the excess water out, and handed him the cloth. "Hold this to your eye while I see from where else you are bleeding. Do you know such things?"

He did as he was told and sighed as the cold cloth pressed to his turgid eye. "I know some, but I can't tell them. You understand that, don't you, Faith?"

"I understand. Besides, once you told them, they would have no reason to keep you alive." She met his gaze. "I'm very keen on you remaining among the living through this ordeal, Nick."

His attempt at a smile failed, but she appreciated the effort. "I shall do my best to not disappoint you."

"See that you do." She lifted the hem of his blouse, tugging it free from his breeches and easing it up his bruised torso. She had to gentle him away from the wall in order to get the fabric over his head. An angry blue bruise marred his ribs and another near his collarbone, but nothing to account for the blood. "I can't find a wound, Nick. How did your shirt get stained?"

"That's Fouché's blood. He got too close and I butted him with my head. I may have broken that perfect nose of his." His voice, though still scratchy, filled with amusement.

Taking back the rag, she washed away the sweat from his chest, back, and arms. Finished, she sat back and plunked the cloth in the bucket. "I wish there was more I could do for you."

Reaching out, he took her hand and pulled her to sit next to him. Slowly, he eased down until his head rested in her lap. "You are an excellent nurse, Faith. I thank you." He wrapped an arm around her thigh and cuddled her.

Faith toyed with the hair at his neck and leaned back. Mr. MacGruder was right about how furious Nick would be if he knew she'd refused to be rescued. She decided to keep it to herself for the time being. He was in enough pain.

If her guess was correct, it was suppertime abovestairs and Jane would be sent for more wine soon. Reaching in the basket, she pulled out a piece of bread. "Do you think you might eat something?"

With a groan, he forced himself back to sitting, picked up his shirt and made several more pained noises as he pulled the cloth back over his head. "If I'm going to obey your orders, I suppose I'll have to try. But may I reserve the right to resume my previous position after our meal?"

Despite all they had been through, she giggled. "You may."

His shoulders relaxed. "What is in the basket?"

Faith's stomach growled as the scent of warm yeasty bread flowed from the bundle.

"Have they not fed you?" Nick's sharp question startled her.

Resting a hand on his arm, she hoped to calm him. "This morning when they took you, but not since."

"I can survive without food. You must eat." It was a command, and he crossed his arms over his chest to further emphasize his point.

Faith removed the cloth from inside the basket and spread it out in front of them. Atop she placed a round loaf of bread hardly bigger than her fist, several slices of meat, and a wedge of cheese. She took the saved bread from her morning meal from her pocket and added that to the meal. "We will eat together, Nick, or I too shall abstain."

She imitated his stubborn pose and cocked her head, waiting for his response.

Sighing, he relaxed. "Will you always challenge my authority, Faith?"

Handing him a piece of the morning bread and a piece of cheese, she couldn't help being amused. "Probably, Nick. If you wanted a girl who did as she was told, you wouldn't have chosen a Wormbattle girl. The entire point is that disobedience got us sent away from home."

He nibbled the food. "One would have thought three years away would have cured you of those habits."

His teasing tones relieved her mind. It gave some proof his injuries were minor. Eating her bread as well, she said, "On the contrary, Miss Agatha teaches women to act as young ladies but to think for themselves."

"Good," he said. "We shall need a great deal of cleverness to get out of this mess, Faith. Come morning, they will take me again and while I will try to stay alive for you, I cannot make any promises. You will need to find a way to escape. And"—he took a pause and stared at her with haunted eyes—"if you find a way out, you must take it and not worry about leaving me or anyone else behind."

"I am not leaving here without you and the servants, Nicholas Ellsworth. You can just put that out of your mind." Her ire rose to a pitch where she had to take deep breaths to control it.

"Do all Wallflowers have such a stubborn streak and temper?" He picked up her hand and kissed the knuckles before returning to his bread and cheese.

"No. Mercy is level-headed and Aurora rarely gives in to her temper. I generally hide my own, but I feel these circumstances warrant some emotion." She ate the last of the morning bread, then broke the new loaf into four pieces.

The key in the lock froze them both.

Joseph Fouché pushed Jane inside the cellar. "Wine!"

Jane ran to the casks and filled a large carafe, then ran back up the steps. All the while, Joseph stood near the door and stared at Nick, unblinking. His eyes were black and his nose swollen, though he still managed to be smug.

Nick faced his old friend and enemy but said nothing and made no move to stand. Perhaps the effort would have been too much, or he might have worried about consequences to Faith if he angered the spy further.

"Enjoy your supper," Joseph crooned mockingly as he stepped out and locked the door.

Nick's shoulders slumped. "I don't imagine they'll return tonight. We are safe for now."

Safe was a relative term. Faith didn't feel safe. She'd seen some horrible things done to her friend Aurora, but she never dreamed she would be so close to the danger. The entire point of the pact she'd made with the other Wallflowers was to make sure they would all remain safe. "Nick?"

He stopped nibbling on the bit of meat in his hand. "Yes?"

It was important to ask the questions that haunted her. "Are we now beyond the point where you intend to keep your past exploits from me?"

Once he'd eaten the remains of his food, he gulped down some of the ale. "I'd say we are quite far beyond that point, sweetheart. Ask your questions."

She liked the endearment more than she should. Even in this ridiculous situation they should behave as a lady and a gentleman. Shaking off the stupid notions ingrained in her from birth, she swallowed the last of her bread. Her stomach finally settled down. "The things being done to you by your old friends. You have done the same to others?"

The swelling in his eyes had lessened and the barest bit of blue stared out at her. "I have beaten people to gain answers."

Her stomach heaved and she forced herself to accept that some things happen in war, things she wouldn't like to hear about. "Do you think they will stop before they kill you?"

Carefully, he wrapped the remaining food in the cloth and placed it in the basket. Then he groaned as he eased himself back to lying with his head in Faith's lap. "No. They will either kill me because I don't tell them or they will kill me once I do tell them. If I told them something, they might keep me alive for the purpose of gaining more information."

"Then tell them and stay alive." She toyed with his hair, careful not to touch parts of his face and neck that were covered in bruises and welts. The cut over his eyes needed some salve or it might fester. The dirt and grime of the cellar would not help that situation.

Nick hugged her thigh and settled in. "I cannot betray England for my own sake, and not even for yours." Regret laced his words, but they were unwavering.

"I know, but can't you lie?" she whispered.

He stilled. "Lie?"

Leaning down so that her mouth was inches from his ear, she said. "Isn't that what you spies do, you lie in the name of this country or that? Tell them a lie, but just one small lie. Make it a good one. They will want to keep you alive, thinking you have more to tell. You may want to faint as well. Aurora use to pretend to faint all the time. Radcliff didn't enjoy beating her if he thought her unconscious already. It was an excellent way to lessen the beatings."

Nick pressed up with his arms on either side of her legs and his face an inch from hers. "I hate that you know this much about such things, Faith. However, this is a rather brilliant idea."

He kissed her hard on the mouth. "Ouch! Lord you taste good, but that hurt more than I'd like our kisses to." He touched his swollen lips.

"Perhaps more gently then," she said, and rubbed her lip along his.

Nibbling her top then her bottom lip, he sighed against her and their breath mingled. "Will you marry me, Faith?"

Her pulse drummed so loudly in her ears, she'd almost missed the question. "Perhaps you should ask me again when this is all over. By then you will be in a more advantageous position and your desires may have changed."

Returning to her lap, he pressed his head against her. Despite his size, he fit with her like two halves long separated and been made to lie in comfort. If they had been on a summer picnic and found a nice tree to rest under, it would have been perfection. "I know what I want, Faith. I knew a long time ago. However, as it is possible my past rearing its ugly head might have hampered any hope of your liking me, you are wise to wait and see if I survive the next few days, before you commit."

"That is not what I meant."

He continued in the same kind, warm tone. "Besides, whatever is left of me if I do live might not be at all appealing to any lady. You deserve a whole man, and I may not be worth a shilling by the end."

Leaning back, she closed her eyes and kept her fingers running through his hair. "Whenever you think you can take no more, you must promise me you will remember three things, Nick."

"Your hand feels so nice." He relaxed against her by degrees. "What three things, sweetheart?"

"Lie about some bit of English politics, faint, and I will grant you favors if you will live through this."

He rolled so he could look up at her. "Just to be clear, you want me to lie and fake losing consciousness?"

"Yes," she said, running her fingers along his stubble-covered jaw.

"Are you lying regarding the last?" The blue of his eyes peeking through his swollen lids glowed in the flickering light.

"I will never lie to you again, Nick." She kissed his mouth but took care not to hurt him. "Now sleep."

He took her hand and kissed it before rolling onto his side and relaxing. "I have quite a lot to live for, it would seem."

A smile tugged at her lips as she let exhaustion lull her to sleep.

Chapter 9

Nick woke in time to light another candle before the light went out and left them in total darkness. He positioned Faith on her side and bundled his coat under her head.

He crouched a few feet away and watched her sleep.

Sore, he knew he'd gotten off easily the day before. Joseph and Jean-Claude would not be as kind when they came for him again. His only hope was that Charles wasn't entirely comfortable with torture. However, he needed Charles to keep the other members of the household safe.

If he died before he could secure Faith's safety, he would have failed his life. The notion sent a shudder through him. Even after lying two nights in a cellar and caring for him, she was the most beautiful thing he'd ever seen. It was unbearable to think of harm coming to her because of the choices he'd made for his life.

No. He would find a way to get her and the three servants to safety. It might well be the last thing he did, but he would find a way.

Faith stretched like a cat and opened her eyes. "You kept the candle lit."

"It was a near thing, but I woke in time." He remained where he was. He didn't want whoever came to collect him to see his affection for Faith.

She sat up. "Thank you. I cannot bear the darkness."

"How will you ever forgive me?" He sat in the center of the floor and crossed his legs. His heart ached with regret.

"This is not your fault, Nick. There is nothing to forgive." She took the cloth from the basket and nibbled some bread before offering the rest to him.

He obliged her without getting too close. "It is all my fault."

"Just remember the three things I told you. We shall discuss anything else when we are all safe."

It was impossible for anyone to be so forgiving. "Tell me about your childhood."

"Why in the world would you want to hear about that?" She scoffed and finished the meager food.

"I want to know how you became so fierce. You look like a lamb, but inside there is a lioness waiting to pounce." Nick adored both the gentle and ferocious sides of Faith.

She smiled and tried to calm her wild curls.

Her joy died as the key turned in the lock.

Jane ran in first. She placed a basket of food by Faith and gathered the empty basket. "I wanted to bring you a blanket, but it was not permitted, my lady."

"I'm fine, Jane. Thank you."

Charles frowned in the doorway. He surveyed Faith and Nick. "Come, Nicholas. Your reprieve is over."

Faith glowered at Charles. "Sir, is there nothing you can do? This treatment is ungentlemanly."

With only the slightest edge of regret in his eyes, Charles nodded. "It is that, my lady. Nothing about war becomes a gentleman."

"We are not at war here in this house." Faith's voice rang with indignation and valor.

Charles shrugged. "On this point, we must disagree."

Before Faith went too far with whatever words stirred in her pretty head, Nick walked to the door and preceded Charles up the steps.

At the top of the steps, Jane scurried toward the servants' stairs while Charles directed him toward an office at the back of Parvus. Before they reached the door, Charles said, "She is quite a woman, Nicholas."

Nick shrugged.

"Are you in love with her?"

The question might have been innocent and born out of genuine curiosity and even care, but Nick couldn't risk that there was another agenda. "I know nothing of love, Charles. Do you?"

"I can see that she cares for you."

"She is a slip of a girl who tricked me into coming here for the purpose of trapping a duke into marriage. I should have left immediately, but planned to toy with her for a few days. In hindsight, I should have followed my first instinct and left as soon as weather permitted." It was a simple thing for Nick to lie to Charles. His pledge to stay honest applied only to Faith. Any other aspiration to be truthful would have to wait for better times, at least where his old friends were concerned.

Charles laughed. "I should have known better than to think your cold heart could be captured."

"Indeed," Nick lied.

Inside, Joseph and Jean-Claude sat on the only two cushioned chairs in the sparsely decorated office. The bookshelves were bare and there was no desk. Since Geb only used the castle for hunting or as a getaway from the city, a proper work space hadn't been important.

Joseph turned, his grin pure evil. His nose was less swollen than the night before, but his eyes were both ringed black underneath. "I see you survived the night. Your injuries do not trouble you much?"

Touching the bruise under his eye, Nick smiled. "It will take more than this to break me, Joseph. You should know that."

"Ah, but we thought perhaps the young lady would persuade you to a more sensible path." Joseph got up and strode to the center of the room. His stare might have been enough to break a lesser man.

The hair on the back of Nick's neck stood up. If they made threats to Faith, he didn't know how he would protect her. The best he could do was pretend she meant nothing and hope that would keep her safe. If Joseph or Jean-Claude knew his true feelings, they would use that information to destroy him, and Faith would suffer for it.

Charles pushed Nick forward. "The girl is insignificant. She means nothing and has no information. She is some kind of pawn in the game between Nicholas and the Egyptian, Arafa."

Always listening, Jean-Claude finally stood and joined them in the center of the room. "Perhaps, but that is a matter for later. Right now, I want to know where the English army plans to move in the next month."

It wasn't easy to hide his relief at the focus moving back to him. Nick felt like a hound dog surrounded by hungry wolves, but that was far better than Faith's life being in jeopardy. "What makes you think I have any contact with Drake, since I am no longer working for the Crown?"

A horrible laugh gurgled from deep in Joseph's chest. "No one leaves the service. You must think us imbeciles to believe such nonsense." His thick French accent rang with derision.

"I am a duke, Joseph. It is not as if my titles came from frolicking to the whims of a king or emperor. My father was the duke before me, and his father, for seven generations. The Crown can command me, but I am not without power. I left the service at the behest of His Royal Majesty. I do not hear from Francis Drake on the comings and goings of the troops as I once did. Do you know nothing of English nobility? Oh, but of course, you wouldn't." Nick knew it was foolish to bait them by deprecating their bestowed titles, but the further their thoughts were from Faith, the better.

Jean-Claude stepped up until he was inches from Nick and slapped his face hard enough to spin Nick's head. "Be mindful of that tongue, lest I cut it out of your filthy English mouth."

Nick's hand fisted of its own accord, but he held back striking the powerful spy. He might kill Nick on the spot and then take his anger out on Faith. Keeping her safe and making sure she and the servants got away unharmed, was the only thing that mattered. Nick held his fist and his tongue in check, but kept his gaze fixed. Faith's plan was sounding better, but it was too soon to give anything away. This would take time, and time was what he needed. Help might arrive, if Nick could hold out long enough without dying.

Joseph ended the staring duel, with a hand on Jean-Claude's shoulder. "Strap him down, and we shall see if his caustic tongue is of any use to us before you cut it out."

The center of the room was empty, save for four ropes looped at the ends. Each one was secured to a spike beaten in to a corner.

Jean-Claude knocked Nick to the stone floor, with a hard swipe to the leg.

Nick went down with a thud and pain stunned his knee, which hit first. He fought briefly against the three men binding his legs and arms but soon found himself facedown on the stone, his arms wide above his head and his legs spread; he likely looked like a prostrate version of da Vinci's *Vitruvian Man*.

Someone grabbed the back of his blouse and tore it down the back.

"Is this necessary?" Charles asked. He never could stand the sight of blood.

"I want the locations and movements of George's army." Joseph's voice was almost as sweet as it was deadly. "If Nicholas would give them to me now, he could spare himself this agony."

Charles knelt on the floor and put his face down to meet Nick's gaze. "Nicholas, be reasonable. Tell us what we ask and your death will be quick and painless. I will even guarantee the safety of the girl."

It was better to remain silent than to risk giving away some bit of his soul where Faith was concerned. Nick closed his eyes.

"Do not say I didn't try to be merciful," Charles said.

Jean-Claude laughed. "I'm glad he is as stubborn as ever. It will give me great joy to rip the information from him one lash stroke at a time."

"Do not kill him before we have what we need, Jean-Claude. I will be very unhappy if he dies too quickly." A chair scraped the stone when Joseph sat.

Nick observed Charles's feet as he rounded the room to watch the spectacle with Joseph.

Unable to see Jean-Claude, Nick knew who would wield the whip. "Where is the English army now?"

The first lash against Nick's flesh likely broke the skin. Searing pain stabbed through him from his right shoulder down to his left hip. That pain stopped when the second strike took its place.

"When will they arrive in Spain?"

The questions and whipping continued. Nick fought to keep his mouth closed, fearful he might accidentally say something important.

Just when Nick hoped one last lash would end his life, the beating stopped. They left him on the floor and exited the office.

Tugging on his bindings gave Nick no release. His pain had morphed into a beast that took over his entire body and there was no escape. He may have lost consciousness. Voices alerted him to their return.

His scalp burned with someone's fingers lifting his head by his hair.

Jean-Claude's pointed nose nearly touched Nick's. "Would you care to speak about the movements of the English army now, old friend?"

"My position is unchanged." Nick hardly recognized his own voice, it was so rough.

Jean-Claude dropped Nick's head and his bruised cheek hit the stone, making him grunt. "Your flesh is already quite raw and bleeding. You might not survive another whipping."

"Perhaps we shall let him rest as he is and come back to this conversation tomorrow." Joseph's voice was a perfect mix of kindness and malice. He really was the ideal spy.

Charles's boot stomped forward until they were inches from Nick's head. "It looks bad. I shall get a tea-soaked cloth to cover him. You would not wish him to die from infection before he tells us everything."

All three left and only Charles returned. "You'll not survive another beating, Nicholas. Tell them what they want to know."

The cool cloth soothed with just a hint of agony. "You know I can't do that, Charles."

"Then you will suffer another long day tomorrow and the next. They won't stop until you are either dead or a traitor to your country. If the latter, then they will kill you. No one can hold on to their secrets forever, Nicholas." Charles tamped the cloth over Nick's skin with the lightest touch.

"Thank you, Charles."

A low huff and Charles stood. "I have instructed the maid to come and add tea to the cloth one time before removing it."

Once again, Nick was alone in the office. Unable to move more than an inch in any direction, his body ached, the cold stone left him shivering, and he prayed for oblivion.

Jane came and did as she was told. "If I free you, they will kill my lady. I'm sorry, Your Grace."

"It's okay, Jane. You must help Lady Faith. I will stay alive as long as I can, but it might not be long enough for help to arrive."

Jane removed the cloth and cleaned him up as best she could. "I wish I could do more for you. This is no way to die."

"We reap what we sow." Nick chuckled. "Tell her, I'm sorry. Will you do that for me, Jane?"

"What shall I tell her you're sorry for, Your Grace?" Jane gave him bread, which probably had not been part of her instructions.

Nick chewed but it was difficult swallowing. When the bread melted to a fine mush, he was able to get it down. "Tell her, I should have paid better attention and never lost my temper. I should have told her everything and kept her safe. I'm sorry I failed her."

Heavy footsteps down the hall, had Jane scurrying to hide whatever food she'd smuggled into the office. "I will tell her."

Alone as the sun left the world, not even total darkness gave Nick peace. Nightmares of a wild-eyed Léonie chasing him with a dagger haunted his night. At dawn her dark eyes metamorphosed into Faith's golden ones, cursing him for his past.

Pain, sharp and sudden, licked up his side. "Wake," Jean-Claude said.

The click of leather against his hand was enough to force Nick to full alertness.

Joseph wore blue slippers more in fashion for a ballroom than a torture chamber. "After a night on the cold stone and your back flayed open to the elements, are you inclined to tell me where the English army is right now?"

Exhaustion, pain, and the fear that any answer could cause Faith harm, kept Nick's mouth closed. Time. He needed more time.

"*Commence*," Joseph said in French.

The lash of the whip cut through both flesh and scabs from the day before. Nick had not realized pain could be worse than what he'd already suffered. He'd been wrong. Only Faith's clear eyes and kind smile, kept him from madness.

The sun was full bright when he finally called out, begging for them to stop. A deep self-loathing welled up in his gut for his weakness. Agony had won the day.

"Where are the English troops now?" Charles sounded nearly as desperate as Nick felt.

"They gather in Plymouth." Nick closed his mouth. It was a lie, but to say too much might end his current pain and get him killed as well. Despite his state of body, his mind remained fixated on getting Faith home safely. Lie and faint, she had said. He let his body go limp and made no move or grunt when Joseph kicked his ribs.

"Lord, have you killed him?" Charles whined.

Jean-Claude's foul breath could wake the dead, but Nick remained still and relaxed. "He lives. Just out."

"Plymouth," Joseph said. "That means our information about an invasion was correct. We must get word to France to take Spain now or postpone for a better time."

"It might not mean that at all," Charles protested. "They might be planning to go directly to France. You'll need to gain more from Nicholas, but you won't do so tonight. He needs rest and care."

"He betrayed us!" Jean-Claude bellowed like a child in a tantrum.

"If he dies, you will learn nothing." Charles called down the hall for servants. He said something in low tones.

Nick remained flaccid on the stone, and despite the agony of his back and pain of lying on the stone so many hours—it might have been days—he didn't move.

"Charles is right. He must be kept alive and we need more information." Joseph paced the floor behind Nick. "Jean-Claude and I will ride out in the morning and send a messenger to France. There is a man waiting at Ellesmere Port. It's a day's ride if the weather holds. You may care for Nicholas as you see fit, Charles. When we return, he will either tell us all, or we shall finish this business."

"If he told us about Plymouth, he will tell more. He merely needs enough encouragement." Jean-Claude loved inflicting pain. Evil lurked inside his calm façade.

"Indeed," Charles said. "Go meet the messenger. Find out what the emperor wishes from us and warn him about Plymouth. When you return, Nicholas will be well enough to begin questioning again."

The door opened and closed.

The rope around Nick's left arm loosened and released. One by one, Charles removed the bindings.

Nick might have been faking his state of unconsciousness, but there was nothing false about his inability to defend himself.

The agony of being lifted from the ground was exquisite, rocketing from his flayed back to every muscle and joint, and Nick expected his head might explode in a thousand bits. His mouth opened on a cry.

"I'm sorry," Charles said. "You're a mess, Nicholas, but this is your own doing."

Chapter 10

Faith had counted nine candles since they'd taken Nick away. It had been more than two days. He might be dead, but in her heart, she felt him still alive. Her body ached and her mouth was so dry she had trouble opening it to eat the last time Jane came with food.

The key turned in the lock and as she did each time, Faith held her breath for whatever was to come. She braced for news that Nick had died at the hands of those three monsters.

Jane stood in the doorway.

There was no sign of Charles or Jean-Claude. Was she to be freed? Her heart sank.

Tears welled in Faith's eyes, but she swallowed her sorrow. It was an effort to form words, and the light from the three candles Jane carried hurt Faith's eyes. "Is he dead?"

"No, my lady. His Grace lives, as far as I know." Jane stepped toward her and reached out her hands to help Faith stand. "I'm to take you to your bedroom."

After so long in the cellar, Faith had trouble understanding. "I'm released from here?"

"From this dungeon, yes. Jamie and Thea will have food and wash water waiting. I've been told you may have a normal meal."

Faith took Jane's hand and followed her out of the cellar. Halfway up the stairs, Faith had to stop and catch her breath. Her legs wobbled on the stairs in protest after so long with little use. "Where is the duke?"

"I don't know. I only know he was alive when the round-faced one sent me to bring you to your room." Jane came to Faith's side, wrapped an arm around her waist, and helped her up the steps.

At the top Faith wanted to sit, but Jane nervously pulled her along until they made it up another flight of stairs to the bedrooms.

True to her word, Jane led Faith to the bedroom she'd slept in before Parvus was invaded by French spies. The sun shining in the window hurt her eyes, and she shaded them with her hand.

The white bedding and bed curtains were a stark, almost obscene difference from the dark filth of the wine cellar. The dressing table had a basin and pitcher for washing, and the round table was spread with white linen and silver.

Jane went to the wardrobe. "I can help you wash and dress, my lady. I was not given a time limit to stay with you."

"Thank you, Jane, but can you draw the curtains? I cannot bear the light as yet." Faith sat in the chair. She longed to lie on the bed and feel the soft down beneath her, but she was so filthy, she couldn't ruin the crisp white sheets.

Once the curtains were drawn and allowed in only indirect sunlight, Jane helped Faith out of her dirty dress. It was the light blue day dress she had picked for the picnic in the hothouse because it had been her favorite and most flattering. She'd wanted Nick to like her and more. Now she never wanted to see the grimy thing again. Though her feelings toward Nick had not changed.

Her hair needed more than a basin and washcloth could offer, so Jane twisted it into a knot atop Faith's head. They scrubbed the grime from her skin and put her into a sensible cream-colored dress that was easy for Faith to get into and out of on her own.

Jane helped her with the last button just as the door swung open. Charles Schulmeister's breath came heavy with the load of carrying Nick into the bedroom.

Nick's arms hung like broken branches from his shoulders and his eyes were closed.

"Put him on the bed," Faith ordered.

Nick's blouse hung on him in tatters. His skin was beaded with sweat.

As if the spy suddenly cared what happened to Nick, Charles lowered him onto his stomach inch by inch.

Faith gasped and her stomach turned at Nick's ravaged back. From his neck to the top of his breeches, he was slashed and bleeding. Some spots had scabbed over and some were fresh and raw.

Nick made no moves as he was placed on the mattress.

"He will need care, my lady. The others have gone on an errand for the day. You may send your maid for supplies. However, should she tell anyone what is happening here, I will kill you both. I may not approve of my colleagues' practices, but I am loyal to their cause. Do not make me regret my decision to offer mercy for Nicholas's sake." Charles bowed.

Faith ran to the bed and sat next to Nick. "Oh, Lord, what have they done to you."

The scratch of his voice was nothing like the strong man she'd come to admire. "I did as you instructed, sweetheart."

"I?" Faith took the washcloth from Jane and lightly patted a square of raw flesh behind his shoulder.

"Come closer," he whispered.

Faith leaned down so that her ear was against his mouth. "You said, lie and faint."

Heart in her throat, Faith let one tear roll down her cheek before she swallowed down her horror. "I did say that and you're still with me, Nick. That is all that matters."

His nod was followed by a cringe.

"Jane, go and fetch clean water, cloths, and bandages. Then go and see if we have some honey to keep these from festering. We must clean him up and keep his blood from being tainted." Faith continued to wash him an inch at a time.

"My lady, you should not be the one to care for a man in such a way." Jane stood close, her eyes filled with terror.

Faith cut her a scolding look. "Go and do what I've said."

The door closed and Faith let her tears go, though not her emotions. She got up, opened the window and dumped the dirty water out. There was some water left in the pitcher and she poured it in the basin before returning to the bed and moving on to the next patch of wounded skin.

"Jane is right, Faith. You are too good for this kind of work. Let a servant care for me now that we are not trapped in the cellar," Nick croaked.

She brushed his hair off his forehead and kissed the unmarred inch of skin below his hairline. "I spent many days caring for Aurora in just this way. Though you would do better with a doctor, I will have to do for now."

"You are more stubborn than I would have thought." He chuckled but the movement made him gasp.

"Be still." She knew that each touch must be agony for him. "I wish I didn't have to hurt you, Nick. I'm sorry."

"Your gentle touch is like heaven, Faith." He hesitated. "Do you think you might help me to rise, so I might clean myself up to some extent before you continue?"

"I will not faint at the sight of you naked." She swallowed down her trepidation, determined to be of help to him.

Even a long sigh hurt him. "It is not a matter of your embarrassment, sweetheart, but my own."

Faith understood and rose from the bed. "Of course."

A knock at the door and Jamie pushed through with a large bucket of water. "I have wash water, my lady. Thea will come with food as soon as she can finish the soup. I said meat pies, but she said you both need something light to start."

"Thank you, Jamie. Just put the bucket there." She pointed to the place near the stand where she'd left the pitcher.

Once the boy had done as he was told, Nick said, "Jamie, would you help me get cleaned up so my lady doesn't have to?"

Eyes like saucers, Jamie ran over and helped ease Nick from the bed. The two stumbled to the chair and Nick sat.

Seeing Nick's mortification, Faith turned her back and walked to the window. She let her eyes become accustomed to the light and wished she could go out into the snow and lose herself in the winter scene below.

It was twenty minutes or more before Jamie said, "I'll fetch a clean bucket of water for the wounds and some clothes, Your Grace."

The door opened and closed.

"You can turn around now, Faith." His voice was somewhat stronger.

He remained on the chair, wrapped from the waist down in the bedsheet.

Aching on the inside for what he had suffered, Faith held back her tears and emotion.

"Are you okay, sweetheart?"

Kneeling before him, she took his hand and kissed it. "I am not bloody and broken."

"Thank God." His groan filled the room as he ran his other hand along her hairline, near her cheek.

Jane shuffled in with a stack of fresh sheets and clothes for Nick. She put the clothes on top of the trunk in the corner before making the bed. If she spared a glance for Faith kneeling with her head in Nick's lap, she said nothing.

More water and a tureen of soup arrived while they remained in the intimate pose. When the servants were gone and the door closed, Nick sighed. "As much as I adore having you near, I wouldn't mind a taste of that soup before I lie back in bed."

Careful not to jostle him, she jumped up and opened the tureen. The warm scent of herbs and chicken filled the room, making Faith's stomach rumble with need.

"Did they bring you food?" Nick's neck turned red.

Faith helped him closer to the table. "They brought me bread with some meat and cheese, every two candles."

"That's twelve hours between meals. God, Faith, I'm sorry. You must eat."

She ignored his command and his apology, and continued to ladle two small bowls of soup. She set one in front of him before covering the white porcelain tureen and sat opposite him. Watching him, she waited.

Eyes narrowed, he spooned a taste of soup over his dry lips.

Faith ate her own soup, but was soon full and put it aside.

It was a shame that neither of them could eat much of the delicious soup, but Nick listed to one side and put down his spoon. "I think that's quite enough for now."

His attempt at rising failed and Faith rounded the table to put her shoulders under his arm and steadied him on the short walk to the bed. She wasn't up to her full strength either, but she was far better off than Nick. Between the two of them they made it to the mattress without incident.

"Lie on your stomach and I will finish cleaning those wounds." Faith dragged the bucket and two cloths over and settled next to him. She started below his shoulders, where she'd left off before. He was clean now, but the wounds would take time to heal.

"You are very gentle," he said on a long breath.

"Those men should be ashamed of what they've done to you." Anger flared in her gut.

He laughed, but then groaned as the jerking must have caused him pain. "They will not feel any shame, I'm afraid. From their perspective, I deserve what I'm getting. After all, I did pose as their friend and fellow French spy, and then turned my back on them to report my findings to my country. It is a dirty business, espionage."

Logic said he was right, but Faith's fury didn't wane. "I don't care what they think is right or wrong. I care only that they have hurt you and I want them to pay for it."

He wrapped a hand around her knee. "I should never like to have you as an enemy, sweetheart."

There was comfort in his touch. She no longer cared about propriety. They had moved beyond such things. "No, nor any of the other Wallflowers, I think. We can be quite ruthless, when necessary. I'm still not convinced that one of them didn't have a hand in Radcliff's death." Faith wrung out the towel, leaving the water pink with his blood. She continued to clean with one cloth and dry with the other until his entire back was free of excess blood, sweat, and grime.

"Do you think so? I thought he was killed during an incident at a gaming hell." Nick stiffened as she cleaned a particularly deep gash.

She stilled until he relaxed, and then continued. "He was. But Mercy had mentioned a week or so before that she'd overheard him bragging about his cheating, and he was sure he would fill his coffers before anyone noticed his system."

"You think Mercedes Heath could have orchestrated Radcliff's death?" Nick sounded affronted, but his smile told a different story.

It had only been four days, but his smile was a beacon of hope after the worst days of her life. "I think she might have found a way to send word to the gambling-house owner. Whether or not she knew it would lead to a stabbing, I can't be sure."

"Have you asked her?"

Faith cleaned the last cut near the waist of his breeches and plunked the towels in the bucket. She dragged it near the door before going to the dresser and gathering the pot of honey. The honey would keep his wounds from festering and poisoning his blood. "I see no reason to ask Mercy about the matter. If she did have something to do with it, I would be putting her in a position where she might have to lie. If she didn't, I might offend her. Though, I suppose there is the possibility she would just tell me the truth."

"Whatever that is, it takes the sting out." Nick sighed and relaxed into the soft down.

"It's honey. It will also keep you from cracking the new scabs as they form, which will mean less scarring and it should stave off any festering." Putting aside the honey, she placed bandages across his back.

"Whoever was responsible for Radcliff's death, I'm glad your friend is free of him."

She had never told her suspicions to anyone else. Somehow, she had come to trust a man who admitted to being a spy. She knew he would understand why one of the Wallflowers might have done such a thing. Faith often wished she'd thought of it herself years earlier. It might have saved Aurora a litany of pain. "I trust you will keep my suspicions to yourself, Nick."

He rolled slightly and looked her in the eye. "I will keep any and all secrets you wish to share with me, Faith."

"I will keep yours as well." She stood. "If you can sit up, I will secure the bandages. Then you can rest."

The bedroom filled with his groans as he pushed first to his hands and knees and then turned himself to sit on the edge of the bed. "If the idea of sleep was not so appealing, I would have refused."

She held a rolled-up bandage. "Can you lift your arms?"

He did, but his face contorted in agony.

"I will be quick." Glad for the wide bandage, she wrapped him quickly from his waist to just under his arms, and then tucked the ends in. Between the sticky honey and his inability to move, the wrapping should hold until morning.

Nick stood and walked around the bed before rolling to his stomach and sinking his head in the pillow. "Lie here with me, Faith?"

Exhausted and haunted by what she'd seen, she couldn't help allowing her tears to finally fall in earnest.

Rolling to his side, he studied her. "Faith?"

"I'm sorry. I'm just tired and…" Sobs wracked her body and she sat on the edge of the bed with her head in her hands.

"Sweetheart, come here, please." Nick's plea slipped through her hysteria.

Like a child, she shuffled around the bed and climbed in. Unable to face him, she lay on her side with her back toward him.

His strong arm wrapped around her and he hauled her back against his chest. "There is no shame in crying after what you have been through," he whispered against her ear. "I wish I could manage a good cry, but my emotions will never permit such a release."

More gales of tears forced their way out and her body heaved with emotion.

Nick held her and kissed the back of her neck. "Let it out, my sweet, brave girl. No one could have handled this better than you have. This is all my fault. I had no right to bring you into such a mess."

Gulping air until she got her emotions under control, she calmed. She loved the feel of his arm around her, and his kisses sent chills through her even in their current state. "I am sorry to be such a ninny. I don't know what's happened to me. I rarely cry, but these last few days have been overwhelming."

"To say the least." He pressed another kiss just behind her ear. "You have every right to cry, rage, hit me, and more. I hope I live long enough to make this up to you."

"Nick?" Her voice trembled.

"Yes, sweetheart?"

"Do you think Charles was telling the truth? Will the other two really be gone all day? I don't want to sleep if you might be dragged away." Her heart pounded with the knowledge that he would not survive another such beating.

"Sleep. He did lie. They will be gone at least two days, perhaps three. They've gone to Ellesmere Port to meet a messenger. They left right after I lied about the location of the English army. They thought I was unconscious when they divulged their plans." Nick rested his cheek against the back of her head.

"I'm glad you lied, but why did you wait so long?" Her eyelids weighed down and it was a struggle to stay awake.

"If I gave in too early, they may not have believed me or they may have killed me once they knew. I needed to buy time."

She yawned. "Time for what?"

"For someone to come save you. We need four or five more days and I think we only have two or three." His voice faded at the end and his arm grew limp around her.

Faith wanted to enjoy the feel of him around her, behind her, and so intimately with her. She imagined what a lifetime of nights as his wife might be, but her body gave in to the need for rest.

Chapter 11

Nick had never been so uncomfortable and delighted at the same time in his life. Waking with all of Faith's soft curves tightly fitted against his body was pure torture and absolute heaven. She was all curves, with a narrow waist, full hips, and delectably plump breasts.

Moving his arm pulled at the scabs forming on his back, but he couldn't resist running his hand down her hip to her thigh and back again until he settled at her ribs.

When he'd asked her to lie with him the day before, he'd expected her to refuse. Then her tears had nearly broken his heart. He'd seen women cry before, but it was usually to gain some favor from him. Faith's tears had built up over days of strain in an untenable situation. She had broken down and let him comfort her. It was the most useful he'd ever felt.

A sliver of sunlight filtered through the curtains. Nick wished he could have remained fitted to Faith's backside for hours, but servants would arrive soon and he didn't know what the day would bring.

With agonizing slowness, Nick pushed back until he could sit up, and slid to the edge of the bed. Still wrapped in the sheet, he made the effort to pull on the clean breeches left for him by Jane. Looking at the blouse, he agonized at the thought of dragging the fine cloth over his ravaged back.

The sheets ruffled and a low feminine sigh followed.

Nick's pulse tripped at the sound and how perfect she was in every way. He turned to find her stretched out with her arms above her head and every inch of her curves arched on the mattress. If the exertion wouldn't have killed him, he'd have seduced her on the spot. As it was, he was in no condition for such activities. "Good morning."

She rolled to her side and opened her eyes. "How do you feel, Nick?"

Having promised never to lie to her again, he said, "Sore but rested."

Faith rolled from the bed. Her cream day dress was wrinkled and her hair a wild mass falling out of her bun. She pointed to the table. "I suppose the servants were here last night and took the soup away."

Noting the empty table, Nick nodded. "I hope we are to be fed this morning or we shall regret not having forced more soup down yesterday."

She slid on her slippers, brushed her curls from her face, and stood. "We must have slept a long time."

Nick stepped in front of her and held her by the arms. "How do you feel?"

Lowering her chin, she gazed up at him from hooded lids. "I am sorry for crying. You have been through so much, and I have no right to tears."

With a kiss on her forehead, Nick smiled. "You have every right, sweetheart. None of this should have happened to you. I am to blame, and if you never wanted to speak to me again, you would be perfectly right."

A scratch at the door was followed by Jamie and Thea entering.

Nick dropped his hands and stepped away. He longed to know how she would have responded to his statement, but it would have to wait. Though, he suspected, she would be well rid of him when this mess came to an end. She needed him for the moment, and her softhearted nature made her care for everyone around her. When she had time to reflect on what he'd put her through, Faith would walk out of his life, and he would be powerless to stop her. He would not blame her. Nothing he could ever do would make up for what he put her through.

Jamie hefted a fresh bucket of water, while Thea placed a tray of food and coffee on the table. The scent of fresh yeasty bread filled the room, along with sausage and coddled eggs with some kind of herbs.

Thea stared a long time at Faith. "Are you all right, my lady?"

"Yes. Thank you, Thea." She took the girl's hand.

"And His Grace?" The cook didn't glance at him.

"His back will need time to heal, but he is better today." Faith offered a hint of a smile.

Thea nodded, then lowered her voice. "It is just the one they call Charles here now. The other two have fled. We are free to move about, but I fear sending Jamie for help, lest Charles take my disobedience out on you."

Wishing he could put on a shirt, Nick stepped closer. "Do not put you or the boy in danger, Cook. We shall find another way. By now, MacGruder would have noted the invasion. I have hope that two days ago, he would have sent for help."

Faith's eyes narrowed with worry, but she forced a smile for Thea's sake.

Jane entered with soap and clothes just as the younger servants were leaving.

Holding a chair for Faith, Nick leaned down and asked, "What troubles you, sweetheart?"

Faith sighed. "I have kept something from you. Mr. MacGruder came to the wine cellar."

"What?" He sat across from her, trying to process what she'd said.

"He came to rescue me, but I refused to leave you and the servants. Surely someone would have died for my leaving. I couldn't bear it." Her voice rang tight with emotion.

She was the most frustrating woman he'd ever met. Lord, but how brave she was, and probably right. When'd he'd pulled himself under control, he spoke calmly. "When was that?"

She stared at the ceiling and pressed fingers to her thumb as if counting before shaking her head. "Time is so confused when in the dark for a long time. The first time you were taken. It couldn't have been more than an hour before they brought you back to the cellar."

Nick stared at his hands. She was right about time getting away when life was suspended by horror. His voice was tight and unfamiliar. "Then my pretty lie to the children might actually have been the truth."

"Are you very angry at me?" She held her breath.

He was, but at the same time he couldn't fault her. "I'm furious that you did not save yourself."

She sighed and turned her gaze away.

"However," he added, "you were probably right, in that someone would have been punished for your leaving. The boy likely would have been beaten or killed as an example and my own death expedited as they would feel pressured for time. But, Faith, must you be so brave?"

Warmth bloomed on her cheeks. "I am not brave, but I do know right from wrong. Still, if Mr. MacGruder went for help two days ago, it will still be four or five before we might be rescued. You will not survive, Nick." Fresh tears welled in her eyes, though she brushed them away.

Touched by her caring, Nick forced a smile. "We shall have to do our best and hope Jean-Claude and Joseph are delayed."

"Perhaps Charles can be persuaded to release us." She sipped a cup of coffee.

Nick shook his head. "That is unlikely. Charles has his own agenda, and I doubt it includes Joseph learning of his duplicity. He would land in my shoes, and that's the last thing he wants."

"Why don't you tell them about Charles? Maybe that will be enough to keep you alive. At least it would divert their attention." Faith's eyes brimmed with hope.

"It might, but it would lose us the one person who does not want me killed. If not for Charles, I might be dead already and you might not have been fed. He will see that you are safely returned home should I die here. I don't know what the others might do to you."

It was a harsh reality and he hated putting thoughts of her own danger in her head, but the truth was what would save them or be their undoing. He would lie to the spies he once called friends, but he would not lie to Faith.

She stared at him, a bite of sausage perched on her fork and frozen halfway to her mouth. "You have that much faith in Charles?"

"No. But he is less ruthless than the others and believes himself a gentleman." Nick shuddered inside at what a fiend like Joseph Fouché might do to Faith if he got a notion that she could help his cause.

Faith blinked.

Jane stood behind her holding a shawl, gaping.

With a laugh, Faith popped the sausage in her mouth. She continued to chuckle while she chewed. "You really meant it when you said you would not lie to me anymore."

"I meant it."

Jane placed the shawl over Faith's shoulders. "I think I would prefer a pretty lie at this point."

Laughing, Nick agreed. The movement sent a spasm of pain across his back and he bit down on a curse. He fisted his hands on the table until the pain subsided. "This will take some time," he said to himself, though both women studied him. "Jane, does Charles keep the keys with him at all times?"

"He gave them to me to release my lady, but other than that, he has kept them. He unlocked the door this morning and let us in. I assume he will lock the door again when I leave." She had come close and kept her voice at a whisper.

"And did he take his wine last night despite eating alone?" Nick forced down a few more bites of bread, and had to rest. He leaned one arm on the table and hoped his rudeness would be forgiven as he sipped some bitter coffee.

"He drank an entire carafe and could barely get himself off to bed." She sniffed and crossed her arms over her chest.

Interesting. Nick worried over what Charles planned for the day ahead. "What has he told you about today, Jane?"

"Only that my lady may have a bath if she wishes."

Nick glanced between the two. "He will ask you to dine with him tonight, Faith. I would bet on it. You should go and see what he wants.

Jane, get your lady a kitchen knife to put in her boot, should his desires be of an amorous temper."

Bright red, Faith put her fork down. "He wouldn't."

Shrugging, Nick said, "I don't think so, but it's best to be cautious. If he touched you and you didn't kill him first, I would have to."

Her blush deepened and disappeared beneath the low dip in her dress. "Get me the knife, Jane."

Pride swelled inside Nick, but his strength waned. "I'm afraid I must return to bed."

"I will go and get fresh bandages, Your Grace." Jane rushed from the room.

Nick stood with less difficulty than before and walked to the bed. He would have loved to rest on his back and watch Faith finish her breakfast, but he had no choice but to lie on his stomach or side. Opting for his front without her sweet body to lean against, he was unable to keep his eyes open.

* * * *

Awakened by a cold blade near his ribs, Nick jerked to the side. Pain shot up his back.

"Shh…You're all right. It's only a scissor. I'm cutting the old bandages away." Faith's voice was soft and soothing.

Nick relaxed but turned his head to see her kneeling on the bed. She'd changed into a soft yellow dress and smelled like roses. "You've had a bath?"

"I didn't want to wake you to change your dressing, so Jane arranged a bath while you slept. I'm happy to have my hair clean again." She put the scissors aside and eased the bandages away from his back.

The odd sensation of honey sliding away from skin was not painful. "May I touch your hair, sweetheart?"

She froze, the cloth halfway across his back. "Perhaps, when I'm finished. If you wish."

"I've been dying to touch those curls since the first time I saw you attempting to tame them back into a chignon," he admitted.

"My hair is impossible." She cut the other side of the dressings and tossed them aside before beginning to clean his wounds.

"I have had many fantasies about your hair and other parts of you." He sighed as his own thoughts caused him discomfort and it was a relief he was facedown.

Silence filled the room for a heavy beat before she asked, "Have you?"

"Of course." The way her hips swayed when she walked had fascinated him from the instant he saw her walking with her friend Poppy across the ballroom that first night they met. He didn't want to frighten her, so he kept that thought to himself.

Busy cleaning his back, she said, "I think I would like to hear about those fantasies when you are feeling better. I have always been told my figure is not appealing to men. I'm not tall enough, nor slim enough. My mother said we were lucky you had not seen me prior to her letters or you would have taken one look at my round hips and run in the other direction."

Rolling to his side so he could meet her gaze forced her to stop her work. She was as red as a summer rose and wouldn't look at him. "Faith." She kept her chin turned down and her eyes on the washcloth in her hands. "Sweetheart, look at me." His erection was certainly evident, but there was no help for that and he was in no condition to relieve his desires.

Faith obeyed.

"Your mother is wrong. I'm sure your stunning figure is talked about amongst men quite often when ladies are out of earshot. However, should I ever hear such talk, I will call out those men and dispatch them immediately. That being said, you should know, I find you distractingly attractive and have since we first met. I love every curve, and should you ever honor me with your body, I shall worship you from head to toe."

Those stunning golden eyes stared back at him in wide awe. "Really?"

Taking one of her hands away from the honey-covered cloth, he placed it firmly over his painful erection. "Very much so." It came out as a groan when her hand closed slightly.

Pulling her away before he hurt himself, he laughed and rolled back to his stomach. His movements were dilatory until he reached a less painful position. "You must give me a short time before I am ready for such actions, I'm afraid."

Returning to her work, she had the gentlest touch and caused him minimal pain. "Then my mother was wrong and all these years I have wished to look more like Aurora for no good reason."

"Your friend is lovely and I mean her no slight when I tell you, it is not her figure that is talked about in gentlemen's clubs." Nick closed his eyes and settled his desires.

She was silent for a long time, and he hoped she was pleased. "Some of these wounds should have been stitched, but they have stopped bleeding and are healing. I see no signs of blood poisoning."

"Due, I'm sure, to your excellent care." Nick reached out and wrapped his hand around her leg.

"I think it's more likely your strength, but either way, it is a good bit of luck. A blood infection with all those open wounds would be a disaster. I'm going to put more honey on and cover them back up."

He wanted to know how she would feel about him when this was all over. If he lived, she would likely run back to London and never see him again. His heart ached with the knowledge, though he couldn't blame her.

When she'd gotten him all bandaged up again, she said, "Mr. Schulmeister has asked me to dine with him, just as you said he would."

The tightness returned to Nick's gut whenever he thought of Faith being out of his sight. "And has Jane secured a knife?"

She nodded. "I don't know if I would have the courage to use it though."

Sitting on the edge of the bed, he took her hand in his and kissed her knuckles. "Only if he acts improperly. If I know you, that alone would put you in enough of a temper to stab old Charles good and deep."

"And then what?" she asked.

"Then you take his keys and we flee as far from here as we can before the others return." Nick kept her hand, rubbing a circle on her soft palm.

"And if he does nothing inappropriate?" There was fear in her voice and he hated hearing it.

"I do not expect you to strike without provocation. Charles is a big man who would likely overpower you. Have dinner with him, answer his questions if you can and you want to, and then come back here and we shall talk about it. Don't provoke him, Faith. He's smart enough to work successfully for two separate governments without detection." Nick wished he could take her place at the table, but he was in no condition to demand anything. He couldn't overpower Charles while his back was agonizing and he was so weak.

She squeezed his hand. "I'm afraid, Nick."

Pulling her into his arms, he hated himself for causing her this pain. He kissed the top of her head. Roses and Faith's lovely warm scent filled his senses. "You are the bravest woman I have ever known. No one could have borne these last five days better."

With her head tucked under his chin, she sighed. "When this is all over, I shall need to sleep for a week."

"I shall see that you are not disturbed, sweetheart." His heart broke with the knowledge that she'd not want him anywhere near once she was safely back in her West Lane home with friends she could trust.

"You should rest, Nick. Your back is healing but you have eaten little and you need to recover more fully."

The key turned and the door opened, revealing Thea with another platter of food. "I've come with His Grace's supper."

Kicking the door closed behind her, she carried the tray to the table and lowered her voice. "It's not as grand as what will be in the dining room, but it will help you gain your strength back."

"Thank you, Cook," Nick said and sat up, away from Faith. "I will do my best to eat it all."

Thea beamed. "Jane is coming to help you dress, my lady."

A long sigh pushed from Faith's lips. "I suppose it is time."

The scabs on Nick's back pulled and the deeper wounds ached with every move. He could not imagine a time when he didn't hurt. It seemed years rather than days. Yet even in his discomfort, he would not trade a moment spent with Faith while she still needed him.

He rose from the bed and made his way to the table. He still couldn't get a shirt on and with only the bandages to cover him, young Thea wouldn't look at him.

The door opened again and Jamie ran in, followed by Rumple.

The dog jumped on Faith and yipped enthusiastically.

"You have grown." Faith laughed and scratched the puppy behind his ears.

Nick sat.

Rumple sniffed the air and approached more cautiously.

"It's okay, boy. I'll live." Nick hoped he was telling the truth.

Bounding over, Rumple's tongue hung to one side and his tail wagged. He jumped into Nick's lap.

His soft fur and enthusiastic tongue were a welcome relief to the serious pall that had fallen over him and Faith. "You are a good boy."

Thea gave him a horrified look due to the proximity the puppy had to her food tray. She stormed over and bundled up Rumple. "I will bring him back when you've finished eating. The Austrian said the beast may stay with you tonight."

"Thank you." Nick watched Thea, Jamie, and Rumple leave and his heaviness returned. He had too many lives depending on him to get them to safety, but he had no means to save them. His stomach churned.

Faith ran her fingers through his hair and pressed her lips to his cheek. "Don't think so much, Nick. Eat and get well."

He marveled at how easily she read him. He was a master of hiding his feelings, yet Faith knew his every emotion before he did.

Chapter 12

Faith let Jane primp and tug until she was in her finest gold gown. The color matched her eyes, and the ribbons in her hair were usually for special occasions.

She sighed as Jane threaded another ribbon through her tamed hair. "It's enough, Jane. I'm not going to a ball. I'm having dinner with my captor."

"Yes, my lady." Jane finished fussing with the last ruby-colored ribbon.

Nick slept through the dressing process, most of which was done behind a screen.

Faith was glad to have had her hair washed, but she wished the occasion was happier. Her nerves were on edge and the knife tucked inside her soft leather boot did nothing to calm her.

Trying to take Nick's advice and not worry about Charles taking liberties was not easy. And thinking of stabbing someone, regardless of the reason, made her stomach heave. However, when she thought about it, she would have stabbed Aurora's horrible husband if she'd ever been given the opportunity. Perhaps she wasn't incapable of such a thing.

Standing, she observed herself in the glass. Her mother would say, *You are too round and too short, but you will have to do.*

Nick appeared in the reflection behind her.

Jane curtsied and stepped out of the room.

His arms came around her waist. "You are the most beautiful thing I have ever seen, Faith. Far too lovely for Charles to gaze upon, or me for that matter."

Putting her hands over his, she tried to see what he saw in the glass. However, she still wished for slimmer hips, less bosom, and straight hair.

"I'm afraid you are biased in some way, Nick. Society tells me I must say thank you and nothing else when a man pays me such compliments."

His lips pressing to the sensitive skin at the back of her ear sent a chill to her toes and warmed all the places in between. He took a deep breath. "I would prefer if you believed me, but I suppose it will have to do."

Smiling at his refection, their eyes met and those tingles she'd begun to associate with Nick flooded her body. "I will be late for dinner and you shouldn't be standing for so long."

Sorrow passed across his gaze and he dropped his hands. "I plan to rest while you eat so I can be awake to talk when you return."

Faith closed her eyes and stayed her emotions. She took a deep breath and headed toward the door. When she looked back, Nick sat on the edge of the bed. He was still pale and his shoulders rounded, but the fire had returned to his blue eyes as he scrutinized her.

With a last smile, she knocked and was released from the bedroom.

Charles waited in the hallway and offered his arm. "Good evening, my lady."

Ignoring his offered arm, she walked around him and down the hall to the stairs. "Mr. Schulmeister, I see no reason to pretend we are friends since you are clearly my captor."

He followed behind. "As you wish, my lady."

The dining room was set for the two of them to eat at one end of the long table. The dark blue curtains were drawn and candles had been lit around the room. The china was not fancy, but it was all that was available at Parvus, as was the serviceable crystal and silver. It was strange how it had all appeared brighter when Faith had planned the picnic in the hothouse.

Faith waited near the chair set for her and allowed Charles to pull it out for her before she sat.

"I'm afraid the castle is not equipped for high society. However, the wine is excellent and as you know, the food quite magnificent." Charles sat at the head of the table.

He poured them each a glass of the dark red wine and drank his halfway down immediately.

Faith sipped hers. "Why have you requested my presence, sir?"

A soup course was brought up by Jamie and Thea. They were children, but knew to keep quiet and do their part.

Spices and herbs wafted through the air in the steam of the white soup. Faith's stomach rumbled and she took a sip. The divine flavors of veal, fowl, ham, and all those marvelous seasonings. It was too good for the likes of a spy who would let those men hurt Nick so badly. It took all her strength not to tell him so.

Charles closed his eyes while he savored the soup. "I wonder if you know that Nicholas was to me Count d'Armon for many years. This was the title he went by. It wasn't until his leaving France that we knew he was a duke."

"I did not know until your friend mentioned it when you first arrived, and I fail to see the importance." Faith took another sip of the lovely broth and put her spoon aside.

He finished his wine and poured another glass. "I suppose it's not important. Perhaps I just wish for you to see my side of things."

"And what is your side?" It couldn't hurt to know more of how his mind worked.

He drank his wine and rubbed his belly while the second course of pheasant was placed before them. The bird was perfectly browned and served with potatoes arranged in a bed around it. "I first met Nicholas in Switzerland. He was charming and knowledgeable and spoke of nothing but the great emperor. We were all taken with him, and his good looks attracted many women when we were about town. Those were good times."

It didn't matter to her what women Nick attracted. She didn't feel jealous as she had when Nick had first told her about his lover, only worried she might learn something that would change her opinion of him, now that she liked him.

Charles devoured the bird with gusto while Faith picked at the succulent dish. She only ate half of it, while he left not a scrap save the bones on his plate.

He wiped his hands on the linen napkin and finished his second glass of wine. "Joseph liked him as well. He being a confidant to Napoleon, he gained Nicholas an audience when we went to Paris. It was quite a bold move, but happily, the emperor was equally taken with Nicholas. We spent years working together and apart. There was an attempt on Napoleon's life, and now I suspect it may have been Nicholas who nearly succeeded in killing him. Of course, I have no proof."

"What does any of this have to do with today, sir?" Faith didn't like listening to stories of Nick unless they came from him. It was ironic after all her attempts to gain information in underhanded ways, but now she only wanted the truth from his own lips.

"You see, we were great friends and he had been lying the entire time." Charles finished another glass of wine and bellowed for more to be brought.

Thea brought fish and an aspic, which she served without a word.

A few minutes later Jane delivered another decanter of wine.

Faith waited until the servants had finished their work. "And have you been completely honest with your friends?" She said the last word with the irony it deserved.

He sighed. "But my flaws are not under scrutiny."

"No. I suppose not, and I'm certain you are grateful for that."

Like a pigeon whose meal was disturbed, he blustered. "I kept him alive for four days. I saw that you were available to care for him. I encouraged the others to go away so he would have time to heal and might live long enough for you to be saved."

"But not him." It pained Faith to know that Charles fully expected Nick to die in the next day to two.

"I'm afraid not even I have that kind of power, my lady Faith."

"Why do you care if I live or die?" There was more here that she didn't know.

Charles drank down the entire glass of wine and filled it. "In Lucerne I was discovered working for the French by an Austrian. I was to be dragged back to my homeland and would have faced the firing squad. Nicholas spoke for me and bought my freedom. I owe him a life."

"But not his?" Faith sipped her wine, but watching him drink to excess made the fine vintage unappealing.

"As I told you, I don't have the power to save Nicholas. I will save you to pay the debt I owe him. He would consider that a fair trade." Charles's words slurred but he drank more. The second decanter was half empty.

"I still don't understand why you wanted to have dinner with me, sir." Faith dabbed the napkin at the corners of her mouth and put it on the table. She'd still not regained her appetite and the company made eating even more difficult.

Charles listed to one side, his arm holding him against the chair. "I wanted you to understand. It's not my fault. This is Nicholas's fault for abusing our friendships. He used us, and Napoleon is not happy. It will probably be another year before Joseph receives the title he is promised. Joseph is not forgiving."

Signaling to Jane, Faith called for more wine.

His speech was less intelligible the longer he drank but, amazingly, he would not fall over. "I will return you to Nicholas now. I hope you understand and do not think too harshly of me."

There was no good response, so Faith kept quiet and followed the wobbling Charles back to her room.

Inside, Nick sat in the chair by the table. His scowl was directed at Charles, who attempted a bow, stumbled and left. The key turned in the lock and German singing followed him away from their door.

Faith sank into the other chair. "I thought for certain he would drink himself into unconsciousness, and I could have taken the keys. We would then all walk out the front door."

"He never falls down. I've seen him drunk for a week, and he wobbles but does not fall," Nick said, his earlier scowl replaced by a smile.

"He said you saved his life."

Nick cocked his head. "I did. I'm surprised he would tell you that."

Relief that Nick hadn't tried to make up some elaborate lie flooded Faith. "He plans to repay the debt by saving me."

"Yes. I suspected that was his plan. I appreciate the gesture more than he will ever know." Nick leaned on the table, his efforts to remain upright clearly taking their toll.

Faith rose and stood with her back to him. "Would you mind undoing this gown? I don't think Jane will be coming back tonight."

The air was sucked out of the room while he made no move to do as she asked. Finally, he untied the bow at the back and unlaced the gown.

The gold silk puddled on the floor and Faith stepped out of it before picking it up and placing over the back of her chair.

Nick observed as she moved in only her chemise, corset, and boots. Returning to the same position, she said, "The corset, if you wouldn't mind?"

"Faith, you are killing me." His hands shook as he pulled the bow and strings.

Breathing a sigh of relief as the binding fell to the floor, she kicked it aside. "Thank you. You can't imagine how uncomfortable those things are."

He slid his hand over her hip and pressed his forehead to her back. "No. I don't imagine I can."

Faith turned, bringing his face to just below her breasts. She ran her fingers through his hair. She reached down with the other hand and slid the knife from her boot.

His head turned in the direction of the steel. "I will not take any liberties you don't allow, sweetheart. Besides, I doubt my body would let me do yours justice at this point and I'm sorry to say so."

Putting the knife on the table, she wished she could run her hands over his body. Someday when he was whole again, she would indulge. "I don't really understand what you mean, but I'm sure I wouldn't stop you."

Leaning back, he met her gaze. Confusion, pain, and longing all registered in his eyes and the twist of his mouth. "Wouldn't you?"

Stepping away, she avoided his question. Faith sat and removed her boots before padding to the bed. When he didn't follow, she walked back and offered her hand. "You can barely sit upright, Nick. Come lie down and we'll talk."

He closed his eyes and sighed. Taking her hand, he followed her to the bed. "I wish I was able to do more than make conversation. I've never wanted anyone so much nor been so incapable of following through."

Pure joy rocketed through Faith. "Is it vanity to be happy that you desire me?"

When they were both lying on their sides facing each other, she said, "I swear I have been through every emotion where you are concerned."

"Tell me about them?" He threaded his fingers through hers but made no move to touch her in any other way.

"Don't you want to hear about dinner?" It was foolish to speak of frivolous things when something Charles told her might help their situation.

He shook his head. "Later. If Jean-Claude and Joseph return tonight, I'd much rather have had time to hear your feelings than the recounting of dinner with a drunk."

Nervous, she wished she'd not mention it. "Perhaps I should change your bandages."

"You did it earlier. The morning will be soon enough. Tell me what you thought the first time you saw me." His startling blue eyes shone with curiosity and worry, but he met her gaze directly.

Sighing, she said, "Honestly, I thought you were too good-looking and impertinent to be crossing the ballroom to introduce yourself to me."

"You made my impertinence very clear, but I didn't realize the first. Why too good-looking?" He used his thumb to caress the palm of her hand.

Faith never would have believed a touch of hands could be so intimate and erotic. She felt his touch over every inch of her body and longed for more. "I never expected to marry someone handsome. Mother said I'd be lucky to find a nice plain-faced man to take me. You are anything but common looking."

Those full lips drew down in a frown, and he thought of how lovely they had been when he'd kissed her.

Nick released her hand and drew her chin up with one finger so she met his stare. "Your mother and I are going to have a long talk. You are beautiful beyond words, and the fact that she filled your head with all this nonsense infuriates me. To be honest, I don't know if I can have a civil conversation with her on the subject. It might take years before I am calm enough to utter any words to that woman. Forgive me. I realize she is your mother and I must be cordial, but Lord in heaven, has she never actually seen you?"

It was funny to have him defend her so vehemently, when she knew her mother was quite right in her depictions. "My mother has certainly seen me, Nick."

He shook his head. "No. I beg to differ. She has looked at you, but I don't believe she has ever really seen you. What do your Wallflower friends say on the topic?"

Heat rose in Faith's neck and cheeks. "They are more inclined to agree with you."

"Well, thank goodness for that at least." He rolled his eyes and regained possession of her hand.

"Why does it matter? I am what I am. I do what everyone does, do my best to hide the flaws in my body and accentuate good teeth and smooth skin." She watched his expression morph from confusion to anger, and then amusement.

Leaning forward, he kissed her nose. "What about your perfect nose?"

"My nose is only passable," she insisted.

He surveyed her hair, still bound, braided, and beribboned. The elaborate style pulled the skin around her forehead. "Is all of that comfortable?"

"Not particularly." She would need time to take all the pins out. It took a platterful to tame her wild tresses.

Nick reached up and plucked one free and placed it in her hand. "Hold this."

One by one, he pulled hair pins from the mass and handed them to Faith. When he had as many as he could find, he drew his fingers through each braid until the ribbons floated to the bed. A few pins made their way to the coverlet as well. "What about your hair? Surely no one can say that it is merely passable."

"My hair is impossible," she cried. "I want hair like Mercy's that flows over her shoulders like silk."

"How can I convince you of how special you are, and not just aesthetically? You are smart, clever, kind, empathetic, and compassionate. Even when all of this was my fault. Even when you were nearly starved to death in a cellar, you took care of me and placed no blame. You are a miracle of nature, Faith Landon. I wish I was going to live to court you properly and convince you of your worth." He kissed her lips like a whisper of wings.

"I like that this is how you see me, and I don't accept that you are going to die. Somehow, we will get out of this together." She wanted it to be true. Needed it to be true. The idea of leaving Parvus without Nick broke her heart.

He smiled. "I'm adding *optimistic* to my description."

She pulled his hand away from her hair, causing her to drop the pins. Threading their fingers again, she said, "You can tell a few more lies and gain us some more time. It can't be much longer before Mr. MacGruder will have gone for help."

A long, sad sigh pushed from the lips she'd come to admire. "Listen to me. You have to live. If Charles comes to take you away, you must go. Do not try to save me." He kissed her knuckles. "Getting to know you has been the most precious time in my life, Faith. If you are harmed, my life will have been for nothing. MacGruder may have been killed already. He may not have noticed our situation for days. It could be another week before someone comes for us, and maybe not at all. I doubt I can hold out that long. Forgive me?"

Faith's temper welled up with the tears. She moved in closer and cried into his bandages. "I will not forgive you, Nick. You have to live. Promise me you'll live."

"I can't make that promise, sweetheart." His voice was tight.

"Then promise me you'll try." She wept against his hard chest and wished she could wrap her arms around him.

He kissed her cheek and neck as he caressed her from her neck to the small of her back. "I'll try. I promise, for you, I'll try."

Chapter 13

Nick loved waking with Faith in his arms. It was the second time, and he wished it were not the last, but he could feel his time waning. It was not yet morning and he lingered with her tucked in against him.

The itching of his healing back kept him up most of the night, but even that was better than the pain that had come before. Unfortunately, more pain was in store, but as long as Faith was safe, it would not be in vain.

She stirred, and he kissed her forehead. "Go back to sleep, sweetheart. It is not yet morning."

Two days of little more than eating and sleeping had helped with his healing. He might be battered, but his shaft still reacted to the amazing woman in his arms.

Cuddling in closer, she sighed, soft and seductive. "How long have you been awake?"

He wrapped a hand around her back, stilling her, but the pressure of her pelvis resting against him in such a delightful way, gained him no relief. "Do you think you might stay still, Faith?"

Looking up into his eyes, she cupped his cheek. In the moonlight, she was a goddess. Her porcelain cheeks glowed and her mass of curls spread out over the pillow. "Are you aroused by me?"

He laughed at the surprise in her voice. "From the instant I ever laid eyes on you."

With her head buried in his chest, he couldn't see the blush he suspected bloomed on her cheeks and neck. In only a thin chemise, she was all but bare to him. "I assumed you were too injured for such things."

Pressing her tighter against his erection, he said, "At least part of me thinks otherwise."

Her head popped up, and she stared at him wide-eyed. "Should I leave you?"

"Only if that is what you want, sweetheart." He must have lost his mind, but wanting Faith had become more important than his life.

"I...I don't want to go anywhere." She stretched her neck and elongated her body. Her lips reached his just as her breasts pressed against his chest.

Forcing aside the agony of his itching wounds, he focused on her sweet lips and the curve of her hip where it fitted against him in maddening arousal. "Then stay."

"And what will you do, Nick?" There was the slightest quiver in her voice.

"Are you afraid of me, Faith? You know I would never harm you or take liberties you did not wish." He must look a monster in her eyes with his open wounds, healing scars, and swollen face. She was smart enough to know he was little better than the men who'd done this to him.

She drew his lower lip between both of hers and then did the same to the upper. "I am not afraid, only nervous and embarrassed."

Curls shrouded her face and he combed them back with one hand while sliding his knee between hers. "Why embarrassed?"

"I'm certain women from your past, like Léonie, will have been better able to pleasure you. I only know the little bit that women speak of in private." Despite her worry, she brought her hips forward until she rubbed against his thigh. A surprised moan punctuated her statement.

"You are the only woman who has ever or will ever matter, Faith." He pressed his leg tighter against her cleft and let her set a pace that pleased her.

"I want to touch you, Nick."

Never had any six words sounded so beautiful. He released her hip and let loose the fall of his breeches. Rising with care, that pain not end this before it had really begun, he removed what few clothes he had on. "I will not be able to lie on my back."

She sat up and gawked her fill of him in the moonlit room. Tentatively, she touched the tip of his shaft, then slid her fingers lower. Her touch was soft and light and maddeningly erotic. "Is it strictly necessary for you to lie on your back?"

Taking hold of her hand, he stopped her seduction. "Not strictly." He laughed. "If you are certain, I'm sure we can make do."

Faith got to her feet on top of the mattress and tugged her chemise over her head, then flung it to the floor. "I am taking your word that you find my form pleasing."

With the moon behind her, she glowed in a perfect feminine silhouette before she knelt down in front of him.

Knowing it would not be what it should, Nick vowed it would be wonderful for Faith. He slid his hands from her shoulders down and let his thumbs rub over her pebbled nipples.

"Oh. That feels nice."

Nick cupped her full breast and tugged her bud into his mouth, worrying it gently with his teeth.

Crying out, she gripped his shoulders. "I'm afraid I'm going to hurt you."

"I'm willing to risk it."

They both laughed.

He offered his hand and helped her sit on the edge of the bed before kneeling in front of her.

Those wide golden eyes surveyed him with trust and interest.

Nick slid one hand between her knees and applied just enough pressure so that she knew what he wanted. An instant later, her legs opened for him. "Lie back, sweetheart."

Staying on her elbows, she watched.

Somehow her constant attention was even more arousing. Nick's body thrummed with need, but he lowered his head and made love to her with his mouth. She tasted like the sweetest honey and threw her head back while biting her lip to keep from waking the house.

Faith collapsed back on the mattress, her head rolling from side to side and her hips pumping against his ravenous mouth.

Nick slid a finger inside her just as her muscles clenched in release. It was spectacular. She was magnificent. He pulled her from the bed and into his arms, holding her until her rapture passed.

Wishing he had the strength to lift her onto the bed wouldn't make it so. Instead, he lowered her to the mattress with her help. When she put her head on the pillow and waited, he joined her on his side, facing her. "Are you all right?"

"Poppy said it was wonderful, but I have to admit I didn't believe her."

Laughing, Nick caressed her from shoulder to hip. "And what do you think now?"

She took his shaft in her hand. "I think there is more pleasure to be had before the sun comes up."

He sighed. "I will do my best, love, but you will have to be satisfied with a half-broken man."

"So far, it has been brilliant. Maybe you shouldn't worry so much. I have nothing to compare you to. For me you are the best lover in the world." Her grin was infectious.

Unable to keep from laughing, he kissed her hard, ignoring his bruised lips, and slid his tongue inside her willing mouth.

She wrapped her hand around the back of his head, allowing him to deepen the kiss, and moaned into his mouth.

Lord, he could listen to that sound for the rest of his life. Unfortunately, that might only be a few more hours. It would have to be enough. He rolled her to her back but couldn't hold his own weight on his arms. Sighing, he rolled back to his side. "We'll have to try this another way."

She faced him with those inquisitive eyes boring into him. "There's more than one way?"

"Hundreds, my sweet. I wish I had time to show them all to you and perhaps discover some new ones."

Frowning, she cradled his face in her hands. "Do not talk like that. Make love to me, Nick, and don't think about anything else. Can you do that?"

His painfully hard shaft jerked, indicating that he could. "I will do my best."

Rewarding him with a long, wet kiss, she bent one leg over his, bringing them intimately close.

Nick lifted her other leg over him but kept hold of it so she didn't touch his back. She rolled onto her back, cheeks flush with desire. She was so wet to his touch he couldn't help sliding his fingers over her sensitive bud until her hips pumped and her eyes closed.

With just the slightest adjustment his tip entered her and he drew her hips down hard.

Eyes wide, she cried out. Nick covered the sound with a kiss and kept them still and locked together. After a moment, he drew his mouth from hers. "I'm sorry, sweetheart. It will never hurt again. Just this one time."

"I know. I should have been prepared. I think I'm okay now." She lifted her hips.

It was heaven and torture to be inside this incredible woman. She should have been his in name as well as body, but he would have to settle for only one. Slowly, they moved together at opposing angles.

Nick thumbed her bud and delighted in her expression as another orgasm wracked her body. She tightened around him, drawing his own climax.

Pulling free, Nick spilled his seed between them. "It is my dream to have another day when we will lie together, my sweet Faith."

A tear escaped from the corner of her eye and wet the pillow.

What he wouldn't give to roll onto his back and pull her with him. He wanted to hold her until all her tears were spent and they were happy. However, he couldn't even manage the first part, and settled for wrapping his arm around her waist and drawing her against him.

In a matter of months, Faith Landon would find a nice nobleman to marry. Nick hated the unknown man with everything he owned, but he would not begrudge Faith a happy life.

The first light of day breached the curtains. Nick sat up. "We had better get cleaned up and dressed, before the servant and Charles arrive. I'm sure Jean-Claude and Joseph will return today and our respite will be over."

In all her perfect naked glory, Faith rose to her knees and blocked him from leaving the bed. "Whatever happens, Nick, I do not regret this. I want you to know, I wanted this and you."

Desperate to keep her, he hugged her tightly to him. "I wanted you too, sweetheart. I always will."

* * * *

Faith changed his bandages and the scabbing tugged and pulled until he thought he was back against the whip. As gentle as she tried to be, it still ached as she pulled the bandages away.

"I think I shall leave this off for a while. Jane managed to get some ointment from the apothecary and we shall use that. Perhaps it will help with the itching as well." Her hands were as gentle as a bird's wing as she applied the ointment.

For a time, it did help his discomfort.

"Nick?" They sat across from each other, poking at a fine luncheon Thea had delivered.

"Yes, Faith?"

"Are you a gambler?"

It had not been a question he'd expected. He put down his fork and studied her down-turned face. Her sweet nose pointed at her plate of meat and her ribbon of a mouth turned down. "I would not say it is a habit, but I have been known to make a wager if the odds were good."

"Odds, yes, that's what you call it when a wager is bad or good. What would you say the odds are that we shall live through the next few days?"

"Faith…"

"Just tell me. I'm better if I know all the facts," she demanded.

Shaking his head, he could see no way to give her hope without lying. "I would guess, your odds are fairly good. I would take that bet."

"And yours?" Her fork clinked loudly against the plate as she studied him. He searched the room for some way out of it.

"Tell me," she said.

It was the earnestness in her voice that won him. "I wouldn't take those odds, Faith. We shall need a miracle to save me."

The key turning in the lock ended the conversation.

Charles appeared more sober than usual. "The other gentlemen are back, and I am to bring you both downstairs."

A knot formed in Nick's stomach. "Why should they wish to see Lady Faith?"

The shuttered look on Charles's face did not ease Nick's mind. "I cannot say."

Nick stood and faced Charles. He gripped his arm. "You owe me, Karl. I have kept my silence about you with the understanding you would protect her. Has that fact altered?"

Jerking away, Charles narrowed his eyes. "I will do all that is in my power to keep her out of harm's way."

"Has your situation changed? Is what you can do less than it was when this affair began?" Nick preferred the upper hand. Not knowing what a French messenger might have told the other two spies, left him at even more of a disadvantage.

"No." Charles stood straighter. "They will not harm the lady, Nicholas."

"If they do, Karl, your life is forfeit." Nick showed anger, but his heart pounded with panic. He'd hoped they would take him away and the last memory of her would be of their night together. It was a fantasy, but he had hoped.

Faith clutched his arm. "Nick, it will be all right."

Jane stood in the door with worried eyes. "My lady?"

"Go down to the kitchens, Jane. Wait there until you are summoned." Faith ordered her maid calmly. The way she made everyone else feel at ease, really was extraordinary.

On the stairs, Nick leaned close. "Say nothing. Be smart and stay alive. Whatever I say to them with regard to you, do not pay it any mind. You know what is in my heart. Let what comes from my mouth be lies."

She nodded as they stepped onto the main floor.

The salon had been cleared of furniture save for a chair in the corner. Ropes hung from the chandelier. Nick's heart sank as Joseph pushed Faith into the chair.

"Have you recovered, Nicholas?" Jean-Claude leaned against the mantel. He toyed with the dagger in his hand.

Joseph placed a similar dagger just under Faith's ear.

She gasped but didn't move or lower her gaze.

"Now, Nicholas," Joseph began. "Stand in the center of the room and slide your right hand into the loop in the rope."

It took a force of will to not look at the point where the dagger could easily pierce Faith's skin. "You intend to appeal to my sense of right and wrong where a lady is concerned, Joseph?" He slid his hand through the loop. "The girl is under my protection. There is no need to be so dramatic. I will comply."

"Excellent. Now, Charles, assist our old friend with his other hand and pull the knots tight. We wouldn't want any accidents that would lead to the young lady being harmed." Joseph waited until Charles had tightened both loops around Nick's wrists before he removed the dagger blade and stepped away from Faith.

Charles's eyes held an apology, but also a promise. He would keep her safe and that would be enough.

Joseph stepped close to Nick, shaking his head. "Lady Faith, I am sorry for what you will witness here today. It is unseemly for a lady to see such things, but I suspect my old friend Nicholas has feelings for you and hope your presence will loosen his lips. Or perhaps you have some knowledge you would like to share. I assume since you are here with His Grace and without a chaperone, that you are lovers. Perhaps he has told you something of the movement of troops in England?"

Faith stared, but said nothing.

"It occurs to me," Joseph continued, "that you should not be here at all. Has Nicholas kidnapped you for some purpose? Do you have a large dowry that he might gain by trapping you into marriage?"

Her expression remained sober and unchanging.

"I see you have nothing to say on the matter. It is puzzling." Joseph moved away from Nick. "You may begin, Jean-Claude."

Pushing away from the hearth, Jean-Claude spun his dagger on one finger. "Do you remember the fun we used to have throwing knives, Nicholas? I was quite good. But for you I will not show off my skills at throwing. I don't want you to leave us too soon. As you know, there are questions that need answers."

Nick remembered very well how good Jean-Claude was with a knife, and he also knew how much pleasure the spy took from torture. With his arms lifted and bound, Nick's back ached anew. He glanced at Faith. Her gaze was fixed on him, but she was expressionless. Only her eyes gave away the worry inside.

"Why don't you tell us when the English army will invade and where? If you do that, I will walk to the doorway and throw this knife with a killing blow. I don't really want to cause you pain, Nicholas. We were friends, after all."

Nick chuckled. "I have already told you too much. I understand my fate, Jean-Claude. Do you know yours?"

Spinning around to face Nick, Jean-Claude approached in a flash. "My only concern is the here and now, Nicholas. And now I have plans to take you apart an inch of flesh at a time until you are begging to tell us anything and everything."

Nick grinned through his pain and fear. "My only regret is that I will not live to see you after the emperor has finished with you. I expect you will wallow in the gutter with not a franc to your name. Will your good friend Joseph Fouché be available to you then, or will his grand titles look down on you as I do now?"

Jean-Claude glanced at Joseph.

Joseph shrugged and tossed his blade to Jean-Claude, who caught it easily with his left hand. "He is a duke, Jean-Claude. Of course he looks down on all of us. He toyed with us and now he sneers. Get the information and we will return to France heroes."

Burying the extra blade in the wood of the mantel, Jean-Claude smiled. He carved a line along Nick's ribs with the remaining blade, deep enough for pain but not death.

Faith gasped, but Nick couldn't look at her while the pain shot through his body.

Chapter 14

Faith wanted to crawl into a corner, put her hands over her ears and cry. Watching that monster Jean-Claude torture and maim Nick was killing her from the inside out.

Each time she looked away, Joseph turned her head to face the horror. "Do not turn away, Lady Faith. You will not want to miss this."

And part of her thought he was right. If Nick had to endure the pain, the least she could do was bear witness.

When she'd first seen the salon with none of its cozy warm furniture in place, it had given Faith pause. The stones held none of the warmth of the room where she had sat waiting for Nick's arrival.

She hadn't understood the meaning of the ropes until Nick had been bound to them. Nick's blood dripped down his ribs in a slow ribbon, staining his tan breeches.

The monster made small slices on different parts of Nick's body and then waited for Nick's pain to subside before moving on to another spot. He dug his knife into the healing wounds on Nick's back.

Faith couldn't see what damage was being done, but she imagined his agony and wished she could absorb some of what he suffered.

"Tell us where the English troops will invade?" Jean-Claude kept his face close to Nick's, taking pleasure from the misery he inflicted. He walked to the fire and placed his knife on the hearth close to the flame, then returned to Nick and kicked his legs out from under him.

The ropes pulled tight and a heartrending groan pushed out of Nick's mouth.

Faith's suffering couldn't compare to his, but she'd have sworn her own back had been torn open with the strain.

Nick got his feet under him and his gaze met hers. Strength and defiance poured from his bright blue eyes even as sweat beaded along his skin. "Send the girl away. She has nothing to do with this."

"She is insurance of your good behavior, Nicholas." Joseph toyed with Faith's hair.

She jerked away from his touch. Nick had told her to ignore what Joseph said, and she did her best. It was not speaking that became the hardest part when she wanted Nick to know she was with him. Not only present in the room, but with him in every way. Did he know? Would thinking it be enough to show him their connection? There were so many things she should have told him and last night had been her chance, yet she'd failed.

Pulling on his glove, Jean-Claude walked back to his blade and picked it up. The heat moved the air around the knife.

Faith bit the inside of her cheek. It was too much.

In three steps, Jean-Claude pressed the heated blade against Nick's side and the skin seared, filling the room with the stench of burning flesh and Nick's wailing protests.

Nick collapsed against the ropes, and while the burn did not bleed, blood ran down his arms from where he was bound. The ropes had cut into his flesh.

The burn blistered and charred.

Tears fell from Faith's eyes; though she tried to blink them away, she couldn't stay the flow.

Even Charles stood from where he'd perched on the windowsill. "For the love of all that is holy, Jean-Claude. Must you stink up the entire castle with the penchant for pain?"

"He knows things, Charles, and he owes us all for what he's done. Do you want to take over the job? We would be here a month and then you would bore him into submission." Jean-Claude sneered and circled Nick like a beast about to kill his prey.

Joseph pulled a lace handkerchief from inside his coat and placed it over his mouth and nose. "In this, I must agree with Charles. It does stink, and we're not out of doors, Jean-Claude. Find another method to gain the knowledge in Nicholas's pretty head."

"Perhaps that is the answer," Jean-Claude said. "Maybe I should cut the information out of his head. I could take an ear first." He held the cooled blade up to Nick's left ear.

Instead of removing the ear, he ran the tip of the blade from just under his ear down his neck and stopped at his collarbone, leaving an angry, bleeding cut in its wake.

Nick gritted his teeth but didn't cry out. Perhaps the pain of the burn was still too severe to pay the slim cut much note.

Gut clenching, Faith could barely keep her seat as blood dripped across his chest. Not so much that he might die from the slice, but enough that the cut should be bound. She didn't know how deep a cut needed to be for a man to bleed to death, but the vein pulsing in Nick's throat loomed terribly close to danger. She held her breath and prayed for the miracle.

A distant and rolling noise sounded like thunder, but the sky was clear. It grew louder, but it was not thunder. The fall of many hooves on the wet roads pounded out the hope of salvation.

Charles spun toward the window facing down the lane in front of Parvus. The blood drained from his cheeks. "We are discovered."

The other two rushed to the window.

Faith was not at an angle to see what was coming. She ran to Nick's side, pulled the knife from the mantel, and cut through one binding before Jean-Claude turned around. Unable to free Nick's other hand, she held the knife in front of herself and guarded him.

"I will kill you both before those troops ever reach the door." Jean-Claude approached.

"Stay away. Run before they lock you up in an English dungeon. I can tell you from experience, you will not like it." Faith sliced from the fiend's chest to his abdomen before he could jump away.

Looking down at his bloody hand where he'd grabbed his cut blouse and bleeding flesh, Jean-Claude's face twisted with surprise. "You bitch!"

"There is not time for this!" Charles grabbed Jean-Claude's arm before he could drive a killing blow. "We must get to the horses."

Joseph was already running toward the door. He stopped and turned toward Nick. "Another time, Nicholas."

"Go," Charles commanded. As soon as the other two were out the door, Charles turned back and glanced from Faith to Nick. "My debt is paid, old friend. I imagine it will be difficult even for Joseph to return to England after this. Stay safe."

Nick managed half a nod.

Charles left at a run. The sound of his boots followed the other two out the back of the house.

Turning, Faith let her tears loose. She could barely see as she cut his other arm from the rope. Holding him around the middle, she did her best to keep him from hitting the floor as they both collapsed in a heap under Nick's weight.

Hooves and carriages approached with the sound of men hollering.

Faith let the knife fall to the stone floor and pressed her hand to the bleeding cut under Nick's ear. "Help!" She'd meant it to be a full scream, but it came out strangled. "Help!"

Dragging her leg out from under Nick's, she grabbed the bottom of her dress and tore off the flowered detail that decorated the bottom few inches. She pressed the cloth against the wound. "Stay with me, Nick. Help is coming."

Shallow breaths puffed against her neck. "I will try, sweetheart. I'm so sorry."

The front door banged open and boots stormed through Parvus.

Jane's screams filled the room.

Faith saw the stricken maid at the threshold with her hand over her mouth.

Geb stood beside Jane looking nearly as shocked, but he recovered first. "Go and send for a surgeon."

Relief flooded Faith and mingled with her panic that Nick's injuries were too severe. The images blurred with more tears as she held him tight.

"They had horses." Faith caught her breath. "They were French spies. They left a few minutes ago."

Geb gave orders to a man in a red coat who was clearly an officer, but the man surveyed the scene and then followed them without question.

More boots on the stone floors and then silence.

A tall shadow fell over Faith. She gazed up into the kind face of Geb's butler, Kosey.

He knelt beside them. "You will have to let him go, my lady."

She understood the words, but she couldn't comply. Nick had nearly died, might still die, and all he wanted was to protect her. Pressing her cheek to his, she wished for half the strength of Nicholas Ellsworth. He knowingly had decided to die for her, and she was not worthy. "I should have done more."

Kneeling beside her, Geb said, "He is alive, my lady. That is a miracle."

"He said it would take a miracle." Faith glanced at Geb through watery eyes. "How did you know?"

Warmth swept through Geb's dark eyes. "There is much to tell on both ends, but you need rest, and His Grace needs a doctor."

Jane helped her stand while Kosey lifted Nick into his arms like he was a child. A head taller than any man Faith had ever seen, the Egyptian servant was formidable yet gentle as he carried Nick away.

"I should be with him," Faith said through more tears that she had no explanation for, other than relief and exhaustion.

Jane wrapped her arm around Faith's shoulders. "Come, my lady. Let's get you cleaned up and in bed. You will be of no use to His Grace if you fall ill."

Safe and unharmed, Faith let Jane take care of everything. She didn't remember changing into a nightgown or getting in bed. One moment she was climbing the stairs and the next she woke from a nightmare. Everything was a blur.

Jane rushed to her bedside. "Are you all right?"

Kosey stood near the door, his eyes bright with concern. The moon shone through the window.

Lying back against the pillow, Faith yawned. "Just a bad dream. But it wasn't a dream, was it, Jane?"

"I'm afraid not, my lady." Jane took her hand.

"How is His Grace?" She yawned again, her eyelids heavy.

Kosey's deep voice filled the room. "He will need much time to heal, but he will live and I believe it is thanks to you, my lady."

As hard as she tried to deny any credit, her eyes closed and she fell into darkness.

* * * *

Blood covered Faith and Nick, or was it wine? They were drowning in it.

Faith woke, gasping for air as she sat up in the bed. The white coverlet was crisp and clean with not a sign of blood. The sun shone defiantly through the clouds and streamed through the window in shards of color.

"It's all right, my lady. You're safe." Jane folded Faith's clothes into a trunk but her eyes filled with worry.

"You're packing." Faith brushed her hair from her face but it tumbled back an instant later. She pushed herself to sitting, with her back against the headboard. "How is Nick? I mean, His Grace."

"He sleeps with the help of a draught the doctor gave. He is in much pain and the burn is quite serious. I think even the doctor was shocked at the damage he's survived. But he is alive and strong." Jane looked up from her task and failed at an attempt to smile.

"We are being sent home?" The answer was obvious, but she asked anyway.

Jane nodded. "Mr. Arafa has arranged a carriage, and the giant will accompany us to ensure our safe return to London."

"He is not a giant, Jane. Just a very tall man." Faith swung her legs over the side of the bed. "Is it morning or afternoon?"

Rushing over, Jane said, "Go slowly. You have been asleep for nearly eighteen hours. It's morning."

Pushing to her feet, she let Jane steady her until she was sure she could manage on her own. "Help me dress so that I can go down to breakfast, Jane."

With a resigned sigh, Jane did as she was told and helped Faith into a dress suitable for travel.

Stepping into the hall for the first time as a free woman, she stopped and surveyed the dim upstairs hallway with only one small window at the end for light. The stairs were to the left, but Faith turned right and found Nick's door open, with a nurse and Kosey inside, watching him sleep.

"Miss, you shouldn't be in here." The nurse stormed over to push Faith out of the room. Her white cap fluttered as she hurried, as did the white apron tied over her blue dress.

Pulling herself to her full height, Faith put up one hand. "Do not touch me, madam. I will see him and I will do so alone."

The nurse toyed with a ribbon of dark hair that had escaped her cap, before tucking it under the fringe. "But, miss, he's not properly clothed for a lady to see him."

Faith sighed, unable to muster a laugh at the ridiculous statement. "I have seen worse. Leave us. I will call you back in a few minutes."

Kosey bowed before shooing the nurse from the room.

"When did you become so formidable, sweetheart?" Nick had appeared asleep. His eyes flickered open and his voice was rough and weak.

The white covers were pulled to just above his waist, and a mountain of pillows had been stacked behind his back. Faith stepped beside him. "I believe I have always been thus, but in private. The events of the past six days have made me see that holding back one's true self is stupidity."

"How will you ever forgive me?" His eyes were half closed, but his sorrow shone through.

"There is nothing to forgive. I arranged our meeting here at Parvus and tricked you into coming. Then I gave you no way to leave without acting ungentlemanly. This is my own doing, and it was you who paid the price."

He closed his eyes.

Whatever the doctor had given him, he fell back to sleep.

Faith leaned over and kissed his cheek. "I will leave you now, Nick. I suppose this was inevitable from the start. Get better and be happy."

Dashing away more tears, Faith took a deep breath and one last look at his face. Though swollen and bruised, he was still handsome and more importantly, kind and loving. Turning her back, she walked away.

She refused to cry anymore and strode down to the dining room. It would do no good and she had to be stronger than tears.

Geb sat reading a newspaper and drinking coffee. He looked up and grinned when she entered. "You are looking well rested, Lady Faith."

"Thank you, and thank you for rescuing us." She sat to his left and thanked Jamie for the cup of coffee he poured.

Thea made her a plate of sausage, toast, and jam and set it before her.

Faith smiled but then turned her attention to Geb. "Mr. Arafa, how did you get here so quickly? It's not that I'm ungrateful, I'm just curious as to how you managed it. Nick believed it would take a day or two at a minimum before anyone could reach us."

Nodding, he folded the paper and placed it on the table. "MacGruder nearly killed himself to get to me in two days. He is recovering in my home near London. After that, it was only a matter of convincing your government I needed a small army to leave immediately. Kosey and I set out with them and it was three days' hard riding to get here."

The servants' door squeaked open and Rumple pushed his head through. Glancing around, he spotted Faith and bounded the rest of the way in. He barked and jumped until Faith pushed out of her seat and met him on the carpet.

"Look at you. I think you've grown bigger again." She scratched the puppy behind the ears and hugged him to her chest.

Rumple whined and licked her chin enthusiastically.

"You know, I missed this little dog more than I realized. So much has happened, I'd almost forgotten he was here. I suppose I was afraid the worst would happen to him." She pulled him onto her lap and hugged him tighter.

Geb laughed. "He obviously missed you as well."

Having thought joy would never return to her life, the bundle of energy and fur was welcome. Faith sighed. "Jamie, come and take him back to the kitchen, will you?"

"Yes, my lady." Jamie picked up Rumple and rushed out of the room.

Faith brushed out her skirt and returned to her seat. She let out a long breath and pushed aside her feelings. "Did you capture them?"

Geb's scowl said it all. "No. The enemy spies managed to get away from Colonel Whitman and his men. I assumed they had an escape route planned all along. They'll be on their way back to France by now. I would pay an enormous sum to get my hands on the monsters who tortured Nicholas."

"Do you think they will try again?" A shudder ran up Faith's spine.

Placing his hands on the table in front of him, Geb cocked his head. "I doubt it. It was a huge risk to come here to take revenge on one man.

Especially when lying to each other is what they all did, still do, I imagine. Nick told me what he could. The laudanum has made a full accounting difficult, and I don't wish for him to suffer so I can hear the story a few days earlier."

"Shall I tell you?" The thought of recapping the past few days made Faith's stomach roil, but she was strong and made the offer with her chin up.

Geb shook his head. "It would ruin your breakfast and you need to eat. You must be quite a woman to have survived. Did they hurt you as they hurt Nicholas?"

Sipping her coffee, she observed him over the rim of her cup. "No. I was not tortured. I was left in the wine cellar for several days and I did what I could for Nick after he was beaten."

Saying nothing, Geb examined her as she ate. He drank more coffee and occasionally asked if she needed anything. When she put her fork aside, he said, "You will return to London. I will see to Nicholas while he recovers. It will take a long time for him to heal."

Sighing, Faith rose and put her napkin on the chair. "I do not wish to leave him."

"It will take much time for him to heal. It would be unseemly for you to remain. I promise he will be well cared for." Geb's smile was warm and reassuring.

Her heart ached at the idea of abandoning Nick after all they'd been through, but she was not his wife. How could she stay? "Thank you again, for arriving when you did. A few moments longer and this might have been a different day, Mr. Arafa."

He rose with her and bowed. "May I give you some advice, Lady Faith?"

"Of course." She placed her hands on the back of the chair.

"When you are home in London, these days at Parvus will not go away. Talk to your friends. Tell them what happened. Keeping horrors locked inside allows them to fester and eat away at a person's soul. Let those nightmares out and they will heal with time." A thousand memories flashed across Geb's eyes and left them solemn.

"Will you listen to Nick's stories and horrors?" she asked.

Geb held his hands out to the side. "I will be here for him should he wish to talk. He can be quite stubborn on such matters. However, you should not follow his example, my lady. Take my advice."

"I will try my best." Faith turned and walked to the door.

"It is all any of us can do. You are, I think, very resilient, Lady Faith Landon. I think you will do well." Geb's voice followed her out of the dining room.

She stopped. "I will leave the puppy here. Perhaps he will bring some happiness to Nick. Tell him that he may deliver Rumple back to me when he is well enough, should he wish to."

"As you wish." Geb bowed and his counsel followed her on the four-day journey back to London.

Chapter 15

"No more laudanum." Nick pushed away the nurse with her spoon. "I've had quite enough."

Nurse Paulette was not used to being told no. She pulled her shoulders back and capped the bottle. "You'll be sorry when the pain begins again and you can't sleep, Your Grace."

A heavy sigh tugged at his scabs. "You may be right, but I'd just as soon have my mind back and suffer the consequences."

"As you wish, but at least let me put some liniment on the burn and your back." Nurse went to the table and picked up her jar of ointment.

He rolled to his side so she could access his back. She didn't have Faith's touch, but he was glad for the itch to ease. "Do you suppose she'll ever want to look on my scars, Paulette?"

There was a long pause. "She seemed a sensible and headstrong woman. It's only been a few weeks, but you're healing well. I don't know her well, but it seems she would be foolish to turn down a duke."

"She's done so before." He chuckled but there was no joy in it.

Paulette raised a brow. "Then you'll just have to charm her, Your Grace."

"And charm her you will," Geb said as he stood in the doorway. "Lady Faith left you something, but I didn't want to bring it until you were better."

Nick had his back to the door. "What is it?"

"Get that mongrel out of this room!" Paulette said.

Stopped a moment by the pain, Nick still managed to turn onto his back. "Rumple?"

"This is a sickroom. There is no place here for a dog. He'll tear open his wounds." Paulette held her hands up to block the intruders.

Holding the end of a short leash, Geb smiled. "I will keep the pup calm, Nurse. It will do Nicholas good to pet something so full of joy and life."

"I give up with you both." Paulette stormed from the room.

Good to his word, Geb kept a tight hold on Rumple, who was jumping and crying to get near to Nick. He lifted the dog to the bed.

The puppy calmed and lay beside Nick, some instinct telling him not to do harm with overexuberance.

Nick ran his hand through the puppy's soft fur. "She left him. Why?" Rumple crept forward along Nick's side and licked his hand.

"She said she wanted him to bring you some happiness while you recovered." Geb sat in the chair next to the bed but kept hold of the leash.

"I would have thought she would have wanted to take him with her back to London, where it is safe." A spark of something akin to hope fired inside him as he scratched behind Rumple's floppy ear. Nick had not felt anything like it in weeks.

"She also said that if you wished to return him, you should do so when you are well enough." Geb lifted both brows and grinned.

Nick sighed and closed his eyes. He lifted one arm over them to block out light, memories…everything.

Rumple whined.

Taking the dog from the bed, Geb held him in his lap. "Jamie, come here, please."

Nick watched while Jamie carried Rumple away. "She left me the dog." He didn't know what to think of such a gesture. Was it her parting gift? He'd been too drugged and tired to respond to her good-bye, but it sounded so final. Now Geb's message from her told a different story. There was an invitation to see her again in the message. "I don't know what to think."

"You should think you are lucky to be alive so that you can do whatever it takes to win that woman's heart."

"How can she want me after what I put her through?" The memory of her stricken face while he hung from the chandelier echoed in his mind. He closed his eyes to try to banish the image.

Geb's footsteps indicated he would leave Nick to his sulking. However, instead of the continued sound of retreating feet, the door closed and Geb returned. He dragged the chair closer and sat. Leaning in, he said, "Tell me what you see, my friend."

In all the time he was a spy, Nick never confided anything. He reported to his superiors, of course, but that never included the effects on him. When Léonie died, he gave Drake the facts and nothing more. Now Geb wanted not the facts, but his experience. It hurt so much to hold it in, he sighed. "I see a pair of amber eyes staring at me as I was about to die, and she would be the witness. She never glanced away. At one point I was so crazed, I thought I heard her mind."

"What did you hear?" Geb urged, eyes alight with interest.

"*I am with you. I am here. We are together.*" He wished it were not just insanity talking. "I was mad with pain. It was only my imagination, but still it lingers with me."

"What kind of a woman would you say Lady Faith is?" Geb crossed his arms over his chest and leaned back. His black hair gleamed in the midday sun. It had snowed several times in the weeks since his rescue, and the sunshine reflected brightly in the room.

Nick loved how gentle yet strong Faith was. Just thinking of her was a pleasure and torture. "What do you mean?"

"You know what I mean. I can see on your face that you were just thinking about her. Is she kind, mean, cold, a whore, manipulative, angry, bitter, thoughtful… What kind of a person is Faith Landon?"

Anger rose at some of the descriptions. "If you ever use *whore* in the same sentence with Faith again, I will cut out your heart."

Geb smiled. "I see. She gave herself to you and you worry if she thinks herself sullied."

"I was in no shape for such things," Nick lied.

"Is she generous?"

Knowing how persistent Geb could be, Nick pushed himself to sitting and let the image of his voluptuous Faith fill his mind. "She is the smartest woman I've ever known, as well as the bravest."

"I was impressed that she survived with seemingly no ill effects, but why do you say she is brave? Because she watched you suffer and didn't look away?" Geb had visited Nick's room every day, but had not asked any questions while Nick was under the influence of laudanum.

"Lord, is that all you think she did?" Nick laughed, but the sharp movement set his wounds aching. The pain subsided and Nick relaxed. "Faith endured nearly three days in the cellar with only one candle. It went out once and she was sent into complete darkness. She refused to leave when MacGruder came to get her, fearing it would go badly for the rest of us. While in there she had to care for me after a beating and she saved bread from the meager meals that were given her, in order that I might have more to eat. She cleaned and dressed my wounds even when they were more severe, and gave me comfort. She is the most magnificent woman ever born. When you rode up, she pulled Jean-Claude's spare knife from the mantel and guarded me like a Valkyrie. She even managed to cut that bastard before he left. No one has ever been less prepared for a situation yet behaved with such honor and courage. No one."

Geb stared with eyes wide. "I didn't realize. I would have liked to have seen her hold off Jean-Claude with his own blade. He will never forget such a thing."

"She is magnificent and I don't deserve her."

"Why do you say that?" Geb leaned forward again, brow furrowed and his hands clasped under his chin.

"I am little better than Charles, Jean-Claude, and Joseph. You know as well as I the things I've done and the pain I've caused." Nick's burned side chose that moment to throb. He took slow breaths through the spasms.

Shaking his head, Geb scowled. "I know no such thing. You have never tortured anyone out of revenge. They didn't need you to learn anything, and they knew full well you would die before you gave them one bit of real information."

Nick pressed his hand over the bandaged burn and tried to will it to settle. "Perhaps, but I have done more than my share of misdeeds. I have much to be ashamed of and very little pride in my time working for Drake and His Majesty."

"You worked for a greater good. If I'm not mistaken, you still do. In fact, when you are well enough, I have the rest of the map you asked for last year. It took a while to gather, but I now know who every one of Napoleon's spies is and which ones are in England. The map shows where each is hiding."

Nick chuckled. It had been so long since he'd met with Geb in the garden during the same ball where he'd first met Faith, he'd almost forgotten. "Did you know my old friends were in town?"

Geb's expression soured. "No. My informants told me they were in Spain."

"Give the list to Drake. Let him sort it out. I'm tired, Geb. I've given my flesh, isn't that enough?" Nick lamented his refusal of the laudanum as each wound pulsed one by one.

"I think you will feel differently when you are well again. These spies are deeply embedded in your London society. They're not going anywhere." Geb stood. "I will call the nurse back in."

"Give the list to Drake, Geb. Don't wait on me. I need no accolades."

"No, just a fiery brunette with wild curls and a noble heart." Geb left the room, his white silk clothes highlighting his heritage and his laugh his friendship.

* * * *

After being in bed through Christmas with only brief walks around the upper floors, Nick was happy to be on the main floor of Parvus playing with Rumple. They sat on the rug in the restored salon and tugged on either side of a rag Rumple had stolen from one of the maids Geb hired.

The previously uninhabited castle was fully staffed, with Kosey holding the position of butler. There were three footmen in white and powder-blue livery and at least five maids, which was excessive for the small castle.

The door opened and a familiar voice said, "Am I disturbing you, Your Grace?"

Francis Drake, Envoy Extraordinary, stood waiting to be invited in. His paunch had grown since last Nick had seen him, and his hairline had receded. Otherwise his sharp eyes were the same as they ever were, even after his embarrassment over some papers being apprehended a few years earlier. The fact that he shared a name with a famous sea captain and favorite of Queen Elizabeth, never fazed Drake, but it had always amused Nick.

Nick scooped up Rumple and gave the puppy a squeeze before setting him aside. With the help of the sturdy chair near the hearth, Nick pulled himself to his feet. "Come in, Drake. I can't say I was expecting you, but I imagine you want something."

Rumple whined and crawled under the settee. The puppy's youth didn't mean he was stupid. He kept his distance from Francis Drake.

Always droll and seemingly relaxed, Drake sauntered in and sat on the chair Nick had just used for support. Black breeches and a ruby coat were part of the gentlemanly façade he used to fool the politicians. "Might I not have just come to see how you are recovering from your episode?"

Nick crossed his arms over his chest. The scars on his back pulled but did not pain him. "No. I'm afraid that I cannot believe."

A slow smile spread across Drake's face. He fussed with the elaborate knot in his cravat. "Humor me." He pointed to the other chair near the hearth.

Nick sat. "I'm recovering nicely. Most of my wounds have healed, though I shall never be as pretty as I once was." He pointed to the red scar showing from his ear down to his collar, since he was in only breeches and a blouse.

"Ladies love a few scars. I'm told it was Fouché who led these men."
Drake inspected his hand as if he'd not seen it before.

"Fouché is in charge of most of Napoleon's policing operations. This may
have been a personal matter for them, but he is still in charge." Nick tried
to speculate over what Drake's visit might be about, but he couldn't guess.

With a long sigh, Drake leaned back and stretched his legs out in front
of him. "Does Fouché actually keep a list of royalists?"

It was starting to come clearer. "It's more of a catalog. But yes, he is
rather obsessed with his record keeping."

"Do you think you might know where he keeps that information?"
Drake remained relaxed, but the intensity in his eyes told a different story.

Warning bells rang in Nick's ears and he kept his answer cautious but
honest. "Not exactly."

In a flash, Drake sat forward. "But in general, you know. Could you
find them and bring them to me?"

Nick sighed. "I don't know, Drake. I don't do that kind of work anymore.
Isn't the list of French spies here in England enough to satisfy you? It was
my last assignment. I realize it took some time to finish, but it is done now."

"We have arrested several from the list and watch the rest. You have
been quite valuable, Your Grace."

"But..." Nick pushed for the rest of this mess.

"But His Majesty realizes you have access to things that no one else
does. You could give England the advantage in this war."

"His Majesty called me home, told me to take care of my lands and
thanked me for a job well done. I have retired from your service." Nick
stood and walked to the window. It had gotten warmer and the snow was
melting, making everything shiny in the garden.

Faith would love how pretty it looked. Until today, she had filled his
mind. He'd tried several times to write her a letter, but couldn't find the
words. How could he tell her to forgive him the unforgivable?

"Now you are needed again." Drake stood, his hands fisted at his sides.

Nick shook his head, wishing he'd never agreed to go to France in the
first place. "I don't know if I can do what you ask. I still need to heal and
would find it difficult to ride a horse at this point. Also, I would have to
do some research as to where Joseph actually keeps his data."

"You should wait for spring." Drake's smile said he'd won. "No one
expects you to cross the Channel in winter."

This was almost as much of a nightmare as the ones he endured every
night when he closed his eyes. "I make you no promises. If I cannot gain a
more specific location, I'll not risk meeting Joseph Fouché again and this

time on his soil. It's not as if he and I are still friends. He came here to torture and kill me. The moment I am discovered in France, I will be arrested."

"Then I would suggest you use all of your skills and not be seen." Drake walked to the door. "I will be joining you for dinner. I shall leave in the morning. Have someone show me to the guest room."

As arrogant as usual. Nick longed to punch Francis Drake in his imperious nose. Instead, he pulled the cord and asked Kosey to see to Drake's comfort.

Once Drake was upstairs, Nick pulled on his overcoat, put Rumple's leash on the puppy and went out to the garden. The icy snow crunched under their feet. He tried to keep to the path, but it was difficult to know where the stones lay beneath layers of winter.

Rumple sniffed every bump in the snow and did his business on several.

Halfway to the hothouse, the footsteps behind him alerted him that he was not alone. Turning brought him face-to-face with a frowning Geb. "You heard, I assume."

Happy barking followed until Geb petted the puppy.

"I'm a man who makes my living on information. Of course, I heard. Are you mad to not have told that fool no?" Geb kept his voice low, but there was no mistaking his anger.

Nick nodded toward the hothouse and they walked in silence until they were inside with the door closed.

Unleashing Rumple sent the bundle of fur scampering through the plants and trees.

Warmth and roses assaulted Nick's senses and brought thoughts of Faith to the forefront. He'd held her and kissed her for the first time in this place. The way she'd let him see parts of herself, who she was and why she reacted to things the way she did, had made him love her.

Nick closed his eyes. Lord, but he did love her.

He shook away the things he wanted to think about and turned to Geb. "I know where Joseph keeps his books. I have seen them."

"Is that worth your life? You will be discovered if you return to Paris," Geb warned.

Nick paced the open center of the hothouse. "They're not in Paris, and I suspect Joseph is nowhere near where they are hidden. He will likely be in Spain or Portugal, gaining intelligence and trying to learn when the English troops will invade."

"And the books?" Geb's eyes flashed with curiosity and possibility.

Shaking his head, Nick said, "It's safer if I keep it to myself."

"If you don't return, where will I look for you?" Geb threw his arms wide.

Nick slapped Geb on the back. "I will get word to you after I go. This way no one can try to glean my whereabouts from you."

Nodding, Geb accepted the response. "Why did you lie to Drake?"

"It wasn't all a lie. I'm several months away from riding for my life." Rumple reappeared and jumped on Nick's leg.

He scooped the puppy into his arms. "Also, I have an errand to run before I leave England, and it will take a few weeks."

"I see," Geb said, grinning.

"Tell me I'm not a fool, old friend." Nick lifted his chin to avoid Rumple's amorous tongue.

A low laugh filled the hothouse. Geb said, "Where women are concerned, we are all fools, Nicholas. She is worth becoming a fool over."

In his daydreams she was standing a few feet away in a white dress and smiling up at him. If only he could rid himself of the nightmares that kept him up, he could believe Faith could be his. "She is worth everything."

Chapter 16

Faith mindlessly sipped her tea. It was too hot in the parlor with the fire blazing in the hearth. Outside it had rained for several days and the snow was all washed away. Nothing felt as it should; uncomfortable in the room as she was uncomfortable in her skin. That white carpet of snow had connected her somehow to the snow at Parvus, and Nick. Now that it was gone and so many months had passed without a word, she was resigned to never see him again.

Her chest ached with her broken heart.

"Are you listening, Faith?" Mercy said, putting aside the newspaper and her spectacles.

"I'm sorry. What were you saying?" Faith hadn't even known someone was speaking. She was lost in her regrets.

Mercy slid her legs out from under her on the chaise and sat forward with her willowy grace, studying Faith. "I was reading the account of the duel between Lord Grandville and Sir Edward Longbottom. The question is, where were you?"

"I'm right here. I was just woolgathering." Faith put her cold tea on the table and sat back on the settee.

Rhys was the only man in the room. He had become part of the Wallflowers the year before during the investigation of Nick, which had begun it all. Of course, as Aurora's brother and now Poppy's husband, his acceptance was inevitable. "You have been doing a lot of that lately, Faith."

"I suppose that's true." The sun poked out from the clouds and Faith stared out the window again.

"Faith?" Aurora brought her attention back to the group. "Do you want to talk about what happened at Parvus?"

A shiver ran up Faith's spine. "I've already told you about the spies and the horrors that followed. I don't see the point in rehashing the entire ordeal again."

Poppy moved away from Rhys. Her dark hair was perfectly tame in a chignon. She stumbled on the rug, but righted herself before Rhys could catch her. Shrugging off her clumsiness, she sat next to Faith and took her hand. "Perhaps if you keep talking about it, you'll be able to let it go and not feel so haunted by the memories."

Faith squeezed Poppy's hand. "I'm fine. The nightmares are few now. My mind is not occupied with anything terrible."

"What then?" Mercy asked.

She just had to forget him. If he'd wanted her, he'd have called by now. "It's nothing."

Leaning his elbows on his knees pulled Rhys to the edge of his seat. "Why don't you just write to him if you still want him, or call off the engagement if you don't, Faith? This waiting and hoping will do neither of you any good."

"I'm not waiting," she lied. "I should call off. I had hoped, but it doesn't matter. Mother will eventually find someone else she thinks will suit, and I will have a perfectly amiable marriage." It sounded calm coming from her lips, but inside she died a little.

"Sounds dreadful," Mercy said under her breath, but everyone heard.

It was impossible to argue. It did sound only slightly better than the abusive marriage Aurora had endured. The idea of marrying someone other than Nick, made Faith's stomach churn. It was out of her hands. Best to change the subject and move on. "So, what did the paper say about the duel?"

They all peered at her with pity.

Faith wanted to run screaming to her room upstairs. Sometimes it was not a blessing to have her friends know her so well.

Mercy picked the paper up and put her spectacles on.

The knocker sounded from the front door.

"Who could that be?" Aurora cocked her head.

A moment later, the butler, Tipton, entered with a silver tray. Always stoic and sedate, Tipton gave Faith an odd glare. His brown eyes twinkled and he offered the card to Aurora. "My lady, the Duke of Breckenridge is waiting in the foyer."

Faith's pulse tripled and she had trouble catching her breath. Hand on her chest, a sound that might be described as a squealing cat caught under the leg of a chair pushed from her mouth. She stood, but then sat. "Oh my." Poppy put her arm around her. "Breathe, Faith. This is no time to faint."

In her countess voice, Aurora said, "Tipton, you may send His Grace in, but go about it slowly, please."

With a bow, Tipton walked back to the door and paused before exiting.

Breathing slowly to keep her head from swimming, Faith didn't know if she wanted to jump for joy or run and hide. He was in the house. Soon he would be in the room. Her breath came too fast.

Poppy rubbed her back. "Slow down, Faith."

Gulping air, but more slowly, she put on the mask of indifference. It was taught to every young lady of breeding from the time they were three, and the Wallflowers had all mastered it.

Mercy stood. "Do you want us to stay or go, Faith? I'm certain he has not come to see any of us."

Unable to think of what she wanted or what to do, she just stared at her hands until the door opened and Tipton announced, "The Duke of Breckenridge." Everyone stood, and Poppy lifted Faith with her.

Faith's legs shook and she prayed the full skirt of her yellow day dress would hide the shimmy. If she didn't look at him, she could make it through this.

"How do you do, Your Grace. What a nice surprise to see you, and looking so well." Aurora always knew how to act in any situation.

"I'm sorry to call without an invitation, Lady Radcliff. I hope I am not intruding. I admit, I knew that Tuesdays are your special day for tea. I used that knowledge to ensure Lady Faith would be at home." His deep, rounded voice cut through the heart of her.

Faith finally met his gaze.

No sign of pain lurked in those bright blue eyes when they locked with hers. His brown hair was longer and combed away from his face. It curled at his collar. The hint of a red scar ran from below his ear to his neckcloth, but he stood straight and tall. His lips turned up in the hint of a smile.

On a short leash at his side, a much larger Rumple barked and squirmed. The puppy was as tall as Nick's knees, but hopped around in obvious recognition of Faith.

"Sit," Nick commanded.

Rumple obeyed, but one paw lifted, ready to jump at the first sign of release.

Suddenly all her fears and worries didn't matter. This was Nick and he knew her. He likely saw right through her nervousness because she could see his in the tight grip of his hand on the leash and tick in his jaw. "Would you all please excuse us? I would like a few minutes with His Grace alone."

Without a word, all four of her friends made a line toward the door. The ladies curtsied as they passed Nick. Rhys shook his hand and then they were gone.

They stared across the parlor at each other.

Faith didn't know what to say, and her brain had taken leave.

Recovering first, Nick said, "Shall I release him? He's been anxious to see you." He pointed to Rumple.

The puppy was dancing on all four feet, not wanting to disappoint Nick, but certainly ready to get to her. His white fur had started to curl and his dark brown eyes lit with excitement while his tail whipped back and forth gleefully.

No words would come, so she nodded.

Nick pulled the leash over Rumple's head and the dog bounded across the room and into Faith's waiting arms. He licked her chin and jumped on her until she had to sit in order to keep from being knocked down.

"Rumple, no."

The puppy sat and put his nose on Faith's knee. He contemplated her with the sweetest eyes.

She scratched behind his ears, noting how his spots had darkened. "He's grown."

Still standing near the door, Nick said, "Jamie was keen on feeding him often."

Suddenly shy, she bit the inside of her cheek and focused on Rumple. "And is everyone at Parvus well?"

"Yes, Faith, and they all send you regards."

She could hardly form words. "And you, Nick? Are you well?"

His smile was slow and slightly sad. "I am mostly healed, though the scars will remain."

She wanted to know more, but she nodded. "Would you care to sit? I can call for tea."

Never taking his gaze from hers, he crossed and sat beside her on the settee. "I do not require tea. I just…"

"Yes?" She longed to hear what he wanted, needed.

"I arrived back in London yesterday." He took her hand and kissed the back.

Rumple sighed and lay down on Faith's feet.

"I'm surprised you stayed at Parvus so long." She suppressed her thoughts of his coming immediately to see her, but it was gratifying.

"I needed time, and the weather has not been good for travel."

Worry overrode anything else. "But you are healed?"

"The scars remain." His neck turned red and his free hand fisted on his leg. Even so, he again kissed her hand slowly and deliberately.

She couldn't imagine why he kept mentioning his scars. He was alive and sitting in the West Lane parlor. "You didn't write."

She was mesmerized by the way his lips moved as he kissed her skin. The sensation of how he had touched her at Parvus filled her.

"I tried many times, but I didn't know what to say, how to say it. I put you in so much danger and you..." He let her hand go, took several breaths.

"I what?" Had she hurt him? She hadn't thought so. "Whatever it is I've done, you must forgive me."

Nick closed his eyes.

Emotion swam in Faith's eyes, blurring her vision. She dabbed it away, not wanting to miss any part of seeing Nick.

A muscle in his jaw ticked. "You should never be sorry. You saved my life. I would not have survived had you not cared for me and protected me. More than that, if you had not been my strength that last day, I could not have managed. I owe you everything."

"You owe me nothing. I did so little and you suffered for us both." The memory of his pain seared within her.

"I came today to return Rumple to his rightful owner and to ask a favor." Nick's voice took on a formal tone.

Faith didn't want him to leave, and she feared once he asked his favor, he would walk out of the house and she would never see him again. "Thank you for bringing the puppy. I hope he was a comfort to you. I'm glad to see you looking so well. Do you think we might just sit here for a time before you say whatever it is you came to say?"

He cocked his head. "We can do whatever you wish, sweetheart."

Faith sighed at the sound of the endearment. Sidling closer, she leaned into him. He wrapped his arm around her shoulders, took up her hand with his other, and leaned them back against the cushion.

The scent of vanilla and the outdoors mixed with Nick's warm scent. She breathed him in, imprinting all of him on her memory. "Has the snow melted at Parvus too?"

"Yes. The grass is already turning green. You would have liked the place once Geb hired on a full staff. It was quite lively. I think Cook has gotten even better at her delicious food preparation with all the practice these months. Jamie has grown several inches, just like Rumple, and MacGruder is as grumpy as ever."

Faith smiled. "It was lucky he saw those friends of yours and came to investigate. He saved us."

Squeezing her tighter, he kissed the top of her head. "He saved you, sweet Faith, and for that I shall always be grateful. However, it was you who saved me. You were my miracle."

Part of her wanted to argue, but she was warm and comfortable in his arms and she didn't want it to end, so she stayed silent on the subject. "Has Mr. Arafa returned to London as well?"

He nodded. "We traveled together."

"You must be glad to be back in your own home." It was small talk, but she loved the normalcy of it.

"Faith?"

"Yes, Nick." Her time had run out. She sighed.

"May I ask my favor now?" He hesitated and there was something uncomfortable in his question.

"What if I don't like what you have to say?"

"I have come here with no expectations. I fully expected you to refuse to see me, so I'm already beyond happy." There was definitely a catch in his voice.

Confused, Faith sat up and studied him.

Rumple sensed the change in emotion, and he sat up too and put his giant paws on Faith's lap.

"Down, boy," Nick said, and Rumple complied.

"What do you mean, refuse to see you? Why would I do that?" Faith blurted it out with less grace than she'd hoped for.

Nick stood and paced to the window, then back again. "I've had a lot of time to think during my recovery. At first, I was delirious with laudanum and could only think in hazy pockets, but over time I refused the drug and regained my senses. You may still toss me from the house, Faith. If my presence is too upsetting to you, I will understand. I will go and never attempt to see you again."

It was possible that Faith's mind was going to explode from lack of understanding. "Why would I want that? What are you talking about? I waited for months for you to write or call and had all but given up. Why would I not wish to see you?"

"I'm certain my presence brings back upsetting memories for you." He stopped his pacing and looked at her, but then began again.

"My memories are intact, whether you are here or not. Do you think the things I saw can be pushed aside so easily? My nightmares will not be dismissed by not seeing you or having you here. Frankly, I don't see how the two are connected." She still wasn't quite sure what he was about.

"I knew I shouldn't come, but Geb said I must." He said it more to himself than her.

Having had enough confusion, she asked, "What is the favor you wish to ask?"

He stopped in front of her and his hands shook as he took hers. "I know you have parents who I should go and see, but as we are still engaged, I decided it was better to see you. Besides, my past dealings with your mother have been confusing."

"Good Lord, Nick. What is it?" Her nerves were hanging on by the last thread.

Nick took a long, deep breath and let it out. "I wonder if you would do me the honor of letting me court you properly. I think perhaps we skipped an important step in getting to know each other and that is entirely my fault."

Heart pounding, she shook her head to clear it. "You want to court me? But Nick, we've been intimate."

Fire lit in his eyes, the memory was crystal clear.

Faith's cheeks heated.

"I have not, nor am I likely to forget that fact, sweetheart." He leaned down and kissed one hand and then the other.

"Why do you want to court me?" Her instincts told her he was looking for a way out of the engagement. "If you want me to call off now, I will do it. My parents know nothing about my being at Parvus with you. They think Mercy and I went to her aunt's country home for a few weeks. No one knows about my being ruined besides you, me, and Jane, and she will never say a word."

He let her hands go and kept his head down. "If you wish to be released from the agreement, I completely understand."

"No. That is not what I want. I want you to be happy."

A second passed and neither one moved. Slowly, Nick's head came up. "I want to court you properly. I only care about your happiness, and I want you to be sure I am the man you wish to marry. The last thing I want is for our engagement to end."

Faith's knees gave out and she was forced to sit. "We have got to get better at communicating, Nick. I shall not survive more of these bewildering exchanges."

His low, rumbling laughter filled the room. "Nor I, sweetheart." He knelt in front of her. "I must demand one thing of you though."

Nerves near the end of tolerance, she saw anger in his eyes. "What?"

"Never again say our night together ruined you. It was the most wonderful night of my life, and I would hate for you to think of it in such terms." His earnest expression broke her heart.

"I have no regrets and one lovely memory of those six days, Nick." She smiled even though tears welled in her eyes.

Rumple took the opportunity to jump on the settee and get in on the embrace.

Faith laughed harder than she had in what felt like ages. "At least you taught him to sit."

Chuckling, Nick dragged Rumple from the furniture and ruffled the fur on his head. "I have one more request, but this is for all the Wallflowers."

"Shall I call them in? I would wager they are not five feet outside that door." Faith felt so full of joy that even her friends' overprotectiveness didn't bother her.

"That is not necessary." He smiled. "You may relay the request. I am throwing a ball on Friday, and if you are not otherwise engaged, I would love for all of you to come."

Excitement vibrated inside Faith. "What is the occasion for the ball?"

His lips turned up in the most sensual smile. "It is part of our courtship. I have written to my sister. She arrived at my house here in town last week, so that a ball is appropriate."

"I would very much like to meet your sister."

Leaning in, he kissed her cheek. "She is going to adore you."

A ripple of worry coursed through Faith. "Would it matter if she did not care for me?"

He was close enough to feel his breath tickle her earlobe. "Nothing and no one can change the way I feel about you."

Cowardice kept her from asking exactly what his feelings were. Longing to know but worried he might say that he cared for her, or something equally benign, kept her silent. The last thing she wanted from Nick was placid emotions. That would kill her.

Chapter 17

Faith had spent hours getting ready to attend Nick's ball. She'd made poor Jane fix her hair twice when a curl worked itself loose. She'd never been more nervous about seeing him. Not even when she'd lured him to Parvus had she been so meticulous about her appearance. She'd chosen a purple gown that was darker than was strictly appropriate for an unmarried lady. Lavender lace around the low neckline and sleeves gave it a sweeter, more feminine look.

Both the Earl and Countess of Dornbury arrived at West Lane to pick her up. Faith was taken by surprise at the sight of her father, who never attended events. While her parents were affectionate toward each other, it had always been Mother's job to find a suitable husband for Faith, and Father wanted no part of the process.

Father cringed as Faith descended the stairs. "That gown is not hiding your overly curved person."

Mother's lips twitched, but she held in her amusement. "You look very nice, Faith."

"But, Melody!" Father blanched.

"We are going to the home of her fiancé. I'm sure by now, Faith knows what His Grace likes and doesn't like about her. If her figure were a problem, she would have chosen a different gown."

Remaining silent, Faith walked the remaining stairs and accepted her wrap from Tipton. It was strange for her mother to take her side in anything, but she was happy to have one parent's support.

Her parents followed her to the door. Father asked, "Where are all those friends of yours?"

"Two of those friends are countesses now, Father. You might show some respect." Faith accepted the footman's hand up into her family's carriage.

Father bristled. "Are they all out gallivanting?"

It did no good to correct him, so Faith held in a torrent of rage to protect her friends. "They already left for the same ball we are attending, Father. Do try to act like a gentleman when you see them. The Earl of Marsden becomes quite protective if anyone insults his wife or sister. Besides, you and Mother have always liked the Countess of Radcliff."

He narrowed his gaze, but said nothing.

Seeming not to notice the tension, Mother smiled. "Do you think His Grace will announce a wedding date, Faith? Is that why he's holding a ball? I understand he brought his sister, the Countess of Dunworth, to London to act as hostess. I've never met her, but she is said to be quite fashionable. I also heard that she never comes to London, so this is a real treat if we catch a glimpse of her."

"Mother, you really should avoid all the gossip. I'm sure the countess is busy with other things and perhaps doesn't care for a season in town." Faith had no idea, but she didn't like her mother gossiping about Nick's sister.

As they approached the Ellsworth townhouse, the carriage slowed to a stop. There was a crush of carriages trying to get close to the house, but none were making progress.

"Damned inconvenient that we must walk from here where all the horses have been." Father slammed his hand against the carriage window but sat forward, ready to exit.

A whistle sounded and the carriage jerked forward.

Mother leaned out the window. It was not at all ladylike. "We are being waved through, Filmore. It seems His Grace had footmen waiting to spot our carriage and now they are directing the other vehicles aside so that we can drive through." She sat back on her seat next to Father and grinned happily. "How thoughtful."

Even Father appeared impressed that anyone would make such an effort for Faith. Perhaps she had moved up slightly on his assessment ladder.

Faith shook off the notions. She was sure to disappoint her father at some point in the near future and would be knocked down again. There was no point looking for his approval when he did not wish to give it. She had managed for one-and-twenty years without a loving father to dote on her; she could survive the rest of her life thus.

Several large men stood like sentinels in front of the house. She studied them, and while they were dressed like gentlemen, they stood like soldiers watching the street.

When the carriage reached the front of the grand stairs leading up to the Ellsworth townhouse, a footman in dove-gray and white livery opened the carriage door. "My lord and lady, Lady Faith, you are welcome. I have been instructed to take you past the line and directly to His Grace. Would you please follow me?"

Father practically leapt from the conveyance, leaving Mother to be helped by the footman. There was nothing Father liked better than to be shown preference in public.

Once Mother was safely on the ground, Faith stepped out of the carriage. "Thank you," she told the footman.

"My lady Faith, it is my pleasure. I am Will, and if you need anything at all, you have only to ask. Everyone in the Duke of Breckenridge's employ is at your service." Will's brown eyes sparked with honesty and admiration.

Faith couldn't imagine why the servant should admire her, since she'd done nothing to earn such regard from Nick's staff. "That is very kind. Has the duke put guards around the house?" She pointed to the men she'd noticed from the carriage.

Will smiled. "It's just a precaution to keep out the riffraff, my lady."

"I see." It was likely more than that, but Faith let it go.

As promised, Will led her and her parents up the steps, past the crowd of people waiting to enter. Inside, the foyer loomed magnificent. A ceiling that soared for thirty feet was adorned with the largest chandelier Faith had ever seen. Its crystals shined in all the colors of the rainbow as the fully lighted jewel gave the foyer the feel of royalty. Black and white checkered marble was beneath her feet, and a curved staircase led up to a grand landing where it was likely the family had their bedrooms.

Faith had never seen such a grand home. Running and hiding was not out of the question. She was not grand enough to be mistress of so much opulence. She would never fit here.

Then she spotted Nick at the bottom of the stairs. His stunning blue eyes locked on hers and he didn't seem to hear whatever the short man next to him was saying, or didn't care. His attention was fully focused on her.

A stretch of silence fell over the din of the crowd as they searched for whatever had captured the Duke's attention so fully. Every head swiveled toward Faith.

Her skin prickled from the unwanted attention, but she stayed focused on Nick and moved through the throng, all the while her heart pounding in her ears.

When she reached him, she made a low curtsy. "Your Grace."

He bowed but kept his gaze fixed on hers. "Lady Faith."

Time stood still for a full three seconds.

Father cleared his throat.

Recovering propriety, Nick rose and shook Father's hand. "My lord, it's good to see you again. Lady Dornbury, you look lovely this evening. Thank you both for accompanying my fiancée to the ball. I'm delighted to have you all here. May I introduce my sister, Elana Trent, Countess of Dunworth?" The woman to Nick's right was as tall as Mercy, her head reaching past Nick's shoulder. Her dark hair and bright blue eyes were exactly like her brother's, and she was elegant in a way that cannot be taught, but must come naturally. She made the slightest curtsy to Faith's parents. "A pleasure to meet you."

Elana turned her attention to Faith. She narrowed her eyes and cocked her head. "I have long wished to make your acquaintance, Lady Faith. I must apologize for not coming to London sooner and meeting you in a more private setting. Would you do me the honor of coming to tea tomorrow so we might better know each other?"

"I would be delighted, Lady Dunworth. Thank you." Faith made a low curtsy.

Looking her over for longer than was comfortable, Elana finally smiled. She took Faith's arm and turned her toward the ballroom without so much as a word to her brother or all the people waiting to get a look at her. "My brother speaks of little else but you, Lady Faith."

When they were out of view of the foyer, she stopped. "I thought you might like to get away from the attention of all those people and your parents. Nick will have to stay and greet people a while longer, but I'm sure he will come and find you as soon as propriety allows."

Faith tried to clear her head. Nick's sister had just left the receiving line to get Faith away from an uncomfortable situation. Elana didn't even know her, but she knew being the center of so much attention was abhorrent. "Thank you, Lady Dunworth. That was very thoughtful."

"I suppose your father will like to stand with Nick for a while." Elana's smile was warm and knowing.

"You have excellent intuition." Faith was astonished by how easily a stranger had read the situation.

With a nod, she shrugged. "I see things about people that would perhaps take others longer to see."

"That must come in handy in London society, with all its intrigue." Faith wished for such a gift.

"I try to avoid London for just that reason. Too much intrigue sets my nerves on edge." She glanced over Faith's shoulder and raised a brow. "Friends of yours?"

Faith turned in the direction of Elana's gaze. Poppy, Aurora, and Mercy were wending their way through the crowd toward her. "Yes."

The Wallflowers arrived, bursting with what they wanted to say. Faith could see it in all their eyes. They all turned to Elana and remained silent.

Faith made the introductions.

"It is a pleasure to meet all of you. I have to return to the foyer and help my brother with the greeting of guests. I'm sure we will have occasion to speak later." Elana smiled and left them.

"Hera's eyes. His sister is so elegant," Poppy said.

"And quite nice," Mercy added.

Aurora nodded. "It's hard to say from so short a visit, but she did seem friendly."

Trying not to commit to any degree of like or dislike until she knew Elana better, Faith said, "She was kind upon meeting me and has invited me to take tea with her tomorrow."

Rhys sauntered over and joined them. "Is this a ladies-only Wallflower meeting, or may I ask my wife for the first dance?"

The musicians tuned their instruments as they readied to play the minuet.

Faith's parents entered the ballroom with Nick as if they owned the place rather than as guests.

Embarrassed, Faith plastered a polite smile on her face and turned toward them.

Nick's sympathetic smile warmed her. "Lady Faith, would you honor me by starting the ball with me?"

Heart pounding and insides aquiver, she took his arm. "I would be delighted."

As soon as they had moved away from the others, Nick said, "You look stunning tonight, Faith."

Her cheeks warmed. "Thank you. My father found the dress too revealing."

"Is it?" He gave her a full look. The gown was slightly low cut, but otherwise revealed nothing of Faith's flesh, though it did hug her curves.

The long look made her blush deeper. "I think it was my figure being revealed that troubled Father."

"I quite like your figure, Faith. Perhaps you should begin ignoring these hurtful comments from your parents. While I'm sure they mean well, ultimately they do you a disservice." He smiled as he took his place for the dance.

It warmed Faith's heart to have him take her part despite his polite regard for her mother and father.

During the dance they didn't speak, but with each pass and touch of his hand Faith remembered the secrets he had shared with her. Despite the horrors of their time at Parvus, Faith loved that he had stopped keeping things from her and shared parts of himself that she doubted even his sister knew.

Geb grinned from the crowd watching the dancing, and Faith returned his smile.

When the dance took her away from Nick, she still felt his gaze following her to her next partner. As the final chords brought them together, his smile was private. "Will you walk with me in the garden, Faith?"

She glanced around the ballroom and found her parents watching from the side, where they stood with Mercy's aunt and Aurora's mother. "I will meet you there in a few minutes. If I retreat now, there will be too many questions."

Nick bowed over her hand, his lips touched her skin and the kiss vibrated through her to a place impolite to think about during a crowded ball. "I will wait for you."

As soon as Nick escorted her back to her parents, he excused himself. Mother pulled her close. "What did he say?"

"There is little time to speak during the minuet, Mother." Faith would try not to lie, but her mother rarely told her the entire truth, so she felt little guilt in a few fibs if need be.

"I saw him speak at the end. What did he say, Faith?" Her mother's eyes flashed with anger as she sensed Faith's reluctance to share anything.

"Only that he would speak to me later in the evening. Must you make drama out of everything, Mother?" It was not entirely a lie, nor was it the truth. Rather pleased with her response, she put on her best blank stare and waited for whatever Mother might throw at her.

Father gripped her other arm. "You had better see to it that a date is set for your wedding, Faith. This absurd length of your engagement is beginning to grate on me in a very unpleasant way. I approved your moving in with those friends of yours because I assumed you'd be married within a few months. If I do not have a firm date by the end of this night, you will be moved back home before the end of the week."

Where he gripped her, pain lanced through her arm. "Why don't you tell him that, Father?"

"Do not test my patience, girl." There was no mistaking that his last word was the worst thing she could be.

She tugged free and faced him. "I will do what I can, Father. You and Mother arranged this marriage, not me. Perhaps you should have stipulated a time frame."

Spinning away, she didn't wait for her father's response. She stormed out of the ballroom, down a hallway, and then down several others until she was thoroughly lost within the townhouse.

Frustrated, she entered a door and found herself in the prettiest room she'd ever seen. Cream walls with arched trim and French doors as tall as the ceiling. They led out to a patio surrounded by trees and lit by torches.

Inside, the three standing candelabras glinted off golden accents on walls and even the thread of the tapestry over the fireplace. Curtains the color of the new leaves in spring hung lushly from the top of the walls and matched a thick rug. Cream and gold chairs made a quartet around a low table in the center of the room, while a lady's desk sat in the corner by a window.

At the sound of the closing door, Faith spun around. Nick stood just inside. "Do you like it?"

"Who could find fault in this room? It is lovely beyond measure. What do you use it for?"

He stepped closer. "It is not in use. My mother used to use it as her study and to entertain her lady friends. I keep it as she left it, in hopes that one day you might like to use it in a similar fashion."

Faith swallowed down the emotion knotted in her throat. "You have been keeping this room much longer than you and I have been engaged, and for much of that time, you hoped I would call it off."

Smiling, he took another step in her direction. "Then let's say, I kept it with the idea of you."

"It is truly lovely. Your mother had a great eye for what would make a person feel comfortable even in an ornate setting." Faith turned toward the fireplace and admired the tapestry depicting animals surrounding a woman sitting in tall grass.

His arms encircled her. "It is meant to be the goddess Diana."

"I thought she was a huntress. Why are the animals so comfortable in her presence?" Faith loved the way he was strong and gentle at the same time.

Kissing her ear, he said, "A good huntress only takes what she needs to survive. Those animals know she is sated and only wishes for their company."

She sighed. "In my experience, people take what they want regardless of their state of satisfaction."

"Not all people. You have your friends," he said.

"That is true. There are some who want only what you are willing to give and take only what they need. People who don't judge." She sighed and leaned against him.

"What did your father say that made him look as if he might strike you?" Nick's tone turned dangerous.

Faith spun in his arms. "You saw that?"

"What did he say?"

The notion of another fib crossed her mind, but lying to Nick felt wrong after all they'd been through. "He wants me to force you to set a date for our wedding or he's threatened to force me to move back to his house."

Nick stepped back, releasing her. He turned and uttered a curse under his breath. "He hurt you?"

Not wanting to whine over a bruised arm after the kind of pain Nick had endured, Faith shrugged. "It was nothing."

"I don't want you under his roof. I know he's your father, but he also has many debts he's run up since our engagement and his fear that he might not get the funds promised might push him to do something foolish." Nick spoke flatly, but turned to meet her gaze.

"He has?" Faith had no idea Father had been overspending in the past year.

Nodding, Nick said, "He bought into a shipping business and two coal mines. He will not be able to pay his debtors, should we not marry."

"He didn't tell me that. Why would he keep that a secret, if he wants me to go forward with the wedding?" Bewildered, Faith struggled to see the logic.

Nick shrugged. "Perhaps your mother doesn't know. Perhaps he holds it as a last card to play with you. I don't know. I only know what I've told you, sweetheart."

"How did you come by this information?" She stared at him, trying to decide if he'd done something inappropriate where her father was concerned.

A slow smile played across his full lips. "I wish I could tell you I came by the information in some innocent way, but I've had your father investigated since your mother first contacted me."

"Why?"

"Because I'm a spy, Faith. I have a difficult time trusting people, and your parents were too eager to rid themselves of a lovely and intelligent daughter. I wanted to know what I was getting into." He raised both brows and waited for whatever her reaction might be.

She couldn't fault him for his mistrust. Not only was he correct about her father, his own experience couldn't help but color his actions. "I see.

I must tell you that my father's debts will not alter my decision. I suppose that is selfish and foolish."

"And noble and charming and yes, foolish. However, I love that it will not force your hand. I do not want you to marry for reasons that are not your own." Nick offered his arm. "Will you walk with me in the garden?"

Chapter 18

The seconds that passed while he waited for Faith to take his arm loomed heavy and progressed slowly. How appropriate that she had found his mother's study. Faith fit perfectly into the feminine surroundings. Mother would have liked Faith's independent nature and warmth.

It occurred to him that he could throw himself on her mercy and beg her to marry him, but he preferred for her to come to her own conclusions. Delivering some facts and his own affection would have to be enough.

She rested her hand on his arm.

Nick let out the breath he'd been holding. He led them out the French doors to the private veranda. "Should I have kept my knowledge of your father's financial situation to myself?"

"Why do you say that?"

"I don't want it to be a factor in your decision, and while I know you said it wouldn't be, I don't see how it cannot." He guided her down the steps and into the sparse garden. It was cool, but spring had arrived in London on the early March night. The grass was green though most trees still awaited their sappy leaves. A great deal of evergreens and the cold ensured their privacy.

She stopped and faced him. "I am fully capable of making a decision based on facts and my own wants rather than those of my parents."

Trying to keep his grin at bay didn't work. "You are a kind, good person who would not like to see your mother, and even your father, suffer if you can do something to prevent it."

A long sigh pushed from her delectable lips. "I wish our courtship had not been so complicated, Nick. Wouldn't it have been nice to have met at a ball and danced a minuet or quadrille? Perhaps we might have talked of politics, or country living versus London. It would have been so normal and nice."

He let loose his sigh. "It might have, but would I feel this fierce attraction to you if our beginnings had been so benign?"

"I don't know," she admitted. "But I know you worry that you have exposed me to things I should not have seen. I am stronger than you think."

His heart ached. "You are a Valkyrie, Faith. I have no doubt about that. That does not absolve me of my errors in judgment. I should have protected you."

"I am tired of this conversation. Can we speak of other things?" She walked ahead of him.

Catching up, he took her hand in his. "What would you like to talk about, sweetheart?"

"Your sister invited me to tea tomorrow. She seems very nice." Faith stopped at the empty fountain. The cherubs stared down on them, their pitchers devoid of water until the threat of any more freezes was past for the year.

"Elana is wonderful. She hates London and came only so I could host this ball. Her husband is also quite nice, but stayed in the country with their children. He also dislikes town." Nick wished it was warmer weather and they could remain in the gardens longer. Faith would look like an angel among the cherubs with water flowing from their pitchers.

Faith shivered and took his hand. They walked back toward the house. "Was theirs a love match?"

"Their marriage was arranged by my father. However, they seem quite happy together." He pulled her up the veranda steps and behind a row of evergreens before wrapping her in his arms.

"Why didn't your father marry her off to a duke or prince?" Faith leaned into his chest and rested her head there.

"Perhaps you should ask Elana that question." Nick rubbed her back from nape to small and reveled in every curve.

She gaped at him. "She would think me impertinent if I asked her that."

He shrugged. "Probably not, but I leave it up to you." He lowered his mouth to hers, no longer wishing to speak about his sister.

Her lips were soft and warm and she responded with a soft sigh. Her supple body was perfection in his arms and he was helpless to keep his desire at bay.

Deepening the kiss, Nick wished he could carry her up to his room and show her what their lovemaking could be. Inside, her mouth was soft and cool and she tasted like heaven. Memories of knowing her carnally caused him to grow uncomfortable in his breeches.

Devoid of fear or hesitation, she reached around his neck and toyed with the hair at his collar. If he'd known how pleasing it would feel, he'd never have cut his hair. Her body formed to his and his responded until it was painful to stand in the cold and not take the kiss further.

Breaking the kiss, he moved her to arm's length. "One day, Faith, I would like to make love to you properly."

"Was the first time not properly done? In my memory, it was quite wonderful." Her smile was wicked.

"I was not able to do a great many things because of my injuries. If you permit it, in the future, that will not be the case." His shaft didn't care that they stood in the cold and fulfillment was not possible.

She shrugged. "You may think what you like, but for me, it was a perfect night."

"I'm happy to hear that." He still wished their first lovemaking had been less inhibited by his condition. However, at the time, they both believed it would be the only time, as his life was forfeit.

"Shall we return to the ball before you are missed?"

"I think you should go inside. I will follow when walking is not so difficult."

A slow grin made it clear she knew what he meant. "At least you are not indifferent to me."

"That is the last word I would ever use to describe my feelings toward you." He straightened.

She cocked her head. "What would be the first?"

"Sir, are you the Duke of Breckenridge?" A man of perhaps twenty, with blond hair and wearing the uniform of an English soldier, stood at the bottom of the steps.

"I am." Nick's desire fled with the practiced alertness of a hardened soldier. "Who sent you?"

The soldier gulped for air. "I'm not to say, Your Grace. I was told only to deliver this message." He held up a slip of folded parchment.

Avoiding Faith's stare, Nick accepted the bad timing. "You had better give it to me then."

In an instant, the soldier was up the steps and thrusting the parchment out in front of him. Nick took the note. "Were you told to wait for a response?"

"No, Your Grace."

Nick cocked his head. "Then you may go."

Almost as quietly as he had appeared, the young man slipped back into the garden and was gone.

"Is something amiss?" Faith asked, her eyes narrowed.

Breaking the familiar seal used by all the agents working for Drake, Nick opened the note. It was a detailed confirmation that Joseph still owned the house in Germany and that he was not currently there. Nick turned to Faith. "No. Everything is fine. I have some business to attend to and will have to leave for a few weeks."

There was no missing the disappointment in her golden eyes. "You have taken another mission?"

He closed the distance between them and whispered, "I cannot discuss it with you, Faith. It is dangerous for you to know too much."

"It was dangerous for me to know nothing. When will you give up this insanity? Was what they did to you at Parvus not enough? Have you some wish to die young?" She stood with her fisted hands on her hips and glared at him.

"The situation is complicated, sweetheart."

She pulled her shoulders back and stood to her diminutive, but full height. "I imagine it would always be thus with you, Nick. I don't know if you can offer me the kind of life I am looking for. I have strong feelings for you, but this evening has been oddly eye-opening. Tell my parents whatever you wish. I will have to give this matter some thought."

A large piece of his heart broke off and he wished he could have the last ten minutes back. But wishing for impossible things like a normal beginning to their acquaintance was neither helpful nor possible. "I understand, sweetheart, but you must also understand that I cannot be someone else to please you."

Wide beautiful eyes stared back at him as if he'd said something that struck a chord with her. When she spoke again, her anger had fled, leaving thoughtfulness and sadness in its wake. "No. You're right, of course. I wouldn't want you to change on my behalf."

"I will handle your father, Faith. When I return to London, we will talk about the future, if there is one for us." He bowed and watched her turn and enter the house through his mother's study.

Freezing, Nick still didn't want to go back to the ball. He couldn't bear Faith's disappointed looks. He walked the garden path and wished there was some other way to get Drake what he needed, but thought of nothing. Finally, his numb fingers forced him inside via the ballroom doors.

Mercedes Heath spotted him immediately and raised one eyebrow as she sashayed the short distance to him. "You look frozen, Your Grace."

"It has grown colder outside, Miss Heath." He needed to toss the note he'd tucked in his pocket into a fire. He'd been so distracted by Faith, he'd almost forgotten.

Mercy was tall for a woman and moved with the grace of a ballerina rather than a debutante. "You shouldn't have stayed out so long. Your guests were beginning to gossip and infer you had left your own ball."

Smiling, he mused over the scandal that would cause. "My sister would have my head if I ever did such a thing."

Mercy laughed. "She does seem formidable."

"Perhaps a dance would warm me. Would you indulge me, Miss Heath?" Nick didn't like standing about while the entire room whispered about him.

"Thank you, that would be very nice." Mercy stuttered slightly as she accepted. Taking his hand, she accompanied him to the dance floor.

When they came together for the first pass, Nick asked, "Why did you seem so surprised by my invitation?"

She shrugged, and even that move flowed gracefully. "Men rarely ask me to dance, Your Grace."

Waiting until they came together again, he asked, "Why is that?"

Her laugh was soft but filled with genuine amusement. "I am an orphan with little to recommend me. I live off the kindness of an aging aunt and a small sum my parents left behind."

Society often enraged Nick. This was a nice woman, smart and witty, yet her lack of fortune or connection would leave her to spend her life alone. "It seems quite unfair to me, Miss Heath, as you dance extremely well."

"My name is Mercy. Life is rarely fair, Your Grace." She grinned as they made the next turn, which took them away from each other. When she once again took his hand, she asked, "Why have you not broken your engagement with my friend? After all this time and all that has happened, I would have thought you'd had enough."

"You are far too bold, Mercy." He let the pass go without answering, but when they arrived together for the end of the dance, he said, "I am not willing to give her up."

Mercy cocked her head. "That may be the first truly honest thing I've ever heard you say, Your Grace."

"My name is Nick. I doubt that is true. However, I admit I have my secrets to keep." He escorted her toward the fireplace.

"If you're not willing to give her up and you are ready to be a good husband, why have you not set a date?" Mercy stopped before they reached the crush of people hovering around the edges of the room.

Nick turned toward her. "I believe you are worried about Lord Dornbury's threat to force Faith back to his home."

"I am." She narrowed her eyes.

"And you suggest I set a date to keep her at the West Lane townhouse, regardless of the fact that she has not officially agreed to marry me?" He put a few things together and could see her logic.

"It seems logical. Faith can always call off later, should that be her decision." Mercy's green eyes flashed with intelligence.

Faith might not like the solution, but it did make sense. "I shall give it some thought. Thank you for your input, Mercy."

Mercy's attention shifted to the other side of the ballroom. "Who is that man?"

Turning his attention in the direction of her gaze, he found the subject of her question speaking to Aurora Sherbourn and her mother, the Dowager Countess of Marsden. The man was broad shouldered, with dark blond hair, and dressed in elegant black with a yellow cummerbund. "That is Wesley Renshaw, the Earl of Castlewick. I went to school with him, but have not seen him in years. I suppose my sister thought his name lofty enough to warrant an invitation."

"Would you mind introducing me?" Her eyes were narrowed and tightness laced her words.

Nick offered his arm. "Of course."

They had to skirt a great many people readying themselves for the next dance. Mercy was far better and nimbler at making a path than he was. Nick asked, "Is the Countess of Radcliff out of mourning?"

"Only just," Mercy said, disgust lacing her words. "Her mother is likely already shopping another abominable husband for her."

"I see," Nick said, and they moved with more urgency. When they reached the threesome, Nick shook Wesley's hand. "How are you, Castlewick?"

"Very well. It's good to see you. I was happy to receive the invitation. I've been at my country home for the winter and just arrived in London two weeks ago. This is the first card I've been inclined to accept." Wesley spoke openly, but withheld any real information.

It was the sign of a man who was into things he didn't want others to know about, but he told enough to keep the questions at a minimum. Nick had seen the tactic many times. "May I introduce Miss Mercedes Heath. She is a good friend of Lady Radcliff's and my fiancée's. The ladies all went to finishing school together."

Wesley bowed. "Miss Heath, a pleasure to meet you."

"How do you do, my lord." Mercy made a pretty curtsy. "I hope you will not think me rude, but I need to steal away my friend. We have an urgent matter to discuss. I'm sure the dowager and our host will be more than enough to entertain you."

A short laugh escaped Wesley's mouth. "I would not wish to keep you from anything urgent."

Aurora took Mercy's arm and the two rushed through the crowd and out of the ballroom.

Lady Marsden's frown said that she did not feel the same as Wesley. "I must apologize for my daughter and her friend. They can be quite dramatic. I can assure you when away from bad influences, Aurora is a perfect lady."

"I'm sure that is true," Wesley agreed, amusement still lingering in his tone.

Aurora's mother made a curtsy and excused herself.

"A perfect lady sounds dreadfully boring." Wesley laughed and slapped Nick on the back. "How have you been?"

The scars on Nick's back were still sensitive, but he managed to only cringe and not call out. "Well enough, Wes."

As alert as ever, Wesley noted Nick's discomfort. "Are you injured?"

"A small accident that is still on the mend. Not to worry."

"I'm sorry. I didn't know." Genuine concern overshadowed Wesley's earlier amusement.

"It's all right. No one knows. I'll be fine. You should know that Lady Radcliff has only been out of mourning for a few weeks and is not looking for a new husband. Her mother is a bit premature in her search for a new match, from what I'm told." The sharp pain was short-lived, and Nick thought it a good time to help a Wallflower, even if it was not his Wallflower.

Wesley nodded. "I'm in no rush. Her mother foisted me on her and I could see she was less than pleased by the intrusion. Still, she is rich and I am as well. It could be a good match when she is ready."

It was hard to argue with that. "I suppose that is true."

"Her friend is a spitfire."

Nick was constantly amazed by Faith and her friends' ability to thwart society. "She is that and quite pretty as well."

"Indeed. Perhaps I will find Miss Heath and beg a dance," Wesley said.

"Good hunting, Wes." Nick laughed and the two parted.

Nick walked to the parlor, where a fire blazed. Several people sat around chatting and two tables were filled with card players. Many of them spoke to him and he made polite conversation. All the while the note in his pocket worried him. He patted it several times to assure himself it was still there.

He continued through to a short hallway that led to his office. He liked the out-of-the-way location, away from the front of the house. Servants and callers rarely bothered him, but he preferred the smaller space facing the garden to the large library his father had used as an office. Inside, pale papered walls surrounded by polished wood molding gave him comfort. He'd missed home when he was abroad. The last week back in London had been delightfully boring. He could stand more boredom in his life.

A small fire in the hearth was the result of a household staff who knew he liked to get away from crowds and think. Nick tossed the note he'd received into the flames and viewed the parchment burn to ash.

"Bad news?" Geb asked from beside him.

Nick hadn't noticed his friend's arrival, but he was used to the way Geb often appeared from out of nowhere. "News is news, neither good or bad."

"Does it take you out of London?"

Nodding, Nick sighed. Faith was never going to forgive him if he didn't stay and make her see how perfect they were for each other.

"Then the news is bad," Geb said gravely.

"Yes. I suppose so." Nick wished he could stay and woo Faith until her feelings matched his own. As it was, this mission would take their relationship in the wrong direction.

Geb sighed. "Will she forgive you?"

It was a fair question. "I would forgive her anything. I suppose if her feelings are as strong as mine, then she will forgive me for leaving town."

"Are you testing her?" The disapproval in Geb's voice was clear.

"Not with intention, but it shall work out that way." Would Faith pass, and would it matter to him if she didn't?

Chapter 19

Faith sat in the ladies' parlor at West Lane and brooded. Not knowing what to think, she sulked and hoped for some sign of what to do. Rumple slept in her lap, his gentle snoring steady and comforting as her mind rushed in a dozen different directions.

"Quite a night last night." Mercy sauntered in and flounced down on the chaise.

It sounded tongue-in-cheek, but Faith ignored the sarcasm. "Why do you suppose he told my father to pick a date in June for our wedding?"

"So that you would not be forced to leave West Lane, of course." Mercy said it with confidence and as if it was the obvious answer.

"How do you know that was his reason?" Faith knew Mercy well enough to know there was more to her matter-of-fact statement.

She shrugged. "Because we discussed the option as the most logical at the ball last night."

"You told him to set a date with my father?" Faith's head pounded as blood rushed through her ears. Her hand stilled in Rumple's fur.

Mercy raised her brows. "I don't think anyone tells the Duke of Breckenridge what to do. I just said it would solve your problem."

Unable to keep calm, Faith jumped from her seat. "But Mercy, I haven't decided if I want to marry him yet."

"What does that matter, Faith? If you don't want to marry him, then you'll break it off with or without a wedding date. This way you get to stay here and not live with your parents. I assumed you would prefer to live here. Was I wrong?" Mercy relaxed back onto the chaise, her left leg bent under her and one arm over her head.

Confused, Faith wasn't sure what to say. "No. I do not want to live with my parents and listen to sermons and censures. But setting a date makes the idea of marrying Nick so imminent."

Unbending from the chaise, Mercy stood and came to sit next to Faith on the settee. "I had the impression you were in love with Nick, Faith. You spoke of him with a great deal of tenderness when you arrived home from your imprisonment. You did not sound then like a woman who was unsure about what she wanted."

"He has not stopped his occupation as a spy, Mercy. I don't know if I can live with the idea of him running off, and not knowing if he'll ever come back." A shiver ran up Faith's spine. Even now she was unsure if she would ever see him again.

Mercy frowned. "Perhaps you should discuss your feelings with him. That is, if you are in love with him."

"He won't even admit to me that he's back to his spying business." She sounded petulant but she didn't care.

"What did he say?" Mercy asked.

"That it would be dangerous for me to know too much about his business."

"It seems it was dangerous for you to know nothing."

"That's what I told him." Faith threw her hands up in the air.

Rumple complained but snuggled in closer.

Smiling, Mercy patted her back. "Don't you have an appointment to have tea with his sister this afternoon?"

Faith glanced at the clock near the door. She sighed. "Yes. I must get ready. Perhaps I can find out something useful from Elana. Though I'm not certain if she knows anything about her brother's activities." Transferring Rumple to Mercy's lap, Faith stood and walked toward the door, thinking about the blue dress she would wear to meet with the elegant Countess of Dunworth.

"May I say one more thing, Faith?" Mercy petted the puppy back into sleep.

Stopping, she turned back to Mercy. "Of course."

"I have always had a romantic belief that if you truly loved someone, you would forgive them almost anything. Nick forgave you for spying on him, even though he was put out by the events of last summer. He trusted you with his care and his heart. Don't you think he deserves the same from you?" Mercy smiled warmly. "Go and get ready. You don't want to be late."

Faith no longer worried about the dress she'd picked. She wrestled with the truth of Mercy's observations. Lord, why did she have to be so logical?

* * * *

Fifteen minutes early for her tea appointment, Faith struggled with whether she should sit in her carriage and wait for the appropriate time to arrive or go up the stairs to the Earl and Countess of Dunworth's townhouse. It was around the corner from Nick's stunning London home, and she'd had a fleeting thought of stopping and seeing if he had indeed left the country as she suspected.

"Oh, dash it. John!" She called the driver.

A moment later John's affable head popped into the window. "My lady?"

"I'm going in."

John's grin showed yellowed teeth, and he had a small scar on his chin that Faith had often speculated about. She'd never had the nerve to ask him how he'd got it, though he was so easy spirited, he would likely tell her. He opened the carriage door and lowered the step before handing Faith down into the street. "I'll be right here when you're ready to go home, Lady Faith."

"Thank you, John." If Faith married and moved away from West Lane, she would miss the life the Wallflowers had created and the loyalty of the people they'd surrounded themselves with.

Pushing aside the future, Faith had a present to deal with. She climbed the stairs, knocked and waited.

An unusually young butler was still fussing with his coat when he pulled the door open. "How may I help you?"

He'd sounded desperate, and Faith relaxed. She smiled at the blond butler with the face of perhaps a twenty-year-old. "Lady Faith Landon to see her ladyship. I have an appointment."

"Of course. Forgive me, my lady. The countess told me you were coming." He babbled an apology but still neglected to invite her in.

"Grant, perhaps you might invite my guest inside the house rather than leave her on the stoop for all the neighbors to gossip about," Elana's kind but forceful voice called from within.

"Yes, my lady. I'm so sorry. Please come in, Lady Faith." Grant opened the door wider.

"Thank you." Faith grinned but hid her desire to laugh. The poor man was already red as a beet.

Not as grand as her brother's home, the townhouse was still far fancier than most. A golden chandelier with dozens of crystals caught the light from a transom above the door and sent tiny rainbows flitting around the foyer. The tiles were white marble with black veins, and a round table stood in the center of the space, adorned with a vase waiting for the first spring flowers. The grand staircase climbed and arched around before disappearing into the upper floor.

At the bottom of the stairs, with her hand resting on the polished wood handrail, Elana stood. Her smile was lit with amusement. "Thank you, Grant. Take the lady's outerwear, and I will take over."

Unable to completely hide her amusement, because she was so relieved to find an imperfection when she expected to feel completely out of her element, Faith giggled. She handed Grant her pelisse, hat, and gloves. "Thank you."

With an awkward bow that nearly sent Faith's belongings flying, Grant made his exit.

Elana approached. Still smiling, she shook her head. "His father was our butler for many years. In fact, the elder Grant was the Dunworth butler when my husband was a boy. We recently pensioned him and he's gone to the country for his health. His son is still learning the position and we are being patient."

"You are most kind to see him through this learning stage. I'm sure he'll be a fine butler one day." Faith had no idea if that were true, but she hoped for Grant's sake she was being honest.

"How are you, Lady Faith?" Elana kissed her cheek.

Taken aback by the show of affection, Faith felt her cheeks flush. "I am well, your ladyship. I'm happy to be here."

A wide smile transformed Elana from pretty to beautiful. "Let's go into my private parlor." Her periwinkle day dress flowed around her as she led the way into a small but comfortable parlor. The fire burned low and two tall windows let in a good deal of light. Every surface was covered in cream and pale blue, and a portrait hanging on the wall depicted Elana sitting on a golden throne with a kind-eyed blond man standing beside her and three children sitting on the enormous chair with her.

"You have a beautiful family, Lady Dunworth." Faith's heart panged with just a touch of jealousy.

"Thank you. That was two years ago. My eldest boy is gone off to school and I miss him terribly. I look forward to summers when all my children are home." She rounded a table, splitting the distance between two overstuffed chairs. "Will you come and sit? Tea will be here in a few minutes."

"I'm sorry to have arrived early. I thought of waiting in the street, but the gossips…" Faith let the word hang, as everyone knew everything that happened in London and a carriage sitting for fifteen minutes outside the Earl of Dunworth's home, would be talked about.

Elana waved off the apology. "I completely agree. But I must insist you call me Elana. After all, we are to be sisters."

Swallowing her immediate desire to add a *maybe* to Elana's statement, Faith forced a smile. "Then I would be honored if you would call me Faith."

With a nod, she cocked her head at the sound of the door opening.

A stout maid with black hair poking out from her white cap bustled in with a tea tray. "Cook baked fresh this morning, my lady, so I added some nice biscuits to the tea tray." She had an accent that Faith couldn't place and her skin was a lovely golden brown.

"Thank you, Maude. This looks lovely."

When Maude had set everything out, she curtsied and strode out purposefully.

Faith had dozens of questions about the maid, but none were appropriate for the first tea with Elana, and she didn't want to be rude. Still, there was something about Maude. "She never even rattled a dish on that heavy tray. What a remarkable feat."

That joyous smile returned to Elana's face. "Maude is remarkable. My husband, Duncan, was in London three years ago meeting at the House of Lords. Maude was starving in the street. Her father is a wealthy and powerful Englishman. He brought her back from his tobacco farm in Antigua where he had fathered several children with his slaves." Disgust rang in Elana's tone. "Maude has never told us the entire story. When her father's wife saw her, she tossed her into the street."

Heart aching for what the poor woman must have gone through, Faith felt her chest tighten. "What made your husband take her in? There are unfortunately many souls begging on London's streets."

Elana sighed. "I think it was because Maude wouldn't beg. She sat outside the House of Lords and waited for her father to come. She had hope that he would see her and do the right thing. Of course, Duncan knew none of the story at that time. He saw her waiting and asked for whom she waited. When she told him, he knew her father would not take care of his daughter. Duncan couldn't bear to see her die in the street, so he asked her to become our ward. Maude said she couldn't accept. She insisted on working if she was to go with him. So, he offered her a position in our home."

"Remarkable." Faith shook her head. "Does her father know she works for you?"

All signs of her earlier smile gone, Elana said, "Oh yes. He knows."

As it was obviously a sore subject, Faith changed the topic. "I'm glad she has found a place with you, Elana. You and his lordship are very kind people."

She laughed. "Most think we are eccentric."

"I have never been one to care what the masses think. It has gotten me in a great deal of trouble over the years." Faith accepted the teacup painted with blue roses that matched the décor of the room.

"Oh. I didn't realize Nick was marrying a rebel. Though, honestly, it doesn't surprise me." She gazed over the rim of her cup and her bright blue eyes smiled.

Faith let the warm, rich brew slide down her throat. The tea was exquisite and likely more expensive than anything they had at West Lane. "I was so disobedient that at fifteen, my father shipped me off to Switzerland for a proper schooling."

Wide-eyed, Elana leaned forward. "Really? How extraordinary. Did you suffer being so far away from home?"

"Lord, no. It was the most wonderful three years of my life. I met three other girls who became my dearest friends. You met them last night at the ball. Being sent to the Wormbattle School for Young Ladies was the best thing that could have happened to me." The memories of learning and playing in Lucerne washed over Faith. Wishing for time to roll back was no more useful than focusing ahead, so she shook off the desire for simpler times.

"What an adventure it must have been. I'm afraid I was educated by nannies and tutors at Breckenridge Manor in Hertfordshire. My parents were strong-minded about education, though, and brought in some brilliant tutors as I grew older."

Faith liked Elana. She was as smart and charming as her brother. "Did you learn more than the average Englishwoman?"

"I think so." Elana blushed, which was even more charming. "But tell me about you, Faith. What do you like to do?"

"I live with two of those friends from my school days. We all moved in together after Aurora's husband died last summer. Poppy has since married and moved to live with her husband, Rhys. But they are at the West Lane house several times a week, so it hardly feels as if she left at all." The notion that her marriage would take her from her friends sent her heart aching.

"You're wrong," Elana said, cutting into Faith's thoughts.

"I beg your pardon?" Faith didn't know how to respond.

"Remember I told you I have a sense for knowing what people need? You were just thinking that Nick would keep you from seeing your friends. I cannot imagine he would do anything that would make you unhappy. I'm convinced he's desperately in love with you." Elana said it all as if it were fact and not just her unusual intuition.

"I'm not at all certain that is true. Our engagement was arranged before he'd even met me." Faith drank the rest of her tea and put her cup down.

Elana sighed, but it was filled with some pleasant memory. "Yes, well, that is often the case. Sometimes fate plays a hand even if it seems contrived."

Nick had said Elana and her husband's marriage had been arranged. "Is that what happened with you and his lordship, Elana?"

"My parents and Duncan's were friends and corresponded often. They did not live close to one another but managed to continue their friendship for years. When I was informed I would be expected to marry Duncan, a man I had never met, I flew into a fit. Mother raged at me. Father was decidedly disappointed. I was furious. Nick was the only one who kept his head."

Faith's insides jumbled with the memory of Aurora being forced into a marriage and how much of a disaster that was. "Well, Nick was not the one being married off."

Elana shook her head. "No. It wasn't that. He was concerned. He proposed that Mother and Father invite Dunworth and his family to our country home. There would be no distractions of the city and we might all get to know Duncan. He made them promise that if I truly disliked Duncan, I could beg off the engagement."

"But you didn't dislike him?" Faith guessed the truth.

Something tender appeared in Elana's smile. "No. I did not. He was as worried as I about the arrangement, and he was so kind and smart. We walked the property in Hertfordshire and talked for hour upon hour. By the end of the first week, we were both begging our parents to purchase a special license so we could marry immediately."

"That is remarkable. If only it were so simple for everyone. I see what you mean about fate, but none of that makes me believe Nick loves me." Faith questioned that all her mother's ministrations had been the work of fate to bring Nick and her together.

"My brother can be a bit of a puzzle. Like now, he has left the country to do who knows what for the Crown. He thinks I don't know he's a spy."

"Have you always known?" Faith was more than a little surprised.

"Of course. He thinks everyone is oblivious, and for the most part he's right. However, I pay attention. I knew when he first left home, he was going into danger. How long have you known?"

Faith took a deep breath. She couldn't lie, nor could she betray anything Nick and she had shared in confidence. "I have suspected since the first night we met."

Elana nodded. "My brother was always hesitant as a boy. It drove my father crazy. Now he makes decisions every day, but he hated change when he was young. Hated going away to school, as it took him away from Mother, and then hated coming home when it took him away from his friends and books. He dearly loves books."

The surprise must have registered on Faith's face.

"You didn't know?" Elana said.

"No. We have not discussed any books that he enjoys." Faith wished the conversation about her reading material had gone further, but he had been angry at her and then their world had turned upside down.

"Well, he loves them and has created an extensive library here in London as well as in Hertfordshire. Father was not fond of books. He said they only gather dust. Nick once told him that without books the brain is the dust gatherer."

Faith laughed.

"It did not go over well with Father, but Mother found it just as amusing."

Not wishing to pry, Faith wanted to know the kind of young man Nick had been. "Nick mentioned that he and your mother were close. Was he close with your father as well?"

Elana's head cocked. "Yes, but in a different way. He and Father spoke of politics and ethics and they debated every point, never agreeing on anything."

"Then they fought?" Faith could understand fighting with one's parents. It was her constant state since she had learned to speak.

"No. They disagreed, but once the debate was finished, they left their opinions behind without rancor. They went hunting from time to time and both had a great love of dogs and horses. Nick was devastated when Father died." Her voice grew tight and she looked away.

"It shows how little I know. I thought men were eager to claim their titles." Faith hoped to lighten the mood with her remark, even though she hadn't lied.

Elana grinned. "I suppose that is true for some. Some fathers are not as kind as ours was."

"So despite his arguments with his father, there was love between them?" Faith said it mostly to herself. "My mother and I have enjoyed periods of affection, but to my father I have always been an inconvenient substitute for the son he wanted."

"I am sorry to hear that, Faith. I have only known you for a short time, but I feel confident your father has lost a great opportunity."

"How so?" Faith asked.

Cocking her head, there was a sincerity to her expression that would keep whomever she spoke to in rapt attention. "My word, Faith, have you no idea how spectacular you are?"

Heat flushed up Faith's neck and cheeks and she had no idea what to say. "You are too kind."

"No. You are special in many ways. I can see why my brother has fallen so completely in love with you."

Faith didn't know what Elana meant in calling her special, but she prayed the rest was true. Her heart was already lost to Nick, and having such a man truly love her, might be enough to make her more than the family disappointment.

Chapter 20

Nick had possibly lost his senses. Traipsing through the German countryside, just east of the French border, his feet were muddy and wet, and spring left him chilled to the bone. He could be back in London, courting Faith and convincing her that he was the right man for her. What had he been thinking?

Just three weeks ago he'd had everything he wanted on the private veranda outside his mother's study, and he'd given it all up for some misguided sense of duty.

He'd left his horse behind at the boarding house, to be less conspicuous, but the spring rain made for a miserable walk through a dense forest.

Joseph used the remote lodge as a retreat when not working. Not many people knew of its existence, but Nick had been his friend and had stayed with him on two occasions when they had time off over the years to relax. Twenty-five years his senior, Joseph had liked Nick and taken him under his wing as a protégé. It was little surprise Nick's betrayal stirred so much rage.

A scraping noise from the thick wood to his left, stopped Nick. He didn't move or even breathe, hoping he had not been discovered when he was so close to reaching his goal.

A doe stepped from behind a tree, gawked at him, and walked off. It would seem he'd lost his menacing scent even to a skittish deer. In his current occupation that was not favorable.

He had never come to Joseph's lodge on his own, and hoped he hadn't gotten turned around. His inquiries had confirmed that Joseph still owned a house in Germany and that the spy's current whereabouts was on the Iberian Peninsula. Hoping to find the house empty, Nick continued through the damp woods.

The dark wood and stone exterior hid the house until, as if out of nowhere, Nick was a hundred feet away. It was a charming place that blended in rather than standing out. An odd juxtaposition from Joseph, who made it a point to be the center of attention whenever possible. While most spies hid, Joseph remained in plain sight, taking in every detail around him and making notes.

The front door was heavy oak, and locked. Nick skirted the structure and found his way in through a servants' entrance. There were no candles lit and the house was cold. The last time he'd been there, fires blazed in every hearth and the place was a cozy retreat.

He'd not find anything, stumbling around in the dark. Nick found the tinder box and managed to light a candle in the parlor. As soon as the wick caught, Charles's bright smile and haughty brow met Nick's gaze from a large chair near the large stone fireplace. "Hello, Nicholas."

Drawing his pistol, Nick pointed it at Charles. "I don't want to kill you, Charles, but that doesn't mean I won't."

Charles lifted his own pistol from the shadows between his thigh and the arm of the chair. "Nor do I wish to kill you, old friend. I didn't keep you alive in England so I could leave you shot on Joseph's floor."

Heart pounding and all his senses sharp, Nick couldn't help the thrill that shot through him. This charge of excitement was why he'd stayed a spy for so long when he could have asked to be sent home to take care of his lands and title. "Why are you here?"

Standing, Charles waved his pistol around negligently. "I've been keeping an eye on you since the unfortunate events in the country. I thought perhaps you would be keen on vengeance, and wanted to make sure your sights were not set on me."

"I have no need for revenge." Nick kept his weapon trained on Charles while making his way around the room. He placed the candle on the table before backing up out of its direct light. A small pianoforte was placed in the corner and Nick sat on the bench.

Charles circled in the other direction, also keen to keep Nick in full view.

It put distance between them and afforded Nick two possible exits if necessary: the door he'd come in, to his left, and the window behind him. It would be a mess, but he didn't wish to be trapped if things went badly.

"What do you call invading Joseph's secret home in the middle of the night?" Charles asked.

"I have an assignment, Charles, as I'm sure you know. I am not inclined to behave as Joseph, Jean-Claude, and you did. It is not revenge, only business." Nick leaned on the instrument's closed key cover.

A wide smile spread on Charles's face. He put one hand on the back of a divan with rich red fabric. "But you'll not weep over his distress after what Joseph allowed Jean-Claude to do to you. And may I point out that without me, you likely would not have survived that little visit, and who knows what would have happened to your lady." Charles shivered and pulled a disgusted face.

Nick didn't let his own shudders show outwardly, though inside he knew Charles was right. The last time Nick had been at Joseph's hunting cabin, he'd lounged on the divan, and now he dueled across it. Life had a strange way of playing out. "Which is the only reason you are still alive now. What do you want, Charles?"

"Ah, that's easy. I want for my country the same information you are collecting for your own." The ease in Charles's manner made Nick nervous. He knew too much.

"Have you integrated yourself into England's network as well, Charles?"

"Let us just say, I have friends in many places." Charles stood.

Nick stood and stepped so that his back was to the door and moved out of the window frame. "To have three masters must be impossible, my friend. Who do you serve, when?"

Waving the gun around the room, Charles said, "Today and always it is Austria, Nicholas. I only serve Napoleon when I must and your King George at his son's whim. That is not to say, I did not use my connections to keep an eye on you and follow you here."

"What is it you think I've come for?" Perhaps a deal could be struck.

"Something I have always admired about you, Nicholas, is your tendency to get directly to the point. It is a rare thing amongst our kind."

Nick didn't like to be lumped in with Charles and the rest of the spies of his acquaintance, but he couldn't deny the truth of it. "And your response?"

"I know you are after Joseph's records of royalists. If you are to gain those names, I want them too." His voice no longer held any whimsy or levity as Charles held his pistol steadily aimed at Nick's heart.

Drake wouldn't like it, but Nick had something worth living for, and he'd be damned if he would throw it all away over some names of people not his enemy. The entire mission was ridiculous. "I will gladly share the information, but you realize Joseph will be displeased when he learns his books have been stolen. Are you certain you wish to be included in his ire?"

"I will take my chances." Charles narrowed his eyes.

"Then I suggest we lower our weapons and get on with it before we're caught, and ruining my boots in these damned woods was for naught." Nick held his breath.

Charles glanced down at Nick's mud-caked boots, smiled, and tucked his pistol inside his coat. "I knew you would be reasonable, Nicholas."

Nick shrugged. "It's a fool's errand, and I should have refused. As it is, I may have ruined my chances to win Lady Faith's heart with this stupidity. I'm not eager to lose my life over it."

"Here is the Nicholas I know. I'm glad you have not lost your good sense with everything you have been through." Charles crossed his arms over his barrel chest, looking happy with himself.

If only he knew how senseless Nick had become where a certain wild-haired, golden-eyed woman was concerned. It was unconscionable to think of so little else but Faith, even when staring at the business end of a gun. Nick rounded the room, keeping Charles in his view at all times. Regardless of what the man said or his past deeds, he was still a spy and not to be trusted. At the stone fireplace, Nick touched several stones until he found one that was loose.

Praying that Joseph's favorite hiding place still held what they wanted, Nick removed the square stone and put it aside. "Charles, do you have the little baton you used to carry back in the old days?"

Charles came forward and peered in the dark hole. He reached back inside his coat and retrieved an eight-inch-long wooden baton. Handing it to Nick, he said, "I don't suppose I'll be getting that back in one piece."

Nick couldn't help liking Charles despite all that had happened. "Unlikely, knowing Joseph."

Holding the baton aloft, Nick waited for further approval.

A nod from Charles, and Nick proceeded to push the baton into the opening big enough for a man's hand.

A loud crack broke the silence and Charles jumped. "*Ach! Gut.*"

Nick laughed and pulled the baton free. It was bitten by the jaws of an animal trap meant to deter foxes from getting too close to the chicken coop. Even so, those sharp teeth and strong jaws could easily break a man's wrist or take off a few fingers. The baton had not survived, but Nick handed it back to Charles anyway.

Safe to put his hand inside the hole, Nick retrieved two black leather-bound books. They appeared harmless enough, but the contents could get many men and women of noble blood or ties to royalist politics hanged in France. "I shall have to have these copied, Charles."

Charles studied the hole where the fireplace had been altered to use as a hiding place. "I need to have a look. Once I find what I think is in there, I can wait for the rest. I trust our agreement is that of gentlemen, Nicholas? I will not have to track you down at some future date to get this copy?"

Nick handed the books to Charles. He then picked up the stone and returned it to its place. Other than the trap, which, now freed from the baton, sat on the hearth, the fireplace was undisturbed. Nick would have given anything to see Joseph's face when he walked in, saw the trap, and knew his hiding place was discovered.

Turning the pages, Charles studied one of the books near the candlelight. "Ah, it is as I thought." He grinned, closed the book, and handed both back to Nick.

Tucking the thin volumes into the inside pocket of his coat, Nick gave a small bow. "I will find a safe way to get the copy to you."

With a shrug, Charles said, "I'm certain you will. You are less given to lying directly than the average spy, Nicholas. Perhaps this is not the business you should be in any longer."

"Perhaps not." Nick didn't think he had ever agreed with anyone more.

Charles tucked away both pieces of his ruined baton. "I think this will mark the end of our association, Nicholas. I hope you will find happiness with Lady Faith. She is quite an amazing woman."

They shook hands.

Nick gave a nod. "Try to stay out of trouble, Charles. Maybe it's time for you to return to Austria and get out of this business yourself."

Charles's lips twisted. "Alas, my country does not enjoy a large body of water to keep Napoleon at bay. You English have time that Austria does not enjoy. I must keep on."

Part of Nick felt sorry for the man, but wartime left little room for those sentiments. "I wish you well, Charles."

Still gripping Nick's hand tightly, Charles met his stare. "And you, Nicholas."

Charles left through the servants' door and turned to the south while Nick headed back toward the village to the west.

The books were not much to carry, but they weighed heavy on Nick. He had already made an enemy of Joseph, and stealing his precious books would create a new level of aggression between them. Still, he could not feel bad about taking them. It had been Joseph's hand on Faith, forcing his angel to watch while Jean-Claude inflicted his punishment.

How was he ever going to make up for such a terrible week? He couldn't. Yet she had forgiven him and even allowed for his lack of communication while he recovered. It was true he'd not known what to say, but it had also given her the opportunity to dismiss him, if that had been her choice. She had not. Did that mean she loved him? He hoped so. But daring to hope left him vulnerable to hurt far greater than any torture he'd endured.

* * * *

"Tell me again why you haven't been to see Lady Faith." Geb made no effort to hide his disappointment. He paced the rug between the round divan and the overstuffed set of English-style chairs in the parlor. Gold, silver, and bronze statues, trinkets, and relics filled every hard surface. The walls were draped in rich fabrics depicting Egyptian scenes. Geb would fit into any of those scenes in his white linen clothes.

"You're worse than a mother hen. I will send her a note as soon as this other business is finished." Nick lounged in one of the chairs, plucking at the rich blue fabric. His leg ached, as he'd not spent enough time with it elevated in the last few hours. It had been six weeks since his ball, when he'd last seen Faith. He longed for her, but he didn't want her near while he was working.

"If you ruin that chair, I will make you have it reupholstered and feel not one bit sorry for it." In a fit of temper, Geb perched his fists on his hips and leveled his dark eyes on Nick.

Stilling his nervous fingers, he left the chair intact.

Geb's expression softened. "Why don't you go and rest that leg?"

It had been bad luck that on his way out of Germany he'd been shot by a French soldier near the border. A random squadron making their way back to camp had spotted him and thought him an English spy, and rightly so. Still, he'd managed his escape with only a small injury to his leg. He would heal. "I can't stay abed when there are things to be done."

Geb carried one of the colorful cushions over to Nick, then lifted Nick's leg onto the soft pillow. "You are most difficult when injured."

The ache lessened, but Nick refused to thank Geb. He hated having need of others and scowled at the cane he'd been using since being shot. He was constantly injured these last months. At least Faith was not there to see him in such a state once again.

"Did you hear from the transcriber? I don't know how long I can hold Drake off." Nick rubbed the side of his thigh, feeling the bandage through his breeches.

"Why don't you just tell him the truth? And why not give him the original books? It might be done already if Kosey's associate had only one copy to make." Geb threw himself onto the divan and rested on his side with his head perched on one hand. It was a decidedly Egyptian pose.

"Insurance," Nick said.

Geb sat up, eyes filled with concern. "You think Joseph Fouché will risk returning to England for those silly books of his?"

Nick had seen Joseph with the books in his hand once. He'd interrupted while Joseph was writing in one of them. The way he'd fondled the pages and then hugged the books to his chest when he was done with whatever he'd written, had made Nick uncomfortable enough to find out what was in the bound treasures. "I'm not sure, but I wouldn't be surprised."

"Then despite your agreement to bring Fouché's books to Drake, you will keep the originals for yourself?"

His friend had a keen mind. There was little point in trying to deceive him. Besides, Geb Arafa was the one person in the world of politics he trusted. They were friends and had been for two years.

"I was thinking about the day we met, Geb." Nick changed the subject and none too smoothly.

A full smile showed Geb's straight white teeth against brown skin. "As you wish, Nicholas. I cannot forget that day. If not for you, I would have lost my head to one of your countrymen."

Nick hated being at sea, and the day he'd met Geb had been a terrible day of rolling waves that left Nick heaving over the rail. It turned out to be a lucky thing since at the same time, a brutish captain had decided he didn't like the look of an Egyptian on one of His Majesty's ships. Geb was not accustomed to being abused, having been raised in a wealthy home. The outcome would have gone terribly wrong if Nick had not pulled rank on the captain.

Luckily, Nick had kept his breakfast down long enough to give the captain a firm set down before he could use his sword to slice through Geb's neck.

After, Geb had helped Nick survive motion sickness for the remainder of the journey and they had remained friends and worked together since. "I think you rushing in with a full regiment at Parvus makes us even on our life-saving account."

"Perhaps," Geb agreed, but frowned. "If I had arrived a few days earlier or refused Lady Faith's request to begin with, it would have ended far better."

"You can't know that. Fouché had me under surveillance for some time. He would have followed me until he caught me off my guard, somewhere with enough privacy to attempt to extract information. It is possible that Faith would not have been present, but my guess is that the lady would have found another way to get me alone. She is quite tenacious." Nick would go and see her as soon as the books were copied, his leg was healed, and he could put this business behind him. He missed her smile and the curve of her neck where it met her shoulder. He longed for the scent of her and her touch. He shook away his baser thoughts. He'd delayed seeing her to avoid distraction, but not seeing her was nearly as muddling to his mind.

"In any event, even if I am no longer indebted to you, I still value your friendship."

Nick said, "As do I, Geb. I think your friendship is the most important of my life."

Geb cocked his head. "I think there is a beautiful young lady whose camaraderie will come to mean more to you. For now, however, I thank you for the honor."

Hoping his friend was right, Nick struggled to rise, took his cane and went to the table in the corner and jotted a letter to Faith. Perhaps letting her know he was close to town was not such a bad idea. It might even relieve some of his obsession to hear from her if she wrote back.

Chapter 21

Faith knew it would be more ladylike to respond to Nick's letter with one of her own. As she stepped down from Aurora's carriage in front of Geb's home, she didn't care about being polite. She wanted to see Nick.

Aurora surveyed the pretty manor house. "You really should have sent a note saying we would call, Faith."

Stepping down and slipping her arm through the crook in Faith's elbow, Mercy made a dismissive sound. "Where's the fun in that, Aurora? This is better. We shall see a true reaction from His Grace."

"I hadn't realized this was a test." Aurora brushed out her sky-blue skirt and tugged her lace-trimmed bonnet into place. "Well, we're here. We had better go knock on the door."

Mercy patted Faith's hand. "Are you all right?"

"I wish Poppy were here. She and Rhys are on far more intimate terms with Mr. Arafa. I feel rude just showing up, now that we're here." Faith took a deep breath and lifted her chin as they climbed the stairs.

"Don't listen to Aurora. Mr. Arafa hardly seems the type to mind an impromptu visit." Mercy kept hold of Faith's arm to keep her from running away.

Nothing was going to stop her from seeing Nick. She might be nervous, but she would have a glimpse of him and know he was well before she returned to town.

Aurora lifted her hand to knock, but the door swung open before she could complete the task.

The butler, Kosey, loomed in the doorway with a wide smile and an elegant bow. He was nearly as tall as the enormous oak door, and in white livery with a turban, he was spectacular. "Good afternoon, ladies. How may I be of assistance?"

Turning her head, Aurora looked to Faith for a response. Raising one curved eyebrow, she smirked.

Faith narrowed her eyes at Aurora for a moment before turning her attention to Kosey. "Lady Faith Landon to see the Duke of Breckenridge with my friends and chaperone."

"Of course." Kosey bowed again. "I will see if His Grace is accepting visitors. Will you ladies wait in the parlor?"

They followed the butler into the grand and elaborate parlor. Faith had admired the room when she'd attended Mr. Arafa's dinner party. He had managed to decorate in the stoic English style, as well as incorporate a fantastic amount of Egyptian art and furniture. Somehow it all worked together to give the room a sense of decadence.

Mercy flounced onto the round divan and sank into the cushion several inches. She attempted to cross her ankles, but rolled back onto her elbows before giving up and crossing her legs under her skirts. "There is really no way to sit ladylike on this, but it's the most comfortable thing I've ever been on. I may never leave." She leaned to one side and propped her head on her elbow.

The door burst open and Nicholas rushed in with his weight supported on a black cane and his handsome face flushed. "You're here."

Mercy gasped, and in her attempt to stand up, rolled to the floor in a heap that was more like Poppy than graceful Mercy. "Oh Lord." She righted herself and all three curtsied.

Nick bowed. "Forgive me. It is a pleasure to see you all."

Suddenly Faith's tongue felt too big for her mouth. She took a breath. "I was delighted to receive your letter."

"I'm happy to hear that." He kept his gaze fixed on hers.

Faith wanted to run across the room and jump into his arms, but she rooted her feet to the floor. Breaking the stare, Faith spotted his cane. "You are injured?"

His Adam's apple bobbed in his throat. "It is nothing and will heal quickly."

"Should I have written?" The awkwardness made her heart pound.

Eyes bright, he approached and took her hands. "I'm elated to see you."

Faith wanted to cry with joy, not only at hearing that he was pleased to have her visit, but just seeing him alive and in England. She'd worried while he was away. She was transfixed by his bright eyes surrounded by dark lashes.

Aurora cleared her throat. "Perhaps the two of you would care to walk in the garden? I'm sure Mercedes and I will find much to amuse ourselves in this parlor."

Dressed the part of an English gentleman, Geb Arafa stepped into the room. His dark jacket and white cravat made his brown skin glow. His eyes sparkled with mischief. "I heard there were guests. What a pleasure to have you ladies here at Aaru." He bowed.

Nick dropped Faith's hands and they both turned toward the doorway.

"Forgive us for not writing ahead, Mr. Arafa. We hope you don't mind our uninvited appearance." Aurora made a pretty curtsy.

A slightly chubby English lady, with housekeeper's keys hanging from her waist and a blue turban wrapped elegantly around her head, came into the room.

"Ah, Mrs. Bastian," Geb said. "How fortunate you are here. Can you arrange some tea for myself and the ladies? I think His Grace will be busy in the gardens, but perhaps will require tea in a short while."

A wide smile played across Mrs. Bastian's round face. "I'll see to it, sir."

When she was gone, Geb narrowed his gaze on Faith and Nicholas. "Are the two of you just going to stand there pretending you do not wish to be alone, or are you going to excuse yourselves to the gardens?"

Mercy laughed. "Oh, I do like it here." She sat back down on the fluffy round divan and promptly leaned over on her side.

Nick took Faith's hand and intertwined his fingers in hers. "If you ladies will excuse us." He made a bow and gently pulled Faith from the room.

Not even bothering to feign disinterest in leaving for the gardens, Faith gave him no resistance. Summer's warm breeze made the elaborate and lush garden a pleasure, but Faith spared only a brief glance at the low maze of shrubs or the large fountain at the center.

She stopped.

Nick turned to face her. Hindered by his cane, the move was not as graceful as the man she saw last at his ball in London. "You are distressed by my injury?"

Looking from his leg to his eyes, she shook in a long breath. "I have a thousand questions about that and other things, Nick, but I'm more distressed that we are awkward in each other's company. I don't know if I should curtsy or leap into your arms."

With only an instant's hesitation, Nick snaked out his arm and dragged her against his chest. "Always leap, sweetheart."

She wrapped her arms around him and breathed in his comforting scent. He'd put some weight back on and felt solid and strong. "Are you finished with that other business?"

His chest lifted and fell and his lips pressed to her hair. "Almost. There is one last item to take care of, but I shall not have to leave England again."

Relief flooded her. It was the first time she'd relaxed since Parvus. Knowing he was safe and would remain so, gave her ease that she'd not known she'd been longing for. "I'm much relieved."

Pulling back, he contemplated her serious expression. "Does that mean you worried over me?"

"Of course." Was he mad to think otherwise?

"When last I saw you, you were none too pleased with me. When I wrote you yesterday, I didn't know if the note I would receive would finally release me from our engagement." A deep frown left those stunning eyes filled with worry.

Holding him tight, she pressed her cheek to his chest. "I was an utter fool. Forgive me. I'll not lie and tell you I'm happy with this odd profession you've chosen, but I love you and I can learn to live with it."

Silence descended on the garden. Time itself and even Nick's pounding heart seemed to stop.

There was a nearly imperceptible beat before Nick's low voice cut through the quiet. "You love me?"

The fact that he didn't know, that she hadn't told him, was appalling. Had she been so foolish? "I love you more than I will ever be able to put into words."

The cane clattered to the stones beneath their feet and he wrapped his strong arms around her more tightly. "I will not take any more assignments."

Faith closed her eyes with the deluge of relief. "Don't make promises you might not be able to keep, Nick. You are the kind of man who goes where you are needed. If England needs you, you shall find it difficult to refuse."

"Difficult but not impossible. I shall be very busy loving you and will have little time for anything else. Let other men do their part. I have something to live for."

Her pulse might pound out of her body. "And I am that something?"

Taking her by the shoulders, he stooped until his eyes were level with hers. "You are everything, Faith. I should have been less the fool and made that clear to you long ago. You saved my life this past winter, but you also saved my heart. I never believed I could feel so much for another person. Every moment I was away from you was absolute torture far worse than what I endured beneath Jean-Claude's whip."

Faith didn't know what to say. It was all she could do to keep her mouth from hanging open at his declaration of not only love, but need.

Nick struggled to his knees. "Tell me that you'll marry me. Not because I'm a duke and not because it's what your parents want. Say you'll be my wife because it will make us both silly with happiness. But, my love, only say these things if they are absolutely true. I want no more falsehoods between us. Never again will I withhold anything from you."

Placing her hands on his shoulders, Faith lowered herself to her knees before him. "I will marry you, not for money or title. As far as I'm concerned, none of those things exist. I would marry you if we had to scrape and save every halfpenny. All I ever wanted was to have a husband who will love me above all else and never do me harm."

Nick palmed her cheek. "You must know, I would never touch you in anger, Faith. Please tell me you don't doubt that."

Resting her hand over his, she leaned into the touch. "I know. Even when I wasn't sure you were the right man for me, with all your secrets between us, I never thought you a monster. I was safe with you at Parvus, even if you were not."

He closed his eyes. "I shall never forgive myself for the danger I put you in. How can one ever make amends for such a thing?"

Joy filled her heart. "Marry me before my mother can turn our wedding into a spectacle for all of London to gawk at and gossip about."

Faith rose to her feet, scooping up Nick's cane as she went. She handed the gold and black handle to him and helped him to stand.

Offering his left elbow, ultimate joy reflected in his eyes. "I thought all women wanted a big wedding with all the fuss."

They walked the path that wound toward the center of the maze. "You should know by now that I am not like other women. I am a Wallflower and we are of a different kind."

He lifted her fingers to his mouth and kissed them. "I shall thank God for that each and every day of my life."

"I hope you will say that when I abandon you each Tuesday to have tea with them, or when I go off on some mad errand because one of them needs me." Worry crept into her voice despite her intent to keep the statement light.

The fountain bubbled as water fell from the mouths of horses. Nick sat on the bench that faced it and pulled Faith onto his lap.

"Your leg!" She tried to pull away even though it was the last thing she wanted.

Keeping her in place, he said, "It's a small wound that causes me little trouble and will heal in a month or so. Now, stop fussing and sit still. I have something to say."

It was no trouble to stay on his lap and wrap her arms round his neck. She toyed with the hair curling at his collar and gazed at the expression of devotion blooming in those eyes. "Say your piece, Nick."

He pulled her bottom tight against him and wrapped his arms around her hips. "I understand Marsden attends these teas. Perhaps I might garner an invitation as well, though I'm sure there are some instances where you ladies will want to be alone, as you were in school. I shall relinquish you to them, but only for short periods of time. I have come to admire this bond you share with those three."

"You and Mr. Arafa are good friends." Faith was blessed with her Wallflower friendships and only wished to make Nick see his good fortune as well.

"Geb is a good friend to me." He nodded and snuggled his head near her breast.

Breath coming faster, Faith kissed his cheek. "Should we return to the house for tea?"

"No."

"Do you want to tell me how you injured your leg?" Faith asked.

"Not at the moment."

She stilled. "Are you keeping secrets again, Nick?"

Kissing the pulse behind her hear, he whispered, "No, I just want to kiss you senseless, and this is a better location for that than the parlor amongst our friends."

Every inch of Faith thrilled with anticipation. She tipped her head to the side to give him better access to her neck. "Well…in that case, you may continue."

A low chuckle rumbled in his chest as he licked and nibbled on her ear. His breath sent shudders of delight directly to the top of her thighs.

Clenching her legs tight, she hoped to relieve some of the tension building between her legs. A sigh escaped her mouth and Nick covered her lips with his. His tongue slipped inside as he made love to her mouth. Lips, teeth, and tongue clashed violently before softening.

With one hand still on her hip, he held her nape with the other, pulling her close and deepening the kiss until she was breathless and wanton.

His shaft pressed, needy, against her bottom, and she wiggled against him.

"I want you, Faith." He dragged his lips down her neck and his declaration dripped with urgency.

"Oh, God. I need you, Nick." Her body thrummed with desire for more, for all of Nick.

His mouth stopped an inch from the top of her scooped neckline. He traced a line with his tongue along the edge.

Faith gripped him tighter as desire flooded her every sense and an ache pulsed low in her belly.

"Shall we make love or shall I return you to your friends immediately? I'm afraid those are the only two choices I can give you in my current condition." He laughed, but the strained sound had no humor.

"We cannot very well make love here." She took in the open gardens with their full view of the back of the house. "Anyone could walk out and see us right now."

Slowly, Nick's head came up and his gaze met hers. "Does that mean you would prefer making love to returning to the house, Faith?"

Between her legs the sensitive bud pulsed and waited for her answer. "I would prefer to have you deep inside me, but not here by the fountain."

His groan rumbled deep inside him and vibrated through her, heightening her want for him. Nick lifted her to her feet and steadied her when she wobbled. He took several breaths while staring at the pebbled ground before rising and taking her hand. "Come on."

Slowly and with the help of his cane, Nick pulled her through the garden and around a line of evergreens. The pebbled path ended, but a dirt path continued toward a paddock. Poppy had once told Faith that Geb used the paddock past the gardens to hold his fine horses after the barn had been damaged by a storm. They entered another grove of trees and a creek bubbled nearby. A small stone house appeared from out of the thick woods. Nick pulled the latch and let them in.

"Where are we?" Faith asked.

Nick struck a tinder and lit a few candles. "This was the caretaker's cottage, but he married and lives in town now. It is not in use, but I'm happy to see it's still kept clean."

Just as Nick said, the quaint two-room home had barely a sheen of dust to indicate it was no longer in use. A chair before the fireplace with fire irons, and a foot stool, made up the parlor, with a tiny kitchen in the corner near the door.

Standing in the only other door, Nick reached out his hand for her to join him. His eyes rang with questions, desire, and love.

Heart in her throat, she joined him. The bedroom was small, with only a single bed and wardrobe. She sank into Nick's arms and wrapped hers around his strong back. "I never dreamed it would be like this."

"I do seem to find less than ideal circumstances for our lovemaking, dearest. I shall do better in the future, but I understand if you wish to return to the house." Nick sighed against the top of her head.

Unable to hold it in, she giggled. "I don't care about that. I'm just happy to be near you. Don't you know I want you just as much as you seem to desire me?"

He kissed her crown. "What did you expect to be different then?"

Always believing she would find a romance that would sway her to marry had not prepared Faith. "Love."

"Oh? What did you expect?" She could feel his smile lift against her skull.

Faith turned her head up and looked at him and ran her hand down his ribs inside his coat. "I don't know, but not this all-encompassing need to be near you, with you, to hear your voice and see you smile. It's much more than I had ever thought possible."

He shrugged out of the coat and placed it on the bedpost before lifting Faith into his arms with her legs wrapped around his waist. His cane clattered to the floor. "Tell me to stop."

She gasped as his shaft pressed against her center. "Oh my."

"Tell me I ask too much of you." He eased her onto the bed and lowered himself on top of her, trailing kisses down her neck to the swell of her breast.

Faith's skirt bunched between them and she wiggled to push it aside. "Don't stop, Nick, but be quick before the others come looking for us."

A wicked grin tugged at his lips as he pulled down the front of her bodice and freed one nipple, which he took between his teeth and worried.

A quick gasp pushed from her lips as the touch of pain forced pleasure between her legs. His tongue lapped and he sucked on the taut pebble until she thought she might jump out of her skin.

Nick leered at her, that same naughty expression plastered on his handsome face as he sank lower, to where her skirts bunched. Wicked grin in place, he tossed her skirts over his head and wrapped his hands under her thighs.

Faith screamed with laughter and wiggled away.

Holding fast, his mouth pressed to her center.

Laughter gone, Faith's body floated above the bed as she arched into his lovemaking. His tongue swirled around her sensitive nub and dipped inside her. Each movement shot thrill after thrill to her core and the muscles low in her belly tightened to a pleasure akin to pain.

She wrapped her legs around his back and wished they were both naked. Then he slid one finger inside her wet sheath and suckled her. In the entire world there was only emotion and pleasure. The rest floated away in a mist of unimportance. His mouth, arms, legs, fingers, the way his hair tickled the inside of her thigh, was all that existed. Her body left her mind behind in a cacophony of pleasure and she tumbled over the edge with abandon.

Nick lapped at her overly sensitive bud ever so gently, kissing his way from one thigh to the other, dipping inside her on the journey. She shuddered with every touch, wanting more, but so sensitive to even the slightest pressure.

If Faith died in this moment, she would be perfectly and exquisitely happy and satisfied.

Chapter 22

Nick longed for all of her and had toyed with a fleeting thought of plunging inside her and being quick about it. Faith was right that eventually the others would come looking for them, but not right away. Aurora would not be a strict chaperone.

As they had time, he lapped up her heady juices like the most addictive drug and reveled in her pleasure. The tiny cottage was a distance from the house and no one would hear her cries, and he loved the sound of each tiny gasp and rapturous scream. He would never get enough Faith, and planned a lifetime of lovemaking in far better settings. On that score he had failed her thus far, but he would do much better in the near future.

Rain tapped on the roof and ground outside.

Her desire to marry, with a special license, had created desire he'd not expected. She loved him. It stood his cock at full attention when he'd only planned to steal a kiss or two in the garden. Knowing that her need was as great as his own filled him with pure joy and excruciating desire.

As her pleasure subsided, he crawled out from under her skirts. His leg ached and he stumbled before righting himself and covering her body with his. Her eyes were closed and a smile tugged at her lips. She was so lovely.

"You look pleased, my love," Nick said.

Her eyes popped open. Those golden eyes filled with mischief. "I will not be fully pleased until you have the same look on your face."

Wrapping his arms around her back, he rolled so that she straddled him. "I would never want to disappoint you."

When he reached to release the fall of his breeches, she rocked against his hand and moaned. Her eyes were again closed and she perched atop him with her neck arched back. She might have been a queen, but she was his. Nothing was as beautiful as seeing her pleasure. His antics under her skirt had robbed him of seeing the last orgasm; he would not miss the next. He pressed his thumb to her wet slit and rubbed that sensitive bud.

Faith rocked back and forth like a goddess in the saddle. Nick adjusted her hips so that his shaft perched at her center but left the choice to her. Without hesitation, she reached between her legs and guided him inside her with one smooth, earth-shattering move.

Her mouth opened on a delighted cry.

Thunder sounded in the distance.

Holding her legs down to keep her in place, Nick groaned with his own pleasure at being sheathed inside her.

She rocked forward, taking him deeper, and he gripped her hips and helped her set a pace to please them both.

As her pace quickened, Nick gritted his teeth, holding back his own release until Faith tumbled over the abyss and then he went with her. He drew her down to lie atop him and held her while still inside her heavenly body. "You are magnificent, Faith."

"Mmm…"

"Are you all right?" He ran his hands up and down her back, wishing they were both naked.

"I'm perfectly content." She sighed against his neck.

"That makes what I have to say even more difficult."

Lightning lit the small room, which had grown dim with the storm.

Propping her chin on her hand where it rested on his chest, she smiled at him. "What is it?"

"We have to get tidied up and go back to the house." Nick wished it weren't so, but thunder rolled louder, almost a stern reminder.

"I suppose we must, and it's raining too." She moaned.

Easing out of her produced the most delicious sound from her. He considered getting right back into the bed and saying damn to polite society.

Another crack of lightning was quickly followed by thunder.

"There's a well outside. I'll fetch some water for washing."

Faith rolled to her side, her shapely legs exposed, and studied him. "You will get the special license?"

Kneeling to retrieve his cane, Nick hovered over her on his ascent and kissed her nose. "I will gladly obtain whatever documents make you my wife the fastest."

A stunning blush pinked her cheeks. "Even though we have behaved like husband and wife already?"

He secured his fall. "Sneaking away to a shed like servants is hardly good enough for you, Faith."

The most musical laugh tumbled from her full lips. "Oh, but it's so much fun. I hope even after we marry, we will still steal away from time to time for a tryst."

Halfway to the door, he turned back to watch the way her breast rose and fell with every breath. She'd not righted her dress and one nipple was still exposed while her arms were over her head. He could gaze at her all day and never tire of the sight. "Every damned chance we get, my love."

* * * *

Once they were cleaned up and Faith's hair coiled back into her chignon as well as possible, they returned to the house. Some of her wild curls had escaped, and they were slightly wet from the rain, but no one said a word when they returned to their friends.

Geb had called in Kosey to play the pianoforte, and the ladies listened to the skilled musician.

Aurora gave her one long look with a raised brow.

Cheeks heated, Faith just shrugged and sat listening to Mozart.

As soon as the piece was over, Aurora said, "Kosey, you and Mercy should play a duet. She is as accomplished as you."

Kosey glowed with delight. "I would enjoy that exceedingly. Lady Mercedes, would you care to join me?"

Smiling, Mercy said, "I'm only a miss, not a lady, but I'd be happy to play a duet with such a fine musician."

In another setting, a servant playing a duet with a lady would have been scandalous, but nothing was out of the ordinary in Geb Arafa's home. Mercy sat alongside Kosey, and the two played a duet by Johann Sebastian Bach.

Faith had to brush the tears from her eyes, it was so beautiful. Faith loved being at Aaru. She was happy and comfortable in Geb's home. A wild thought flew into her head. "Mr. Arafa, perhaps I am overstepping, but I wonder if I might ask a favor."

"You may ask whatever you like. I cannot promise a favorable answer, dear Lady Faith, until I have heard the question." Geb leaned back in his overstuffed English chair.

"Nick and I have decided to marry immediately. He will try to obtain a special license and inform my parents of our plan…"

She didn't get to continue as she was swept into a group hug between Mercy and Aurora. "You should have stopped the music and told us immediately," Aurora scolded.

"I'm delighted for you," Mercy said. Her grin stretched from ear to ear.

Geb slapped the arm of his chair. "I am delighted as well. What is the favor?"

Nick watched her, his head cocked to one side and a question floating in his eyes.

"Do you think we might marry here in your gardens? I adore your home."

"Not to mention the state of fitfulness she would be sending her mother into." Mercy laughed loudly.

Aurora hid her amusement behind a gloved hand. "It would send both your parents into fits, Faith."

Waiting for Geb's response, Faith shrugged. "Mother and Father have had their way in every other aspect of my life. They get a daughter who is a duchess; I want this one day just for Nick and I to be perfectly at ease and happy. If Mr. Arafa will permit it, Aaru is where I'd like to marry."

Geb leaped from his chair and pulled Faith into a brotherly hug. He swung her around and landed her back on her feet. "It shall be the greatest event of the year. Whatever you want, we shall see to it. Kosey," he called toward the door. "Get parchment and ink, we have lists to make."

Nick was beside her a moment later. He leaned down and whispered, "This is what you want?"

Looking up into his eyes, she realized she should have consulted him before making the request. Geb's enthusiasm might make it awkward to change their minds after the fact. "I'm sorry. Is this a bad idea?"

"Not at all. If you want to marry in the gardens here or in Hyde Park, I shall be proud to be the man standing at the front waiting for you." Nick kissed her cheek.

"Will you come with me to tell my parents?" A prick of nerves rumbled low in her gut and she worried that she'd made a mistake.

"Not to worry, my love. They will be elated, or they will not receive an invitation. Either way, you and I will be spending the rest of our lives together, and that is all I want." He moved them toward the sitting area where Kosey and Geb made a list with the help of Mercy and Aurora, who also talked about stopping in to see Poppy on the ride home.

Faith couldn't wait to tell her other friend her news, and she slid into the space between the ladies on the divan and joined the chatter.

When they finally rose to leave Geb's home, Faith's heart soared with curiosity and excitement over her future.

Nick walked them to the door. "I will call in a few days, when this business is over."

Aurora and Mercy had made their curtsies and walked to the carriage, but Faith stayed behind. "I forgot to ask one thing, Nick, and it's a critical one."

Closing the distance between them, he took her hand and kissed it. "Whatever it is, I'm sure you need not look so grave, Faith."

"If you disagree, it might be a problem between us. Still, I think it best to get these things out in the open now rather than find out later when you are stuck with me for the rest of your life." She pulled her hand away and gnawed on her thumbnail.

Taking her hand back, he kissed the thumb and smiled. "Just tell me."

Pretending she was brave like Poppy, she lifted her chin. "I have always dreamed of having a lot of children. Now, I realize that is not always possible, but it is still my dream. We never discussed if you like children."

If it was possible for him to be more handsome, his smile did the trick. "I do like children. My sister's children and I are very close. I'll not have you risking your health, but we shall have as many as you like within reason."

Unable to remember a better day in her entire life, Faith thought she might burst with happiness at any moment. She threw her arms around Nick's neck and nearly toppled them both.

Nick righted them and his cane dropped once again.

Kosey cleared his throat from his post by the door and turned away.

"You have made me very happy today, Nicholas Ellsworth. I hope you do not regret matching yourself to a Wallflower." She kissed his cheek with a wet smack.

His laugh rolled and bounced around the wood-lined foyer. "If this afternoon with you, and then with your friends, making plans, was an indication of what is to come, I think we shall have an animated life."

"It shall never be dull, that is certain." Faith stepped back, full of bliss as she had never known before.

"No, never that." He feigned horror with a hand to his heart and wide eyes.

"You'll tell me when you've obtained the license?"

He bowed. "You will be the first to know."

It was hard to leave him. If she could have crawled inside his chest and stayed safely with him always, she would have done so. With one last look into those stunning blue eyes, she turned and joined her friends in the carriage.

As soon as she was seated, John put up the step, closed the door, and started them back to London.

"You look extremely happy," Mercy said, wrapping her arm around Faith's shoulders and giving her a squeeze.

Faith glanced from Aurora to Mercy. Trepidation lurked in Aurora's eyes. She still had her doubts about any of them marrying. Her golden-blond hair was perfectly coiffed and her gown had not a single wrinkle. To a stranger she would look content as a widow. However, Faith saw the pain and fear lurking in her friend's eyes with all the scars left by her late husband.

Aurora hoped Bertram Sherbourn was rotting in hell, where he belonged. "It's going to be fine, Aurora. He loves me and is a good and kind man." She hesitated to bring up the other subject she'd been holding tight to. "You know, he has been through something similar to you, Aurora. Perhaps if you and he spoke, you both might benefit from it."

Her composure shattered, Aurora appeared ready to jump from the moving carriage. "I cannot see how rehashing terrible things does anyone any good."

A long sigh came from Mercy. "Of course you do, Aurora. We Wallflowers have done our fair share of baring our souls, and it always helps. You are just afraid. I think Faith's idea has merit and you might consider it rather than tossing it aside."

Aurora bit her lip. "I will consider it."

Faith leaned forward and patted Aurora's knee.

More relaxed, Aurora said, "I'm glad you found him worthy, Faith. I'm also so happy for you. I can see the joy he brings you. However, should you need to get away from him, should things change, you can always come home to West Lane."

Faith knew she meant well, but the notion was preposterous. Nick would never hurt her. She tried to lighten the mood. "Did you give that speech to Poppy when she married Rhys?"

One eyebrow rose over Aurora's right eye. "Rhys is my brother. I would flay him alive should he behave as an animal. However, Poppy knows she can find refuge with me for as long as I live."

Mercy pushed her spectacles up onto her nose and smiled. Her green eyes sparkled with mischief. "As I shall never find anyone who would marry me, you may provide me safe harbor for as long as you can stand me, Aurora."

"Why do you say that, Mercy? You are lovely and accomplished. Any man would be lucky to have you for a wife, if that's what you want." Faith hated the stigma put on her friend for things not of her own doing. It wasn't Mercy's fault her parents had died and left only a small allowance due to the entailments on their home.

"Ha." Mercy wrapped a curl of red hair around her finger and twirled it. "They don't seem to know that. Besides, I like my life. I come and go as I please. My aunt is happy to be rid of me, though it's nice that she still checks in from time to time to make certain I am well. Everything is as it should be. Of course, should Aurora ever remarry, I shall have to find employment as someone's nanny or lady's companion."

"Remarry!" Aurora screamed. "That is one thing I shall never do. What possible reason could I have to strap myself to another man? No. Being a widow suits me just fine."

Faith wasn't certain that was true, but she kept her opinion to herself. There was no sense arguing with Aurora once she'd set her mind to something.

The carriage bumped and shifted.

Faith grabbed the window to keep from falling on Mercy. "What on earth."

The horses brayed and John yelled before there was more jostling and then silence.

"John?" Aurora called to the coachman.

Joseph Fouché's face appeared in the window. Handsome, dripping from the rain and oozing evil, he grinned at them. "I'm afraid your driver is unable to answer at the moment. My man will drive you home, where you will instruct your servants to remain passive or I shall kill every one of them before taking the strap to you ladies. I'm sure Lady Faith can confirm that I mean what I say."

Heart in her throat, Faith thought she might be sick. "What do you want?"

He opened the door and leaned in. "I have what I want for the moment. Your fiancé will provide the rest. May I say what a pleasure it is to see you again, my lady. Perhaps when we arrive back at West Lane you might introduce me to your friends."

Faith didn't know what to say.

Joseph's smirk was nauseating. He closed the carriage door.

"Go!" Joseph yelled up to his driver, who immediately snapped the horses into a trot.

Out the carriage window lay John, with his face down in the grass.

"John." Aurora covered her mouth. "Do you think he's dead?" She appealed to Faith.

"I don't know. Joseph Fouché was the man in charge when Nick was tortured. He would have no guilt over killing anyone. He'll keep us alive to get whatever it is he wants from Nick." Faith shuddered at the thought of again being under the thumb of such evil, and this time without Nick or even Charles to protect her.

"What do we do?" Mercy's eyes were wide and she searched the carriage for some answer, which might be hidden within.

"He knows where we live, which means he's been watching us. He may already have men holding the servants hostage. All we can do is go along and hope Nick has and is willing to give Joseph what he wants."

Mercy stilled. "Would he withhold some item when our lives are in jeopardy? When you might be harmed?"

A dozen scenarios flew through Faith's head and many of them did not end well. "I believe with all my heart that Nick will do everything in his power to keep us safe. More than that..." She shrugged.

"And you intend to marry a man who lives this way, Faith. Will you constantly be in danger?" Aurora scolded, her brows pulled together.

None of the danger mattered. She loved Nick and would risk anything for him. However, the idea that this might continue after they had children was something she would address some other time. "This is all related to whatever took Nick out of England recently. Once this matter is at an end, our lives will be less interesting. Besides, wars don't last forever."

"You must really love him," Mercy said with more amazement than Faith had ever heard from her.

"I do, but we can put that aside until we find a way out of this mess."

"I shall not have this man, whatever his name is, harming my servants." The fire was back in Aurora's voice.

"No. We must do what we can to get them out of West Lane." Faith had to devise a plan while they waited for rescue. "It will be a while before we reach home. Perhaps we can think of something."

Chapter 23

Tipton opened the front door, his expression strained.

Each Wallflower was held by a large man, who pushed them into the foyer. Two more henchmen stood guard inside, one holding a pistol against Tipton's ribs. "I'm sorry, my ladies." Tipton's lips pulled into a thin line.

Faith had been right to think the West Lane house was under attack before they arrived home. Joseph Fouché didn't strike her as a man who left things to chance. The foyer table was in pieces and the servants' door, which normally blended into the woodwork, was cracked and opened. "Was anyone harmed, Tipton?"

"We have not been injured, my lady." Tipton narrowed his eyes on the man gripping Faith's arm.

"Put them in that parlor, then two of you stand guard outside the windows." Joseph pointed to the ladies' parlor.

The guards shoved them inside and closed the door.

Tipton walked inside a moment later. "I have been instructed to inform you that none shall be harmed if you stay in this room without making a fuss."

Aurora rushed over and whispered, "Tipton, John was hurt and perhaps worse. They left him on the side of the road out of London. Do you think there is a way to send someone to help him?"

Normally stoic, the butler chewed his lip. "They have not noted the kitchen boy. He can ride a horse well enough for the task. I'll try to send him."

"Should we send Benny to get help here in London?" Mercy asked.

"We cannot leave John lying, perhaps dying, in the rain. Send him to John. We shall fend for ourselves." Aurora's voice cracked but she held her head high as a queen.

Faith leaned in. "Tell Benny not to come back here. John is closer to Aaru. He can get help there and tell His Grace what has happened."

"Can we send a note to Marsden? Surely Rhys can help." Mercy wrapped her arms around her slim torso.

"I will do what I can, my lady." Tipton exited, with the guard outside the door glowering down at him.

"Where did he find so many giant men to work for him?" Mercy sat on the chaise like a statue.

"He has a good deal of funds from Napoleon, I would imagine." Faith sat next to her. "I'm sorry to have dragged the two of you into this mess."

"It seems to me your fiancé is to blame, not you." Aurora crossed her arms and sat in the chair adjacent to them.

It was strange for their feminine retreat from the outside world to have become their prison. This was the place where they always gathered to gossip and catch up. Ever since they came home from school, Faith had cherished this room. Now Aurora glared with anger over Nick. Tears pressed at the back of Faith's eyes.

Mercy took a deep breath that made her seem frail rather than willowy. "Aurora, you can't blame His Grace and Faith, this is not your fault. Whatever the Duke of Breckenridge is involved in must be quite serious if it would put this Fouché fellow to so much trouble. I just hope whatever England is getting from this is worth it."

It was amazing the way Mercy could always see to the heart of a thing without letting fear or other emotions cloud her judgment.

"Who in the name of Zeus are you?" Poppy's voice rang out from the foyer. "Where is Tipton? Don't you touch me."

"Oh Lord. Poppy." Aurora stood so fast she nearly toppled her chair. "We said we'd stop on our way home and tell her what happened with Breckenridge."

The door burst open and one of those gruff-looking guards shoved Poppy inside. "You stay in there with the others while I find Fouché." There was no sign of a French accent, only the rough tones of a poor Londoner. Joseph must pay a fortune for His Majesty's loyal subjects to be working for him.

Her russet dress had a tear at the hem and a smudge of mud just below the breast. "What in the name of Hades is going on here?"

Faith ran to her. "Did they hurt you?"

Poppy's narrowed eyes grew wide, then she followed Faith's gaze to her torn dress. "Oh no. I tripped up the stairs to the carriage and didn't think it necessary to return to the house for a change since I was only coming here to see you three. Then I tripped up the steps here and some mud found my bodice." As Poppy was often less than graceful, she was not bothered by these events. "Who are they and why was I tossed into the parlor like so much baggage?"

"They work for a French spy who wants something that Nicholas has," Mercy said in an unworried tone.

Poppy walked with Faith to the divan and sat. "What does he have?"

"We don't know." Aurora returned to her chair, the only sign of worry the way she toyed with a string of blue thread along the piped cushion.

"What does it have to do with us?" Poppy's tone grew conspiratorial and she leaned in. Her dark eyelashes framed bright blue eyes filled with interest rather than fear.

Mercy flounced onto the chaise and pushed her spectacles up her nose. "Nothing really, except that Faith is engaged to Nicholas and I think we are to be used as bait or ransom."

Fouché stormed into the parlor and stopped short at the sight of a fourth Wallflower. "Who are you and what the hell are you doing here?" His thick French accent did nothing to smooth over his state of distress.

With a cock of her head, Poppy examined the spy without response. Then, slowly, she stood and propped her fists on her hips. Leveling her gaze on Fouché, she said, "I am the Countess of Marsden, these are my friends, and you now have a ticking clock, Frenchman."

Faith's heart pounded with the truth, though she was not at all certain that boded well for the West Lane household. "You had better write to His Grace and ask for whatever it is you want, Monsieur Fouché. If this visit lasts much into the night, the Earl of Marsden will come to fetch his wife and check on his sister." She gave Aurora a pointed look.

"Damn all of you royal scum. I should kill the four of you just for the sheer joy of it. Your heads rolling on the plush rug would be no hardship for me." His handsome face twisted with desire that turned Faith's stomach.

Mercy sighed. "You will never get whatever Breckenridge has if one tiny hair on any of our heads is harmed. You know that, or you would have done your worst on the road. Whatever he has is important, or why go to so much trouble?"

He strode across the room, the high polish of his boots catching the candlelight. "You are smarter than I expected. Though I suppose I should have known Lady Faith's friends would be clever. You are the orphan, if my information serves me. No parents or money to speak of. Kept in good standing by a maiden aunt who had had enough of you and passed you off to Lady Radcliff."

Keeping her expression passive, only the other Wallflowers would have noticed the hurt in Mercy's eyes. She stood and curtsied. "Mercedes Heath, and nothing you have to say is important enough to me to do me any harm. I can assure you that my lack of title will not make me less valuable to His Grace, if that is where your perverse mind has led you."

He leaned close to her. "That mouth will get you in trouble, mademoiselle. You should mind that tongue."

Mercy sat and stared back without blinking.

Before one of her friends said or did something that might cause them injury, Faith said, "You should go and write your ransom note before the hour grows too late."

Fouché narrowed his gaze, but then turned and strode from the room.

"He is rather terrifying," Poppy said once the door was closed and the footsteps faded. "Is he the one who tortured Nick?"

Shaking her head, Faith tried not to let the visions that still haunted her sleep push into her waking mind. "He gave the orders, but no. I don't think he likes to do the dirty work as much as to watch it. He's still a vicious man and not to be toyed with. Let's hope this kidnapping is of short duration."

* * * *

Nick signed his letter to the archbishop of Canterbury. He would need to gain an audience in Doctors' Commons and beg to obtain a special license. Perhaps he'd better go to his banker first and gather extra funds for the church.

Someone pounded on the front door.

Kosey's deep voice barked orders, and boots thundered in the foyer.

Pulse jumping, Nick rushed to see what was happening.

A boy of perhaps thirteen stood on the white marble floor, dripping from the rain and telling an animated story. His light brown hair was plastered to his head and hung long around his neck. He twisted a cap in his hands and fear marked his blue eyes. Accent thick from the London streets, he babbled, "I didn't know what to do. Mr. John was alive, and I worried he'd drown on the side of the road before I could get back to him, but the ladies— I couldn't go fast with him so out of sorts."

Two footmen in Aaru white livery carried the Wallflower's driver, John, into the house and placed him on the floor. He shivered and his eyes were heavy-lidded.

Kosey said, "Put him by the fire in the parlor and get blankets."

The footmen complied quickly.

Panic pounded inside Nick's chest. He gripped the boy by the thin shoulders and lowered to his level. "Who are you? What happened to John?"

The boy swallowed and stared as if Nick might slit his throat.

Easing his grip, he asked again, softer. "What's your name, boy?"

"Benny, sir. I work on West Lane for the Countess of Radcliff and the other ladies. I'm the kitchen boy. That's why Tipton sent me, 'cause no one ever notices me, but I can ride a horse just fine, and knows how to sneak about, so he sent me to see if John were alive and then to bring word here, and John was alive, but I didn't know if he could ride and had to go slow, and then the rain, I couldn't leave him to drown, but the ladies…" The words all tumbled together as Benny's story got more urgent.

"Benny, be calm. We will see to John. You did well. Tell me what happened to the ladies." Nick used every muscle in his body to keep still and not frighten Benny.

Benny gulped and nodded. "There were these men who came and made all of us sit in the kitchen. I stayed in the garden out of sight, but close. Didn't really know what to do. Then the other man with the fancy clothes and funny accent came with the ladies and put them in the parlor. Tipton told me to sneak off and see if John lived and bring word here."

"Did you hear the man's name?" Nick wanted to shake it out of Benny, but kept his own fear in check. The boy was doing all he could.

A deep scowl marked Benny's young face and he stared at the floor. "It was strange, like his accent. One of his brutish fellows said it. Fish, fatch…I'm just not sure, sir."

"*Fouché*," Nick said with a perfect French accent.

"That's it!" Benny hollered with a wide smile. Then he observed John being carried away. "Is Mr. John going to be okay? I did my best, but he jostled a lot and only said a few words all the way here." Tears sparked in Benny's eyes.

Kosey wrapped his arm around Benny. "You did marvelously. Come and get dry and warm. We will see to John. A doctor is already called to fix him." He guided Benny toward the servants' stairs, a deep look of concern pulling his mouth taut.

Nick had no idea when Geb had come into the foyer, but when he straightened, his friend was there. "We will need a plan," Geb said.

"We need those books," Nick replied.

Shaking his head, Geb led the way into his study. The desk was stained to a dark rich brown with gold inlay around the edges. Books and scrolls from every part of the world lined the shelves, and dark pine-green fabrics covered the comfortable chairs. The rain made it look later than it was outside the tall windows, but still time was of the essence. Geb rang for Kosey. "You really think Fouché would come all this way and kidnap ladies of substance for the purpose of getting his silly list of royalists back?"

Kosey stepped into the room and closed the door. "The boy is exhausted, but unharmed. The driver has a bad knock to the head. Time will tell if he will recover. Mrs. Bastian is with him now and the doctor is on his way."

Nick nodded, then turned his attention back to Geb's question. He had been shot, stabbed, tortured, betrayed, and seen dozens of horrors in his military career, but he hadn't known blinding fear, until that moment. "I think he would kill everyone in that house if that's what it took to get his books back."

"Shall I go to my transcriber and get the books?" Kosey asked, arms folded over his wide chest, his expression still, though worry shone in his dark eyes.

"Get the original books, Kosey. Fouché won't settle for the copy. His attachment is strange, but I know he will not give up the ladies for copies." Nick had seen the way Joseph fondled the books. It would have to be the real thing.

"And if there is resistance?" Kosey raised his brows.

Rage filled Nick's chest to capacity. "I don't care if Drake himself is waiting in the room. Get those books."

Kosey looked to Geb, who nodded. He made a low bow and left.

"So, we go to London, my friend?" Geb stood behind his desk, hands pressed to the surface. His dark eyes lit with such fury, it might have been his own family taken hostage.

Nick needed to rid himself of the anger before he did something rash. He sat with his head in his hands. His mind, racing with possibilities, needed clearing. It was a few deep breaths before he could respond. "It is obvious that Joseph knows where I am. He will send a message with his demands. He may not know that Benny came here so swiftly. We must assume he knows nothing of the boy and he left poor John to die in a ditch. He thinks he has time."

A knock at the door was followed by Mrs. Bastian stepping inside. Her blue turban was askew, keys rattled against her hip, and her usually pleasant expression was serious and stern. "Kosey left for London. The doctor is here, and this letter just arrived by messenger."

She handed the note to Nick. He recognized the handwriting as Joseph's and practiced keeping his cool. "How is John?"

A long sigh preceded a shrug. "Time will tell. He took quite a bang to the head and then lay in the weather. The boy is fast asleep, poor lamb."

Once the housekeeper left, Nick opened the letter from Joseph and forced his hands to stop shaking. "He demands his books in return for the lives of all in the West Lane house. He will begin killing members of the staff one hour after dark."

"Not much time." Geb rounded the desk.

"No. Something must have rushed him. Generally, he likes to take his time to get his way. The trouble he went to at Parvus was more to his liking." Nick stood. "I wish I had an hour to rid myself of this fury racing through my veins. But whatever has shortened Joseph's time has done the same to ours."

"You can beat the devil out of a punching bag when this is over, or Kosey will fight you on the mat. Now we must go. I shall call for horses." Geb opened the door.

"Have someone wake the boy. Benny may be needed." Nick stood and swallowed emotion like a sour pill. A level head was what he needed to keep Faith and the others safe.

Benny slept in the saddle in front of Nick. The child was exhausted and rightfully so, as he'd probably never ridden so far on his own before, then had to get John on the horse and tell his tale at Aaru.

They stopped at the home of the Earl of Marsden. His sister was involved, and he might be willing to help. A footman took care of Benny, who leaned against the stone rail.

"See that he remains here," Nick said.

"I won't wander off, sir. I need to save the ladies." Benny tugged on his worn gray coat.

Rhys sat in his study in a large overstuffed chair, dozing. He stood quickly when they walked in with barely an announcement. "Your Grace, Mr. Arafa, what brings you here?"

They were splattered with mud from the long dash to London and must look a sight. Nick bowed his head briefly. "It seems your sister's home is under duress and the fault lies with me, my lord. The ladies left Aaru and were abducted by a French agent whom I provoked. We need your help and the help of your wife to retrieve the ladies and servants, if that is possible."

Rhys blinked several times. "My wife went to see her friends at West Lane when they didn't stop here with details about their visit."

"Ah, this is why Fouché is rushed." Geb nodded his head.

"I beg your pardon," Rhys said.

Nick should have known. "The arrival of your wife means that Joseph would have to rush his plans. He knows when Lady Marsden does not return home this evening, you will come looking for her."

Eyes narrowed, Rhys's fists clenched at his sides. "What does this Frenchman want?"

"Some notebooks I stole from him." There was no point lying and it would take too long to do so. "He is quite attached to them, but the English government wanted them. I had sent them to be copied, but Kosey has gone to retrieve them regardless of the state of transcription."

With a moment to process what he'd been told, Rhys examined Nick and then turned to Geb, who nodded. "I'll get my coat and have my horse brought around. How long do we have?"

The rain had stopped, giving way to a few late shards of daylight. "An hour, maybe more. I think my arrival at West Lane will give us some extra time."

Rhys's butler stood in the doorway with the coat without having to be called. Rhys tugged it on. "I wonder if this Fouché had any idea what he was getting into when he took those four hostages. They can vex a saint when provoked."

"Do you think they will do something foolish?" Geb asked.

"I can almost guarantee it." Rhys stormed toward the door.

Following in his wake, Nick shuddered at what kind of mischief the ladies might get into.

Chapter 24

"You realize this man is a murderer." Faith had seen what Fouché was capable of, but she also hated sitting and doing nothing in their own home. This was not like Parvus, where they had few resources. They were in the middle of a London neighborhood with a houseful of servants.

Poppy walked to the door. "One of those thugs told Tipton they will begin killing our people in less than an hour, Faith. We need to distract him and stall until help arrives."

Mercy stood and joined Poppy at the door. "And if help does not arrive? It is possible that no message was sent and Benny did not make it to Aaru. What if we are on our own?"

Taking a deep breath, Faith cringed inwardly. "I think that is what we must assume, though I'm sure Nick will come."

"I cannot risk the staff on hopes related to a spy." Aurora joined them at the door.

Poppy gave them all a nod and yelled, "You will open this door this instant!" She banged on the closed door.

The door pulled open and the hinge protested loudly. The oversized guard grunted. "What do you want?"

Faith steadied her pulse and narrowed her eyes at the brute. "We are ladies locked in a room with no privy for three hours. What do you think we want?"

His eyes widened for a moment before his cheeks pinked. "I'll take you down to the servants one at a time."

Stepping forward, Aurora said, "Surely a large man like yourself can manage two of us down one flight of steps."

"Fine, you two." He pointed to Faith and Aurora.

They didn't give him time to reconsider and dashed out of the parlor, through the foyer and the broken door, down the servants' stairs. The guard barked for another of Fouché's men to watch the parlor door, and followed them down.

At the bottom of the stairs the room opened up into the large kitchens. The long table was used for food preparation and was where the staff took their meals. Tipton, Jane, Kathy, the upstairs maid, Anna, the newly promoted housekeeper, Gillian, three footmen, the cook, and her assistant all turned and stood.

"Sit!" yelled a guard.

They obeyed but stared at Faith and Aurora.

"Tim, I've got to go back upstairs. You watch these two. They need the privy."

"A'right, Dick." Tim scratched the long scar running from the corner of his mouth back to his ear.

"We'll need our maid," Aurora commanded.

Tim scoffed and spit on the floor. "You swells can't do nothin' on your own, not even take a piss." He glowered. "Well, one of you go help the helpless then."

With the scrape of her chair, Jane rushed toward them. "I'll help you, my lady."

Aurora, Faith, and Jane scurried down the hall to a small room the servants used for privacy. It was near the outside door for ease of cleaning. Inside the unadorned white-walled room were a chair and two chamber pots.

Aurora said, "We must get all of you out of here, Jane."

Eyes wide, Jane shook her head. "I'll not leave you ladies, and I can't imagine Tipton will either."

It had occurred to Faith that the servants might refuse to go. While it warmed her heart, her frustration built. "Then Gillian must take all the others with her and get out of this house before something terrible happens."

"How will we get around that Tim?" Jane pulled a disgusted face.

"Is he the only guard down here?" Aurora asked.

Jane nodded.

It wasn't the cleanest plan, but it just might work. Faith took a breath. "One good wallop from one of cook's pans should do the trick. Then tie him up and put him in the larder for now."

"But wait until Lady Poppy and Mercy come down," Aurora warned. "One guard you should be able to handle, but Dick is a big man and might not go down with just a frying pan."

Jane gave a worried nod and took a breath. "You two go out. I'll pretend to clean up here."

Pulling Jane into a hug, Faith wished she could have spared the woman all she'd endured on her behalf. "Stay safe, Jane. I'm so sorry to have brought all of this on you."

With a tight squeeze, Jane said, "This is not your fault, but I'll be glad when it's all over."

Not looking back, Faith took Aurora's hand and they sauntered down the hall toward the kitchen.

Tim opened his mouth and took a deep breath to call upstairs.

Aurora put her hand out flat. "There is no need to bellow as if we were in a gaming hell, sir. We can find our way back to the parlor without escort."

"See that you do, milady." He spat out the last word.

They climbed the stairs to the foyer.

Faith stared Dick down as if he were her prey and not the other way around. Best to appear bold even if you felt small. She and Aurora stepped past his hulking figure and into the ladies' parlor.

Letting out a long breath, Poppy stomped over with Mercy just behind. "How did it go? Were you able to deliver the message?"

Aurora hugged Poppy. "Yes. Now you two go down and refuse Dick's help. That's the one outside this door. Hopefully he'll think you harmless and let you down the servants' stairs without an escort."

"Be brash and forceful." Faith paused. "Well, just be yourself, Poppy. That should do nicely."

Poppy cocked her head with her hands on her hips. "Thanks for that." She laughed. "I knew my bad manners would eventually come in handy."

Kissing her cheek, Aurora said, "We would not change a thing about you. Now be quick. I can't imagine we have much time to spare."

Faith took Mercy's hand and gave it a squeeze. "Be careful."

With a nod, they knocked and were let out of the parlor.

There was nothing to do but wait and listen for trouble. The sun peeked through the heavy cloud cover for a moment before it set. Even in the summer, there would usually be a fire in the hearth, and a chill fell over the room.

Taking a few candles from the small gold and silver chest on the table, Faith lit them before the old ones guttered out. Her memory of total darkness in the cellar at Parvus was too fresh to allow herself to be left without illumination if she could avoid it.

Aurora rounded the divan and took a candle from her. "This will all turn out fine, Faith."

In her heart Faith knew Nick would do everything in his power to keep them safe, but her head screamed that he might not be able to do anything. She nodded. "We are Wallflowers, we can manage our way out of anything."

Smile weak, Aurora nodded. "This waiting is worse than sneaking around below."

The door opened. Poppy and Mercy strolled in, looking bored.

As soon as the door closed, they ran the rest of the way over. Mercy whispered, "It's done. Tim is in the larder, tied up like a goose at Christmas."

"Tipton and Jane refused to leave." Poppy shook her head. "It was none too easy to get Gillian out of the house, but she took responsibility for the other servants and they've gone. They'll call for help as well."

"Good work," Faith said. She knew any help the servants could bring would be too late, but it didn't matter as long as they were safely out of West Lane.

"Now what?" Poppy asked.

Aurora smiled. "Now we do what Wallflowers do best."

"We make trouble," Mercy finished. "I closed the flue in the kitchen oven. A fair amount of smoke should be filling the rooms just above by now."

Masculine yelling across the foyer sounded through the door.

"The house is on fire!" Dick's voice rang out.

Smoke wafted through the parlor.

Mercy opened a window and gave the guard a scathing glare. "It would seem we're all going to burn to death. You might want to scurry off before the fire brigade arrives. There's likely to be men from Bow Street with them to investigate."

A second guard appeared in front of the house. With one look at each other, the two ran off.

The Wallflowers stepped toward the window, skirts in hand.

The door burst open behind them. Joseph Fouché growled, "Get away from that window." He rushed over, pushing Poppy aside. Seeing his guards were no longer at their posts, he narrowed his eyes on them. "You four are going to be a joy to take apart piece by piece."

Dick stood just inside the parlor, shifting from foot to foot. "We'd better get out before we all burn to death."

Joseph's hand snaked out and grabbed Mercy by the upper arm.

She cried out in pain.

"Take this one downstairs with you and check the kitchen." Joseph thrust Mercy across the room toward Dick. "And open some damned windows."

Dick grabbed Mercy and groaned, but followed the orders.

Joseph rounded the seating area and pulled the poker from the stand near the fireplace.

Despite lamenting the chill earlier, Faith was now glad there was no fire in the hearth as she stared at the end of the metal rod in Joseph's hand.

"Now, the three of you will walk slowly and calmly into the foyer. Just in case you actually were foolish enough to set fire to your own house, we should be near the door." Joseph raised the poker and shooed them in the direction of the parlor door.

Smoke filled the air above them. Faith took Aurora's and Poppy's hands and pulled them to sit on the foyer floor where the air was clearer.

Coughing and gagging, Mercy and Dick came up the servants' stairs beside the grand staircase with Tipton and Jane behind them. Dick's eyes watered. "The flue was closed. This should clear soon. I didn't see Tim, and only these two remained below."

Joseph swung his poker around. It swished through the air until it was level with Faith's throat. "Where is my man from downstairs?"

"I haven't the faintest idea. Perhaps he ran off like the men outside. You might think of hiring more reliable workers." Faith held in her terror and sounded calm and composed.

He leaned in and pressed the tip of the poker to the base of Faith's throat. She met his stare directly.

Both Aurora and Poppy gripped the poker and pushed it back.

Eyes so filled with hate they made Faith's heart pound, Joseph Fouché said, "Your hero has failed you, Lady Faith. Once again, the great Duke of Breckenridge is brought low. Really, what you see in him, I cannot imagine." He pulled the poker away with a jerk. He pointed it at Jane. "Kill that one and toss her in the street for Nicholas to find."

Dick raised his pistol and pointed it at Jane. She screamed and huddled against the wall.

Mercy covered Jane's body with her own.

Faith, Aurora, and Poppy rushed Dick. They tugged his arm and scratched at his eyes.

"Get 'em offa me!" Dick pulled the trigger and shot the ceiling near the chandelier. Plaster rained down on them all.

With the fire poker raised above his head, Joseph went after the Wallflowers.

Tipton blocked the descending iron and raised his arm to absorb the blow. He grunted, but he stood his ground, using his other arm to hold Joseph back.

The front door crashed open with enough force to jar it from its hinges. It boomed nearly as loud as the gunshot, but with more effect.

The occupants all froze.

Faith's breath caught.

Nick stood in the doorway, flanked by Geb and Rhys with Kosey close behind.

With remarkable swiftness, Joseph snatched Faith from the skirmishing people and drew his dagger. The iron poker cut a suffocating line across her middle while the tip of the knife pricked at her throat. "No one move or I will cut her from ear to ear, Nicholas."

Holding up both hands in a sign of peace, Nick stepped forward. "No one wants that, Joseph."

"I wouldn't mind. She and her friends are nothing but trouble, but I need my books back, so she will remain breathing for the moment."

Faith stared into Nick's eyes and where she had seen love, hate, resignation, and pain before, she now saw only fear. He feared losing her more than he had losing his own life. She swallowed down her own worries. "What insurance do you give that you won't kill me as soon as he hands you the books?"

"My word as a gentleman." His lips touched her earlobe.

Faith shuddered at his touch. "That seems of little value."

The look on Nick's face screamed, *Don't provoke him.* He kept one hand out and pulled two slim leather volumes from inside his coat. "Just give me Lady Faith and I will give you your books. Then you return to France and never come back, Joseph."

"Do you know they nearly set this house on fire?"

A twitch of a smile tugged at Nick's lips. "We saw the smoke."

"You will have me followed and arrested. I cannot risk capture. I will keep your woman but let the others go. Give me my books. I will set her free when I am far from London." Joseph's hold tightened.

His grip was worse than the most painful corset, and Faith struggled for breath.

Already shaking his head, Nick's lips pursed. "You know I won't allow that. You would kill her before you reach the Channel."

"How do you suggest we solve our little problem, Nicholas?" His voice lilted with pleasure.

Faith's heart lodged in her throat. Two men showing their dominance could bode badly for her, trapped in the middle. Nick's gaze shifted to her and she knew he would do whatever it took to keep her safe. It gave her ease—well, as much as was possible with a dagger at her throat and a fire poker strapped across her ribs.

Nick stared at Joseph. "I will go with you. You hold Lady Faith and I will hold the books. When we are far enough away that you feel you can make your escape, we can make the trade. I would not risk chasing you with Lady Faith to protect. All I want is my fiancée."

The air was sucked out of the room in the moments Joseph thought over his options. "No one else will follow." His warning was for the other men, but he kept his sights on Nick.

"You have my word. I will ride alone, but if any harm comes to Lady Faith, I will take you apart piece by piece until there is nothing left for your countrymen to bury." The ferocity in Nick's voice and the set of his jaw, sent a chill through Faith. Nick took the pistol from Geb's hand and motioned for the doorway to be cleared.

Rhys, Kosey, Geb, and Benny shifted to the left, entering the foyer. Rhys pulled Poppy in with one arm and took Aurora's hand with the other while keeping his gaze fixed on Faith.

Nick moved to one side as well, allowing Joseph to put his back to the open door. All the while holding Faith painfully tight. He dropped the fire poker on the steps.

Faith tried to give them all a reassuring smile, but feared it had come off as weak as it felt.

As she stumbled down the steps, Nick followed. The sight of him was the only thing keeping her sane. The day had begun so beautifully, with them declaring their love for each other, and now the end was a possible disaster. She swallowed her panic but screeched as Joseph tossed her onto a horse. She grabbed the saddle and mane and barely kept her seat before he was behind her, gripping her again.

Nick was still mounting when Joseph kicked the animal into a gallop.

The streets of London whizzed by in a blur as they sped southeast toward the Channel. By the time they reached the River Thames, Faith thought she might vomit from the pace and jostling, but over Joseph's shoulder she saw that Nick rode hard, just several paces behind them.

Only the panting horse forced Joseph to finally slow near Blackheath, but as soon as Nick closed the gap, the poor beast was forced into a canter.

"Will you run this animal to death?" Faith yelled over the hoofbeats and wind.

Pain seized her ribs from his brutal grip.

In the woods, somewhere near Bexley, she guessed, he finally stopped either because it was enough distance that he felt safe, or because the horse was spent and could run no farther.

Grabbing her by the hair, Joseph lowered Faith to the ground.

Faith screamed.

Without letting go, he jumped down and pressed his knife to her throat.

Nick appeared out of the darkness just as the moon appeared from behind the clouds.

The point of the dagger touched her flesh and warmth trickled down Faith's neck.

She gasped but held still. "If you kill me now, Fouché, you'll never see those precious books of yours."

"I should kill you both and take my property. It would serve you right, Nicholas." Fouché's voice near her ear rang with longing.

As if the ride had been of little consequence and the situation were normal, Nick sauntered closer, his gait marred only slightly by his injured leg. With his right hand he drew the pistol from his coat and with the left he pulled out the books. "We have an agreement, Joseph. Let her go and take the books."

"I'll need your horse as well. This one will not make the miles." Joseph tugged on Faith's hair.

It was not the first time she had wished for tamer locks, but now she just wanted to shave her head bald and be done with it.

"Put the knife away, Joseph. Give me Lady Faith and you may have the books and the horse." Nick limped forward until he was just out of arm's reach.

The dagger disappeared from Faith's view, but her hair was still tightly gripped in Joseph's fist as the two men circled each other. They stopped when Nick's horse was behind them.

Nick put his pistol inside his coat. He put his hand out for Faith and the books out for Joseph. "Time to go, Joseph. I told the others to stay at West Lane, but if this takes too long, they will come looking for us."

"I really did think you my friend, Nicholas. When this war is over, perhaps I shall think so again." Joseph snatched the books and let go of Faith's hair.

With a quick move, Nick grabbed her hand and pulled her to his chest. "When the war ends, I think it best if we keep our distance. What you did today and in the country ended any possibility of any future association."

Joseph shrugged, leapt into the saddle and dashed into the thick wood.

Nick tipped her head back and touched where Joseph's blade had cut. "Just a scratch." Crushing her in his arms, Nick peppered kisses in her hair, on her forehead and cheeks. "I thought I'd lost you."

Freeing her hands from between them, she wrapped him in a hug. "I knew you would get me back."

"I'm sorry, Faith. This was all my doing. I should have told Drake to go to hell." Nick kissed her cheek again before he kissed her mouth, hard and demanding.

Tears mixed with their kisses, as Faith finally let her emotions loose. She gripped his coat and opened her mouth to his. Their tongues warred and made peace a dozen times before they drew breath.

When they finally broke the kiss, Faith leaned in. "I think the next time this Drake fellow demands your services, you should send him to speak with me."

Laughing, Nick gave her a squeeze. "I'll do just that." He stepped to the frothed, panting horse and took up his reins. "I'm afraid we'll have to walk to the nearest village. This poor boy is in bad shape."

Faith petted the horse's nose, but groaned at the thought of a long walk. "Do you think he'll live?"

"Let's see if we can ease him into a slow walk. Carrying two people at such a pace, may have worn his heart out, but he's a hearty fellow. I have high hopes."

Leading the horse with one hand and holding Faith's hand with his other, they limped through the woods until they reached a small village. No one stirred at the late hour, but Nick woke the stableman for assistance.

The dropping of his title and the promise of a large payment, assured them a fresh horse and the care of the one Joseph had nearly spent.

Wrapped in Nick's arms atop the new horse, she was in no rush to get home. Nick was content to walk the main road toward London without haste.

After a long silence, he said, "I cannot imagine you still wish to marry me."

Faith strained her neck and looked him eye to eye. Her heart stuck in her throat. "Is that your way of saying you've changed your mind?"

He pulled the horse to a stop, lifted her by the waist, and turned her so she straddled the horse, facing him. "I have never wanted anything more in my life than to marry you, Faith. I love you. Nothing will change that."

The position was quite provocative, and she wrapped her legs around his hips, pulling them closer. "Then we are in agreement, since that is all I have wanted for some months now."

"I do hope we're not interrupting anything?" Geb said from the road in front of them. Kosey rode beside him on an enormous beast.

Faith's cheeks caught fire and she buried her face in Nick's shoulder.

Nick's low laugh was like music. He kissed her cheek and turned her so that both her legs were on one side of the saddle. "Not at all, we were just making our way home."

Kosey gave Faith a wink. "We shall escort you."

"Where is my horse?" Geb asked.

Nick relayed the story while Faith pressed her cheek to his chest. The sound of his heartbeat lulled her to sleep, but nightmares woke her several times. Not even exhaustion could keep her demons at bay.

When Nick carried her up to her room at the West Lane townhouse, she begged him not to leave. He pulled a chair close to the bed, but she eventually lured him into lying beside her. Though above the covers while she was beneath, she finally slept in his arms.

Chapter 25

Faith woke to an empty bed. Jane arrived to help her wash and dress. Her peach and cream room was oddly quiet and empty compared to the bombardment of thoughts shooting through her mind.

"Are you all right, Jane?" She hugged her maid.

"Just fine, my lady. What about you?"

Other than sore ribs and a scabbed-over nick to her throat, Faith felt fine, if somewhat stiff from the hard ride. "I think all my bits and pieces are in the correct places."

"It's a miracle," Jane said.

She slipped her arms through the sleeves of the day dress. Her stomach growled. "Jane, why is the house so quiet?"

"Everyone went down to break their fasts and didn't want to wake you after recent events. You've been asleep an entire day and night. His Grace said you were exhausted." Jane quickly worked the ties at the back of the dress.

"I slept an entire day away?" That explained why she was so hungry and stiff.

Jane pulled Faith's hair into a loose bun and pinned it before going to the window and opening the heavy cream drapes.

Sitting on the chair by her writing desk, Faith pulled on her shoes. "I'm going down. I don't like all this quiet. It seems wrong for West Lane."

Tender muscles forced Faith to take the steps more slowly than she would have liked, but she made her way and found all three of her friends, plus Rhys, seated around the breakfast table, chatting. They silenced when she walked in.

Everything was as it should be. The newly decorated breakfast room was bright and cheerful with light pouring in the front window. The rose-colored curtains had their femininity tempered by a dark maroon border that matched the rug. The walls had been changed from floor-to-ceiling wood to wainscoting below and crisp white paper above. Aurora was redecorating her husband's abominable house one room at a time and turning it into a home where Wallflowers were comfortable. The sideboard was draped in white, as was the table. White china and crystal gleamed.

"Were you talking about me?" Faith asked, happy to see them all hale and hardy.

Aurora stood and hugged her. "Only good things, of course."

Faith returned the hug. "I never had any doubts."

With a bow, Tipton cradled his left arm in a white sling. "Would you like me to make you a plate, my lady?"

Faith hadn't eaten in a long time, but food didn't appeal. "Just toast and coffee, but only if you can manage it, Tipton."

"It is my pleasure, my lady." Tipton slipped into a grin before donning his stoic repose.

Rhys had stood when she entered and sat as soon as she took her place at the table. "You should eat more, Faith. You look quite pale."

Around a mouthful of food, Poppy said, "She'll eat when she's hungry. Don't bully her."

"I heard you had to walk a long way to get home," Mercy said.

"Too far," Faith agreed. "And you know how I hate walking. But, after the ride bounced me about for miles, I didn't complain about the walk. I will eat more after I manage the toast. I'm quite famished."

Tipton put a plate with toast, butter, and jam in front of Faith and then set a steaming cup of coffee beside it.

"I'm just glad you both made it home in one piece." Aurora cut a link of sausage and put half on Faith's plate.

It was like old times. In school, Faith was always trying to slim down to please her mother, and her friends were constantly making sure she ate enough. "Thank you all for being so brave yesterday. I hope that part of our lives is now at an end."

Faith ate the toast and the sausage while her friends observed.

Rhys read the paper. "The only thing about the incident that has been reported is the smoke pouring from this house. It just says a servant left the flue closed and caused no damage, though it sent neighbors off in fear."

Laughing, Mercy choked on her tea. "I think they must have seen those two guards I scared off, running from the house."

"Where is Nick?" Faith finally asked.

Lips still twitching, Mercy said, "He went to meet with someone in government and then had an appointment with the archbishop of Canterbury. He said to tell you he would return with news this afternoon."

"Oh." Nerves flitted around in Faith's stomach and she put her coffee down.

Rhys sat forward, a line of concern between his eyes. "Have you changed your mind about Breckenridge, Faith?"

"No." Her voice was weak.

"Because if you have, we'll send Rhys down to Doctors' Commons right now and stop everything." Like a ferocious mother lion, Aurora's eyes lighted, ready for action.

It was all so perfect: her friends' loyalty, Rhys's rushing forward, Tipton standing ready. Faith wanted to cry with joy. "I want to marry Nick more than I've ever wanted anything in my life. I'm just a bit overwhelmed by how normal everything seems this morning."

They all nodded.

Aurora sighed. "Soon it will be just you and I living here, Mercy."

Nodding, Mercy sipped her tea. "I think Faith and Poppy will come back from time to time."

Nerves rattled Faith. "Every Tuesday for tea at the very least."

"And what about me?" Rhys added. "Does no one care if I return or not?"

Poppy kissed his cheek. "We adore you and you know it. After all, we made you a Wallflower, and have you to tea. What more can you want?"

He laughed. "Not one thing." He stole a kiss from his wife.

The front door knocker sounded and Tipton rushed from the room.

"Should he be working with his arm injured?" Faith asked Aurora.

Aurora lifted her hands in defeat. "I tried to get him to rest. Luckily it is not broken and only badly banged up, but I still would have liked for him to take a few days off to recover. He wouldn't have it."

"His Grace, the Duke of Breckenridge," Tipton announced from the breakfast room door.

They all turned.

Expecting Nick to be happy, Faith rushed to him when he looked like a man who'd lost his best friend.

Rumple escaped the kitchen and bounded across the breakfast room to leap on him.

Faith reached him at the same time. "What's happened?"

Kneeling down, Nick scratched Rumple behind the ears.

Benny arrived to take the puppy back below. "Sorry, he got away from me."

Nick ruffled Benny's hair. "I'm glad to see he's doing so well."

Puffing up like a pigeon, Benny said, "When those men came yesterday, I locked him in the root cellar so as he wouldn't get kilt."

"That was wise," Nick said.

With a wide grin, Benny dragged Rumple out.

Hand shaking, Nick touched Faith's cheek. "The Archbishop denied my request. We did not get a special license. I'm sorry, once again I've failed you, Faith."

Looking around, Faith found everyone staring. She turned back to Nick. "Nonsense. After all we've endured, I'll not have anyone decide our fate, not even the Archbishop of Canterbury."

"Oh?" Nick raised his brows. "What do you suggest?"

"That Tipton needs to rest and we shall all go to Gretna Green." Faith stomped her foot, but immediately regretted the sharp movement as her joints still ached.

Nick had given up on his cane, but still limped as he took her hand and they returned to the table. "My word, and I was told by your friends that the appearance of propriety was important to you, Lady Faith."

She shrugged and sipped her cooled coffee. "It seems I have changed."

"Then we had better pack for Scotland. Someone must inform Mr. Arafa. He will wish to join us, I'm certain, and he must know the nuptials will not be taking place at his home." Aurora placed her napkin on the table. She stood, forcing the men to stand as well. Halfway to the door, she stopped. "Your Grace, may I have a private word?"

Nick's mouth opened and closed, before he recovered. "Of course, but I hope by now you might call me Nick."

With a nod, she exited.

Nick followed.

Faith's heart pounded as she watched them walk out. She looked to Mercy and Poppy.

"I'm sure it's nothing," Poppy said.

"Or something." Mercy winked.

Faith shook her head. "I suppose he must get used to the Wallflowers at some point." Still, her small breakfast threatened to reappear.

* * * *

Nick had thought nothing would surprise him after the last few months, but Aurora asking to speak to him alone was completely unexpected. He followed her into the ladies' parlor. "Is something wrong, Aurora?"

"No. I'm pleased for you and Faith. I can see that you love each other. That is all I've ever wanted for my friends." She paced to the window, stopped, and paced back.

"Can I help you in some way?" Nick had no idea what she wanted, but it was clear whatever it was gave her some difficulty.

Aurora took a deep breath. "Perhaps, and perhaps I might be of some service to you as well. It seems we have had similar negative experiences. My friends suggested that speaking to someone who understands might help."

Pain and panic tightened inside Nick. Aurora's eyes were so filled with worry, but she trusted him. He said, "Let's sit."

Chapter 26

Faith's gown fluffed all around her like a meringue when she flopped backward on the bed. "I never thought it would happen. We're actually married."

Back in England, they had stopped at an inn only an hour south of Gretna Green. After a fun dinner with their friends, Nick had coaxed his wife to their room. It wasn't as plush as he would have liked, but the white walls and clean bed were enough. Other than the bed, one chair and a wardrobe were the only furnishings. None of it mattered, as Faith was his wife. Nothing else mattered.

The wonder in her voice made Nick smile. "Trekking to Scotland was your idea, my love. Why didn't you think it would work out?" Easing down beside her, he slipped his hand around her waist and settled it on her hip.

She rolled to face him. "Look at all we've been through: misunderstandings, imprisonment, separation, kidnapping, denial of a license. Didn't you think some monster would pop out of the anvil and keep us apart?"

Leaning in, he took her earlobe tween his teeth. "Nothing could ever keep me from you, once I knew you."

She moaned and threw her leg over his. "I'm glad to hear it, Your Grace. I'd hate to think I had fallen so far by myself."

Gripping her bottom, he pulled her forward and wished she was already out of the layers of fabric making up her wedding gown. "Never. I shall fall as low or climb as high as necessary to keep us together, my duchess. I never wish to be parted from you and will do all in my power to stay as we are right now."

She wiggled against his already hard shaft. "Just as we are right now?"

Nick slid his hand down her leg, found the bottom of her skirt, then slid back up her stocking to her bare thigh. "We may have to change positions, to eat on occasion, and I would like to make love one time unhurried, naked, and without injuries hindering me."

Stricken with laughter, Faith was an angel. "We have made do nicely. But now we are married, Nick. I'm yours for a lifetime. There is no need to rush."

Pulling the ties at the back of her gown, he said, "I shall treasure every moment, Faith. I will spend a lifetime showing you how precious you are and worshiping you with my body and worldly goods. You shall want for nothing."

Faith stood and let the dress puddle on the floor. She pulled the ties at her shoulders and her chemise flowed over her curves. "I want right now, husband."

"Oh, Lord, so do I." He pulled her back onto the bed and kissed her until they were both senseless with need. "I love you, Faith. I love you more than I ever thought it possible to love someone."

A slow smile pulled her full lips and lit her eyes. "It fills my heart to overflowing to hear you say so, Nick. I love you so very much. Did you know we Wallflowers once believed men incapable of romantic love?"

He brushed her wild curls back from her face. "I don't think I would have argued the point before I met you, but now I know."

Kissing his palm where it cupped her cheek, she asked, "What do you know?"

"I was only an empty vessel until you filled me up with so much emotion, it will take my lifetime to release it all." Nick's heart ached with all of it.

"I will love you for a hundred lifetimes and shower you with all the love you give me in each one." Faith straddled his hips, her hair hiding half her face.

Eternity was what she promised. He closed his eyes against the onslaught of emotion mixed with desire. "A hundred lifetimes may be just enough."

Leaning down, she sealed their pledge with a kiss.

In the beginning she had misled him. He would follow her hereafter.

Keep reading a special excerpt of the next book in The Wallflowers of West Lane series!

CAPTURING THE EARL
The Wallflowers of West Lane
A.S. Fenichel

The friendship of four young ladies has created an indestructible bond to protect one another from the perils of love and marriage . . .

After the demise of her friend's disastrous marriage, Mercedes Parsons isn't about to let the widowed Wallflower of West Lane undertake another perilous trip to the altar. At least, not before the bridegroom-to-be is thoroughly investigated. If only Mercy could stop her uncharacteristic daydreaming about Wesley Renshaw's charm, his intellect, his dashing good looks. After all, the earl is already spoken for! She must keep her wits about her and avoid giving in to temptation.

Wesley is both irritated and intrigued by the machinations of Mercy—who is she to decide whom he can and cannot marry? Yet while he admires her unwavering loyalty to her friends, he decides it's high time the misguided noblewoman had a dose of her own medicine. Two can play at this spying game. But they are both embarked on a dangerous charade. And it won't be merely Mercy's reputation at risk—or her heart on the line—as Wesley comes to the inescapable conclusion that he has found the right woman at long last . . .

Look for CAPTURING THE EARL, *on sale soon.*

Prologue

Mercedes Heath shook her head. She must have heard him wrong. After all, why would Wesley Renshaw, the Earl of Castlewick, want to dance with her?

The ballroom was loud and awash with activity. The Duke of Breckenridge lived in one of the largest townhouses in London, but it was still enough of a crush that she might have misunderstood the charming earl.

"Miss Heath?" Wesley's light brown eyes sparkled with some amusement only he understood.

"I beg your pardon, my lord?" Mercy tried to be polite, but it came out sharper than she'd planned.

Mercy was tall for a woman, but the Earl was still a few inches taller with the broadest shoulders she'd ever encountered. She had a fleeting thought about what he must do to stay so muscular, but brushed the wayward notion aside. His dark blond curls fell over the golden tan of his forehead, but his bright eyes hinted with browns and golds, at least she imagined they did. Mercy has spent so much time admiring him that once again, she had missed what he said.

Her Aunt Phyllis had urged her to put her spectacles in her reticule and stop hiding her pretty face. She had done so to appease her only living blood relative, but found herself out of sorts with her vision blurred.

However, she saw well enough to note his offered arm, indicating he did indeed wish to dance with her.

As she had missed the opportunity to give some excuse for why she couldn't possibly dance with him, she placed her hand on his arm and they joined the other dancers.

The conductor tapped his wand and a waltz began. Mercy tried not to notice the missed notes and out of tune second violin, but the sound grated on her nerves.

Wesley placed a hand at the small of her back a bit more firmly than was strictly necessary.

Turning her attention to him, she asked. "Have I been rude?"

His smile sent a shot of attraction from Mercy's head to her toes and it stopped in a few interesting places along the way. "Not at all. You are seemingly distracted. Is the music not to your liking?"

It would be more polite to say nothing or deny any issues with the orchestra, but Mercy didn't care about such customs and she had no reason to attempt small talk with this earl. He was nothing to her. She looked from the ornate arch ceiling with its frescoes to her Aunt Phillis who watched from the furthest corner of the ballroom before settling her attention back on the handsome man whirling her around the room. "The second violin is out of tune, the pianoforte is being played by a complete oaf and the flutist has missed no less than two notes of every eight."

"I see." He grinned as if perhaps he did actually understand, but perhaps he was just amused by her in general. That could explain his desire to dance with a girl of no means and little relations.

"I realize I am likely the only one to notice such things and that the Duke and his sister have hired one of the most popular orchestras in London." Mercy shrugged as she also knew no one cared what she thought of the music.

A robust couple bounded across the dance floor laughing and smiling as if they were part of a circus. Neither seemed capable of waltzing but neither did they care as they pushed several couples out of their way and headed directly for Mercy.

In one graceful move, Wesley lifted Mercy from her feet and out of harm's way. Her body crushed to his with an embrace that felt almost tender before he released her and in the same instant fell back into the perfectly balanced steps of the waltz. "You are a musician then."

She laughed and it surprised even herself. She rarely laughed in the company of strangers. Girls of her kind were not supposed to show outward enjoyment in public. It was grotesque in Aunt Phyllis's opinion. But the way he dismissed saving her from a pummeling as if it never happened and took up the conversation without a hitch amused her. "I would not call myself as such, but I do play."

"Yet you hear every nuance. I think you might be modest." His firm hand on her back guided them easily around the room and sent heat through her in way no other man ever had.

Mercy had no response. If she said she was an accomplished musician, she would be a braggart and if she denied, a liar. Remaining silent was her only choice.

"I would like to hear you play some time, Miss Heath." He cocked his strong chin to one side. "I think I would enjoy that very much."

The music ended. "Perhaps you will, my lord."

She turned to walk away, but he touched her elbow. "Will you not stay for the Boulanger?"

It was common for partners to stand up for two consecutive dances. Mercy just assumed he would have had enough dancing with a girl of no consequence and politely let her find her way back to some quiet corner or to her friends. "If you wish, my lord."

He offered his hand and they joined a circle of dancers.

The Boulanger left little time for chatting, but it did give her a moment to observe Wesley and how he interacted with others. He smiled politely at every woman who he partnered, though never so wide as to give someone the wrong impression. When they were once again hand in hand, his eyes sparkled with something tender.

Mercy assumed she was imagining things. With her blurred vision, she could easily imagine anything in the place of the truth. He couldn't care about someone like her. If he showed special regard it was only because he wanted something. In most cases what men wanted from her she was not willing to give. Her wicked body responded to the earl without regard for the fact that he was unattainable. Heat flushed up her neck and face while parts lower suddenly came alive with desire.

Quashing the thought, she focused on the music, noted every mistake and even a few nicely handled stanzas.

Moving around the floor to the beat of the music and occasionally coming together with a man who had asked her specifically to dance with him, was a rare delight. It was easy to glide around the floor, but she wished she had clear sight so she could see all the nuances of his expression.

His full lips were turned up, but she couldn't tell if the expression touched his eyes. Fumbling for her reticule, she decided that she would put her spectacles back on just as the music ended and catch a glimpse of Wesley's true gaze before it was likely she'd never see him again.

Gripping the wire rim between two fingers she turned toward Wesley.

The final notes were played.

Applause erupted from the dancers.

The man with the paunch on her other side bumped her, pushing her into Wesley.

Wesley's arms came around her before she tumbled to the floor.

The spectacles flew from her hand as she gripped his arm.

A sickening crunch followed.

As the dancers dispersed and the musicians put down their instruments, among the clatter, Mercy crouched beside her crushed spectacles. She picked up the twisted frames. One lens was crushed to splinters on the wooden floor, but the other was still in the frame with just one crack diagonally across. Mercy put the one lens to her eye. "I suppose it could be worse."

"I'm sorry, Miss Heath. I hope those are not a desperate need."

She had expected him to walk off when the others had, but he'd stayed with her and stood just behind. She drew a long breath and let it out. "I shall survive, my lord."

Firmly he gripped her elbow and drew her back to standing. He studied the crushed wire and glass in her hand. "Do not injure yourself on the glass, miss."

Ladies of worth didn't care if they could see or not. It was more important to be lovely and snare a fine husband with money and power. Mercy preferred to see and read. She needed to read the music of the masters as much as she required breath. Still, her weakness was too obvious in his presence and heat crept up her cheeks. Plunking the ruin spectacles back in her reticule, Mercy forced a polite smile. "Thank you, my lord. I am uninjured. I enjoyed the dance."

She turned and strode toward the hallway where she could rush to the ladies' retiring room and recover herself.

Wesley stayed at her side. "To whom may I deliver you, Miss Heath?"

Halfway across the wide grand foyer, she stopped and turned to him. "You need not concern yourself, my lord. I am a grown woman and can manage to keep myself safe. My friends and my aunt are here tonight."

Stepping until he was inches from her, his warmth spread through her. "I can see you are upset and I only wish to help."

It was impossible he could know her mind. She had practiced the indifferent mask she wore to these events and it had never failed her. The fact that she couldn't afford to replace the spectacles was bad enough. His knowing she was distressed was unbearable. "I am not upset. They are only a meaningless object. You need not worry."

"It is too late for that, Miss Heath." His soft voice brought her head up.

Even slightly blurred he was more handsome than was good for her. "I thank you for your concern, my lord. I shall just retire for a few minutes and be right again."

He shifted from one foot to the other, his frown obvious. "Shall I find your friends and send them to you?"

"That is not necessary." Though she had to admit, it was a very kind idea. "I am fine. It was a vigorous dance and I need to rest."

The air thickened in the moment where he made no reply. He bowed. "As you wish, Miss Heath. I thank you for the dance."

After making a quick curtsy, she tried to think of something to say, but instead rushed away and closeted herself in a small parlor to catch her breath.

Once she had thoroughly inspected her ruined spectacles, she returned them to her reticule with a sigh. Perhaps she could ask her aunt for a few extra pounds to replace them. No. She would see if she could take on a few new music students and earn enough wages to buy a new pair.

That decided, she left the parlor and popped out into the cool night for some air. She was in a part of the house unused by the ball attendees and reveled in the quiet. The gardens were lit and she heard voices on the other side of a tall hedge. Several couples were hidden from her view, but she heard them chatting on the larger veranda that flanked the ballroom. Staying hidden, she circled a baluster and stepped onto a stone path.

A perfect night, Mercy took a deep breath. She had to return, but not yet. Her mind bustled with questions about why the Earl of Castlewick would ask her to dance, care about her broken eye-wear, or her state of distress. It was all very odd.

Another set of footsteps sounded from behind.

Mercy spun around to find Wesley quickly approaching. "My lord?"

"Miss Heath, when you didn't return, I became concerned." He bowed.

She stepped back. "Why would such a thing concern you?"

"I beg your pardon." His tone sharpened.

Keeping her distance, Mercy regretted stepping so far from the safety of a crowd. "I mean you no offense, my lord, but why should my state of being be of any concern to you? I am nothing to you save a dance partner. To be honest, I'm still trying to fathom why you asked me to dance in the first place."

It was rude. She should have kept her questions to herself, thanked him for his attention and walked away. Yet she wanted to know and had little to lose.

Another man in his position might have walked away or become affronted and given her a setting down. Wesley smiled. "I asked you to dance because you are a lovely woman and I thought it might be a pleasant way to spend part of the evening. As for my concern"—his face grew serious—"I should have protected you better during the dance and after. What happened to your belongings should never have occurred."

He felt responsible. How odd. Mercy hadn't met many men of his ilk who were so solicitous of their dance partners' feelings. He likely wanted to steal a kiss or more and had followed her to get her alone. Mercy feigned patting her hair, but pulled a long hat pin she kept tucked in her elaborate bun. "My lord, I appreciate your attention." It was difficult to not sound sarcastic. If necessary, she would jab him and run. "You may rest assured; I am in no immediate danger. I just wanted some air."

The way his laugh rolled around the garden and caught on the breeze brought Mercy nothing but delight. "I think the weapon is a fine idea, Miss Heath. I shall instruct my two sisters to have exactly such an item placed in their hair for balls, trips to the theater and the like."

Mercy raised her brow and smiled, but didn't sheath her weapon against overly amorous admirers. "You might tell them picnics and walks in the park are better suited to several pins in one's stays or actual hats. One never knows when a man of means will try to take advantage of a woman below his station. Of course, your sisters have your title to protect them."

She had no need for spectacles or better lighting to see that her words had angered him. His fists clenched at his sides and his shoulders went rigid. "I have no intention of taking anything that is not offered freely from any woman, regardless of her station."

"Then you had better go back to the house, my lord, before someone sees you and me in the garden alone and I am ruined. Or do you intend to marry me, should we be discovered?" She made a scoffing sound that was not very ladylike.

The moon shone on him like a god of old as he crossed his arms over his chest. "I have no intention of marrying you, Miss Heath. Though I have to say, your candor is refreshing after so many inane hours of debutantes who connive after my attention."

"Conniving is not really in my nature. And in any event, I am not of your station. I am only Miss Heath, an orphan whose father had no title and whose lands were entailed elsewhere. If not for my aunt's kindness, I would be someone's governess or worse. You may be sure I have no designs on a man like you." She carefully and deliberately put her pin back into her hair without poking herself.

"I'm not sure I like the way you say, 'a man like me.' In fact, I didn't like any of what you just said." He scowled.

"And yet it was all true."

Giving her a nod, he said, "Good evening, Miss Heath."

She made a quick curtsy and rushed back toward the house.

Meet the Author

A.S. Fenichel gave up a successful IT career in New York City to follow her husband to Texas and pursue her lifelong dream of being a professional writer. She's never looked back. A.S. adores writing stories filled with love, passion, desire, magic, and maybe a little mayhem tossed in for good measure. Books have always been her perfect escape and she still relishes diving into one and staying up all night to finish a good story. The author of The Forever Brides series, the Everton Domestic Society series, and more, A.S. adores strong, empowered heroines no matter the era, and that's what you'll find in all her books. A Jersey Girl at heart, she now makes her home in Southern Missouri with her real-life hero, her wonderful husband. When not reading or writing, she enjoys cooking, travel, history, puttering in her garden and spoiling her fussy cat. Be sure to write visit her website at asfenichel.com, find her on Facebook, and follow her on Twitter.

Printed in the United States
by Baker & Taylor Publisher Services